First Edition May 2022

ISBN 978-1-7350329-2-4 (ppr)
ISBN 978-1-7350329-3-1 (ebk)
ISBN 978-1-7350329-4-8 (hdbk)

I dedicate this story to God; may He continue to bring Light in the darkness.

Thank you to my husband, Nick, for inspiring me to finish. Thank you also to my children and family who support my dreams.

The Light Within

By: T. Emiller

Cover Art: Donovan Howard Sr. (Artistic Peace)

Contents

Chapter 1

The Box

Darkness; a cold, silky blanket of it rested over her. With a sudden pull, her lungs drew in the stale air around her, breaking the eerie silence. As her gasps echoed into the shadows, the scents of copper and sand swirled about her, accompanied by the taste of iron on her lips. Though Liana lay unmoving, her mind raced on and replayed the events leading up to this moment. Images of her as she searched her backyard for her beloved canine companion, Striker, gave way to a horrific scene of Casimir as he ripped her away from her world and ended the lives of those around her.

Casimir, as his memory flashed by, his name repeated in her head and ignited a fire within.

Liana opened her eyes only to be met with far-reaching darkness. She knew she had to escape and quickly; for at any moment, he could be upon her. Sharp pains stabbed through her chest as she filled her lungs with another deep breath and tried to focus on anything around her.

Through the darkness, she began to pinpoint the blurred walls as they curved upward to support the low stone ceiling. With the slightest movement, a fiery pain lashed through her and extended to every fiber of her being. Her head swirled as the room spun and she struggled to raise herself from the cold ground.

As her vision adjusted, a small pool of water came into focus only a short distance from her. Next to it lay the crystalline blade that Casimir, just moments ago, used to restore her power before he cruelly dumped her into the water and transported her from the world she once knew, to another realm. Her breath, held hostage as she braced through the zaps of pain that accompanied each jerk or twist, came in slow, unsteady draws as she crawled toward the knife.

With each extension of her arm, her sweatshirt tugged painfully and pulled at the cotton fibers that fused with the open wounds on her back. As soon as the dagger was in her grasp, she shakily pulled herself to her feet. Stashing the blade in her sweatshirt pocket, she quickly searched for a way out. A quiet whisper of a breeze blew through the low cavern and drew her attention toward a small seam of light in the darkness. Her legs wobbled as if brand new to her and screamed out in protest as she stumbled toward the small opening in the cave.

Liana pushed her way through dense, blue, and green vines that fell like a curtain over the entrance of the cave. They clung to her, tearing slightly at the exposed flesh of her face and hands as she moved through the overgrowth into a strange forest. The air, eerily quiet and oddly heavy around her, amplified every movement of hers and sent an echo off the tightly packed, slender trunks of the nearby trees.

Time wasn't her friend at this moment and Liana was desperately aware of it. With each pain-filled step forward, she pulled herself along the trunks of the trees as the forest floor spun around her. Her labored breathing reverberated up the pale bark, into the canopy of branches where boughs distantly creaked in a far-off breeze.

Liana's heart leaped in her throat as twigs snapped and cracked behind her. Desperate to put some ground between her and Casimir, Liana released the tree's support and ran with intensity. Her feet pounded on the ground

The Box

several times before they found an unearthed root and sent Liana tumbling to the forest floor. Amid her fall, her head connected with a nearby outstretched branch and opened the sizable wound on her temple that was previously created by Casimir. She lay still and clutched her head as the forest floor spun around her.

"Liana!"

The haunting voice slithered across the silent landscape, instantly striking her, injecting its venom through her core. It wriggled into the depths of her and doused the little flame that dared to rise within. His shout manifested a crippling fear and suddenly, it was as though the shadows themselves held her in place.

"Get up! What are you doing?" Casimir spat angrily as he closed in on her.

In a matter of seconds, he was at her side. He gripped her arm above the elbow and harshly jerked her to her feet. Clutching her chin, Casimir lifted Liana's face and inspected her temple briefly. She blinked as the trees spun around her and gradually the four Casimirs she saw before her, merged back to one. As he twisted and turned her face, Liana kept her eyes on the ground. His touch repulsed her, making her sick to her stomach and the thought of being taken again only intensified her condition.

"Look at me," he growled angrily in her face through his teeth.

She knew now wasn't the time to run, for she surely couldn't escape him in her current state. As her eyes met his, she swallowed, understanding the necessity of her submission at this moment. A smug grin spread across Casimir's face as his eyes connected and he released her from his grip.

The Light Within

"Liana, Liana," his tone shifted to a gentle reassurance as he raised his arm over her head. He rested it on her shoulder and used it to pull her into his side. "Please don't run off," he lectured while he steered her through the trees. "I am the only one who can protect you now."

She nodded slowly; her blank expression fixed on her feet as she fought back the razor wires of panic that tightened across her chest and demanded her attention.

"Now, give me the blade," he spoke slowly, in a quiet whisper and extended his open hand in front of her as his other hand gripped her tighter to his side.

How did he know, she questioned herself, *I had it? What am I doing?*

Without hesitation, Liana absently reached into her sweatshirt and pulled out the long, quartz-like blade. In the mere seconds it took for her to reach into her hoodie and hand Casimir the blade, the internal war waged on. As she freed her grip on the blade, she felt the pull to obey Casimir diminish.

He quickly tucked the blade under a strap at his side and turned back to Liana. Her shaking hand lingered in the air where his once was. His clutch on her shoulder eased as he resumed guiding her through the darkening woods. His presence was unsettling to her, yet the blank look on her face remained fixed as she followed along.

"We must get you to the castle, quickly." Casimir urged Liana on, though her pace didn't change.

Liana remained lost in thought as she reflected on her situation. There was something present in his remarks Liana could sense. Underlying angst and the air of desperation in his voice could be felt in every word he spoke. This didn't seem like the calculated Casimir she had experienced previously. Liana worried he was far more dangerous.

An annoyed sigh echoed from Casimir through the air. "K," he called over his shoulder to one of the many individuals of his group that escorted Liana through the trees.

"Yessir?"

The voice boomed from directly behind Liana. Her eyes widened in response to its familiarity.

"Help Liana," Casimir paused for a moment, as though searching for the words, "pick up the pace."

"Yessir." The voice barked back obediently.

Instantly Liana was lifted into the solid arms of the man behind her. Once the group resumed their trek through the woods, Liana looked to the man's face to confirm her fears.

"See?" Casimir spoke down to Liana over his shoulder. "A simple yes and do what you're told. No one gets hurt, no messes to clean up."

As he spoke, the grip of the man tightened around her. She swallowed uneasily, as her mind busily raced to the dead-end of every plan of escape she could conceive.

"Though unfortunate about your beast, K. You will be rewarded for the sacrifice." Casimir's voice trailed off as he waved a dismissive hand in the air.

"Anything for the Kingdom," the man said as he made eye contact with Liana.

Fury ignited within as their eyes connected. Of all the people she suspected of betraying her, she never would've thought Khius would be the one locking eyes with her in a moment such as this.

How could I, she thought as her jaw clenched in anger, *have been so oblivious?!*

The Light Within

Her eyes remained locked on Khius as his widened. He dropped her to her feet and reached desperately up to his neck. His face turned from red to purple as he grabbed at an unseen force.

"Liana," Khius choked out, gasping for air as he fell to his knees. "Please!"

Liana jumped as the slender fingers of Casimir connected with her skin and slid along the back of her neck before they gripped securely to the sides of her throat. Her eyes fell from Khius and as she focused on the numerous leaves resting on the forest floor, her hold on him eased. Her heart raced on as the trees began to spin and she grew faint. She leaned her shoulder into Casimir for support.

How dare he betray me, the thought crept up in the back of her mind, though it sounded unlike her own. *He can't get away with this!*

Infuriated, Liana redirected her attention back to Khius. As their eyes connected again, she detected a far-off sense of remorse. Though no words escaped his lips, she could feel his eyes plead for her to let him explain. Through a narrowed gaze, she swallowed the huge lump in her throat and turned her attention back to the ground.

Maybe, she thought again, *he has a plan. No! I don't care anymore! I can't trust him. How can I trust anyone?*

Tears welled as her frustration mounted and she was suddenly very aware of everyone that stood there and stared at her.

"Casimir," she whispered as she turned to him.

"Come now, you need rest," Casimir spoke softly in Liana's ear as he lifted her into his arms.

The ground swirled into the sky the harder Liana tried to concentrate on the scene around her. She pulled

The Box

the hood of her sweatshirt over her face, tucked herself into Casimir's chest, and tried to blot out most of the scene from her view. She could feel Casimir's pace quickening the further they went. His rhythmic steps and the accompanying darkness Liana had surrounded herself in, lulled and begged for her slumber. Fighting the urge to rest her eyes, she peered through the small opening of her hood.

The slender white and silver trees gradually thinned out the further he carried her until only a few scorched trunks jaggedly cut into her line of vision. The smell of sulfur and ash progressively choked out any breathable air as they neared the city gates. Liana pulled her sweatshirt up over her nose and attempted to block out what she could.

As they approached the gate, guards covered fully from head to foot in black uniform, stood armed and unwavering. When they turned their attention to Casimir, his face reflected in their mirrored goggles. With a nod, they turned and pushed the creaking, rusted gates open just enough for them to enter one by one. As they passed the guard, the mirrored goggles turned their gaze to Liana and peered curiously before they caught the attention of Casimir and went back to their prearranged position.

The group stepped through the dark, vine-covered gates and what met her eyes made her bury her face into Casimir's torso. A brief glimpse of the once pearly stone streets and smiling faces found only scorched and lifeless ruins, littered with unresponsive expressions and embers that smoked on incessantly. Casimir pulled Liana in closer and shielded her from the sight as they quickly made their way to the castle. As they moved hastily through the side streets, onlooking citizens murmured when they caught glimpses of Liana.

Shouting from guards soon broke out as they cracked canes over heads and barked, "What are you looking at? Get back in line!"

Outraged, Liana looked up from between Casimir's arms but found they were now secured in the castle. Instead, her eyes immediately fell on a massive tree trunk and wandered up to the far-reaching branches of the tree that stood towering in the entrance hall. She recalled the powerful aroma of the gorgeous blossoms and excitedly pulled her nose from beneath her sweatshirt. A short inward breath left Liana crinkling her nose in disgust. The stale air resonating around her was laced with the violent odors of what lay beyond the castle walls.

A frustrated sigh echoed around her; it echoed from Casimir as he kicked fallen leaves from the tree out of his way. Upon second glance, Liana noted the distressed state of the once glorious tree. The white and golden bark that wove through the branches quickly gave way to a hardened, withering, grey rot at the base of the tree, where all but a few of its leaves now rested.

As Casimir rounded a corner and blocked the tree from Liana's vision, she noticed it wasn't the only thing that had changed since she'd last been here. The atmosphere around them was quite different inside the walls. Endless beautifully decorated faces of all different types of individuals walked about in ornately decorated, silky clothing. They all spoke to one another and laughed merrily as they strolled or lounged around. It was as if they were oblivious to what was happening just beyond the castle.

The Box

Even the servants, clad in uniforms of a royal blue velvet, adorned smiles on their faces. They bowed and greeted Casimir as he walked past and whispered excitedly as soon as his back was to them. Casimir nodded to some and scowled at others as he went. He hastily moved through the castle, taking several twists and turns through passageways before he reached a long corridor with guards at both ends.

Casimir motioned for the group of men following them to leave. His pace slowed as he entered the hallway. Angst and disgust churned in Liana and grew as they neared the door at the end of the hall. It felt like ages before they finally entered the large room at the end. She knew the room quite well; it was the King's Chambers. Her heart sunk, for in the time it took for him to cross the threshold of the room, her memories raced and endlessly tormented her.

"Why don't you take a moment. I'll return for you soon." He said with a strange tone Liana couldn't quite pin.

He set her on her feet and ran a finger down her cheek. Instantly, she jerked her head from his touch. His insistent glare burned into the cheek that so rudely rejected his precious affection; if he were the one with the power, Liana knew she'd be dead by now. Every second felt like a century as his presence persisted. He paused for a moment as if he debated speaking before he finally turned to shut the large wooden doors between them.

A huge breath of air, held captive by her fear, escaped Liana and with it, countless tears. Broken by the weight hanging over her and exhausted from trying to survive, Liana fell, face in hands, to her knees and wept.

The Light Within

"Help me, please!" She cried out into her tear-filled palms, to the Light within her as she searched for guidance.

Her cries gradually yielded to silence and slowly, crushing failures stacked high in her mind, toppled only by hopeless thoughts, laced in fear. As the tears rained on, Liana's breath failed her. She fell backward and leaned against the large wooden doors, gasping in between the moans of her cries.

"So...s-stupid," she said in between sobs, simultaneously striking her head back against the door.

Breathe, the word whispered through her thoughts, slowly consuming the toxic ideas that swirled inside as her lungs filled in response.

Liana closed her swollen eyes and concentrated solely on the air around her as it filled her nostrils. Countless deep breaths later, Liana finally opened her eyes and took in the room around her.

The bed linens and immaculately decorative tapestries all looked the same as she remembered them so long ago, yet everything was darker. The room, once vibrant and glowing, was full of shadows that pressed in on Liana, as they whispered and reached for her. She stood slowly, holding herself against the door for stability. After a few calculated breaths, she slowly made her way from the door; the shadows shifted about her as she crossed the distance of the sizable room.

Though she could have sworn she just showered, she was in desperate need to be clean. The touch of Casimir on her cheek and his lingering grip on her, made her cringe and hate her own flesh. She was grateful that, even after all this time away, her familiarity with the room helped guide her mindlessly to the shower.

The Box

Without a second thought, she turned the taps of the water and let the hot steam surround her. She stepped into the stream of the shower. As she leaned her head against the tile wall, she felt her mind clear. She knew she had to think of a plan and quick.

Slowly and painfully, she separated the sweatshirt from the wounds on her back it so desperately clung to. Through the tears, she scrubbed and washed away the bloodied traces of the hours she had just survived. Determined to continue to survive, she shut off the water, drew a deep breath inward, and threw open the shower curtain.

The fleeting gift of peace vanished instantly as her gaze fell on none other than Casimir. His usually smug grin was wider than ever in his victory-perceived state of mind. He stood several feet away in the bedroom beyond the open bathroom, eyeing her exposed, dripping figure intrusively. No words left his lips, he simply motioned for her to follow as he walked out of her line of vision.

Shivering, she stepped from the shower and in the absence of a towel, wrapped her arms around herself. Calculating each step so as not to slip, she made her way to Casimir, who stood proudly near a large box displayed prominently on the bed at the center of the room.

As she approached, he wrapped her in a towel and moved her to stand in front of his offering. She remained, unmoving and eyes fixed on the box as he moved the towel along her skin in an attempt to dry her uncooperative form.

The seemingly harmless box held a beautifully decorated gown and several jeweled accessories to match. Had Liana cared about any of those things in the slightest, she would've been overly impressed. Suddenly aware that she may not be giving Casimir the reaction he was searching for, she cleared her throat and reached for the gown.

"It's very beautiful." Her voice lifted into a half-convincing rhythm that visibly pleased Casimir.

"Only the best for my Queen. Now let's see it!" An air of excitement rang in his words, trailed with a hint of something Liana couldn't quite decipher.

His hand found his chin, and his eyes never left her form as he walked across the room. Gradually, he rested in the shadows and lounged back on a sofa that stretched along the wall.

Liana turned her attention to the dress and swallowed slowly. She lowered the heavy gown and stepped inside. The thick beading and coarse fabrics yanked and tugged her skin as she pulled it over her hips. Steadily, she slid her hand into the sheer sleeve and pulled it up to rest on her shoulder.

She turned to her left to find she struggled with the same gown in a long mirror that leaned against the wall. After she slid the remaining hand into the open sleeve, she turned and sighed as she examined herself. Her lifeless eyes, unresponsive to her attempts to control them, begged for anyone to see the truth.

From behind her, a murmuring breath on her neck asked the question that could give her away, "Well?"

Eyes on the floor, she barked back responsively, "It's gorgeous. I... I just."

She paused and held her breath as she stifled the need to scream while Casimir tightened and yanked at strings on the back of the gown, closing it over her fresh wounds.

The Box

The fabric loosened below her waist and fell to the floor with a large slit that ran up the side and exposed the majority of Liana's thigh. Dark blue fabrics squeezed in at her waist and pressed along her breasts, making her look like some sort of provocative porcelain doll before it trailed off along her arms like dark tendrils that held her in place.

Liana blinked back at the woman in the mirror as she began to grasp what her new life as Casimir's toy may hold. Swallowing uneasily, she looked up and noticed Casimir looking at her over her shoulder. Regretfully, she locked eyes with him in the mirror.

"You'll get used to it," he said with a hungry smile while he stared back at her through the mirror.

She shivered uncomfortably as he moved from her to the box sitting on the bed. As he fiddled with items in the box, he flicked his hand behind him. Suddenly, a fire roared in the large open fireplace that lay next to the door, behind Liana. Its warm glow reflected onto Liana's face through the icy mirror and held her attention.

"Whatever you desire, ask me alone. I am the only one who can take care of you." He smiled at her in the mirror, though her gaze remained on the fire's reflection.

Not until Casimir placed the cold, white-golden metals of a weighted necklace around her bare neck did her attention shift. As his fingers brushed her skin while fastening the loops of the necklace, his fragmented emotions and thoughts seeped into Liana's being. A sense of nervous haste clouded his mind, interrupted periodically with a sinister excitement as he'd glance at her.

Drawing in a gradual, deep breath, Liana tried to block Casimir from her mind and concentrated on the

The Light Within

walls and floors that surrounded her. As he placed the last of his decorations, a pair of white-gold bangles, tightly around her wrists, she felt the weight of it all come together.

"Come," he said and lifted a hand to her.

Suddenly aware of her utter exhaustion, compounded from her previous battles and weighted by Casimir's preparations, she unquestioningly obeyed. He guided her down the hall from the King's Chambers to the many eager faces who waited. They all greeted Liana with a sense of exuberance.

All through the night, they cheered for her accomplishment, for the gift of being at his side. All night long she smiled and nodded as she danced with the beautiful faces, drank their drinks, and filled herself with their food. As the night came to a close, her mind eased and she thought she could breathe again, in moments like these.

Though moments are fleeting, for after the formalities came darkness. All of the beautiful faces wanted what they came for, and he so eagerly accommodated. Liana focused on the walls; she admired their strength to stand as she slid into the darkness.

Chapter 2
Darkness

Frozen toes wiggled uncomfortably in luminous blades of white grass. Liana squinted and looked up over the bright lawn. Her arms wrapped around herself as the shadows whipped in every direction. Just as she turned her attention forward, the wind burst from behind and urged her ahead.

Rough stone steps protruded from the earth in a jagged staircase that twisted off to her left. Liana lifted her foot to the step and froze just before her skin met the stone. With her hesitation, the shadows thrashed back and forth, over, and around her. She followed the staircase with her eyes and frowned as it dissolved into the dark winds out of her sight. Suddenly, a cold sting raced across her foot as it connected with the stone step.

Liana's eyes shot open as the morning light broke through the lingering shadows and gradually reached across the cold, hard floor. The hushed footsteps of Casimir as he slipped from the room brought the relief she desperately anticipated. A click of the door as it latched shut echoed across the walls around her. It signaled her temporary breather and allowed her the reassurance to safely open her eyes.

Aching from the restless night, she stretched out. As her arms moved, she heard the familiar tinkle that reminded her of the ever-present shackles of beautifully woven bangles. Though the nights faded with the morning light, the shackles remained, a constant reminder of her role. With narrowed eyes of determination, she tried, yet again, to wretch the pervasive bracelets from her wrists. Several tireless minutes passed but her fingernails dug and clawed with no sign of opening or removing them. A heavy sigh reverberated from Liana across the room as she sat up and beat her fists on the bed in front of her.

Liana sluggishly pulled herself from the hard bed and drug the fogginess of her mind onto the balcony. She stood as Casimir had many nights and ran her hands along the banister as she looked out over the gardens below. Something wet caught her attention and she squinted down at her hand. Barely visible in the morning light, she rubbed her fingers together as a faint red stain moved around her skin.

Shallow breaths rapidly filled her lungs as she rushed across the floor and plunged her hand under the taps into scalding water. She scrubbed impatiently and as the taunting color faded from her pale skin, she looked up to the steamy mirrors. The blurring reflection of a woman she once knew stared unblinkingly back at her. Disgust filled her eyes for this woman who, hair caked in blood from one of his favored guest's darker preferences, allowed others' wills to consume her.

Never, Casimir's threats echoed in her mind, *speak of the night, or it will be your last.*

Shaking the previous nights' violent recollections from her attention, she turned toward the shower and let the taps flow. The searing water lashed across her flesh, but she didn't flinch. She welcomed the cleaning sting of the waters as they washed over her. Her skin soon glowed a bright red as she plunged her head into the water's path. Liana leaned over and watched as she let the water wash through her hair.

A sudden hand on her hip turned her while her fist instinctively flew at the intruder behind her. As her knuckles stopped short, she looked from the hand that suddenly held her wrist, to its owner. Defeat immediately overtook her. In a split second, an angered face of fury shifted to one of a vacant ragdoll.

Before her expression had even shifted, he had her free wrist snagged and pinned with the other against the shower wall above her head. His free hand slowly slid down her arm as he held her captive with a kiss. His hand reached her hip and pulled her into himself forcefully before he released her from the kiss. He drew back to study her. She immediately turned her head to the side and fixed her eyes on the water.

The shower was the one place she thought she could escape him, but he followed her now, even here. Angered that he dared to steal what precious seclusion she was allotted, she yanked on his grasp in a feeble attempt to free herself. Her wrists slipped in his hold at the sudden movement, but he quickly secured them and diverted his attention to the clanking bracelets.

She swallowed nervously as she realized his focus remained fixed on her bangles for an extended time. Gradually, she turned her head just enough to see his narrowed, suspicious eyes inspecting her. As soon as their eyes connected, he dropped her wrists forcefully from above her.

"Stupid girl," Casimir seethed through his teeth. "What are you doing?" He gestured to the deep gouges visible on her wrists where the bangles rested.

"I..." Only pitiful squeaks escaped her mouth as fear gripped her and held her speech hostage.

She hadn't rehearsed for this encounter as she now did with so many of their others and it showed. She stood, shaking and voiceless, mouth hanging open as the words failed her. An amused look spread across his face as he watched her silent struggle transpire. His eyes remained fixed on her as he pulled a towel from the wall and wrapped it around his waist. He lingered a moment longer, as she struggled to provide the answer he looked for before he turned to walk away.

His voice, followed by amused laughter, echoed through the room as he crossed it, "I seriously insist you stop with such stupid ideas."

Liana shivered silently in place. Moments passed until she heard the loud clamor of the heavy door. Almost instantly, the suffocating grip that rested over her began to ease, and she slowly moved to shut the water off. She yanked a towel from the wall, wrapped it around herself, and quietly walked through the room to the balcony.

"Ahem," a voice interrupted the silence from behind her.

Startled, Liana turned to face the individual. Her eyes grew wide as they fell on the face of Arietta. Relief and hope washed over Liana. It took every fiber in her being not to fling herself at Arietta's feet and sob. She swallowed the lump in her throat as she caught Arietta's eyes motioning to another individual present with them.

The other woman, nearly the same height as Liana, wore a short, black dress, almost identical to Arietta's but cut to fit her curvy frame precisely. Liana's eyes were instantly drawn to her smile; a lasting, sincere beacon that shined from her glowing, flawless face. Her hair was kept in tiny, tight curls, which she twisted and secured back from her face with one large, purple flower. Approaching Liana with an air of excitement, she smiled patiently as she came to a silent standstill in front of her.

"Um, hi," Liana said awkwardly.

"Good morning!"

Darkness

The exuberance in her voice was overwhelming and a bit startling to Liana, who had grown familiar with the facade, followed by contrasting sharp words from all the others.

"You must dress. The King will be addressing his subjects shortly," she said with a smile as she stared at Liana.

"Oh…" Liana said with a half-hearted tone and a half-smile on her face as she dropped her head.

"Come on, it'll be fun!" The woman bounced on the balls of her feet as she tried to contain the excitement from bursting forth. "I'll pick you out something to wear!"

Liana nodded and almost instantly the woman was across the room and through the door that led to a hall of gowns. Arietta let out a loud laugh as she watched the woman half-skip, half-shuffle across the room and once she was out of sight, she turned back to Liana. Crossing the few feet between herself and Liana in seconds, Arietta jumped and grabbed Liana in a strong, welcomed embrace.

"You're alive!" she whispered excitedly in Liana's ear.

Though Liana felt anything but 'alive'. Arietta quickly released her and stepped back slightly to come face to face. An earnest smile shone back at Liana. As Arietta's outstretched arms lingered, her hands ran down to Liana's wrists.

You, Arietta's voice echoed in her mind as their eyes connected, *are going to be okay*.

As she came in contact with the bangles on Liana's arms, her smile immediately faded, and she took a step back from Liana. Suddenly, the cheerful woman burst through the door.

The Light Within

"So," the woman called to them as she crossed the room. "There's this really nice blue one."

As she spoke, she held out in front of her, a modestly cut, floor-length, sky blue dress with long sleeves, before hanging it on the post of the bed. Liana left the balcony and crossed the room slowly while she eyed the dress with quiet contemplation.

"This is one of the King's favorites," the woman continued as she held out a heavily jeweled, strapless, navy-blue gown.

"Surely we'll avoid that one then," Liana spoke absentmindedly.

The women both snickered in response, followed by Liana with the realization of her words. She quickly shook her head as Casimir came across her thoughts and they all immediately composed themselves.

"And this is one of my favorites!" As she spoke, the woman held the floor-length gown in front of her and walked toward Liana.

The bright cobalt gown had several silvery designs along the silken material that fell to the floor and was held in place with sheer, blue material that reached from the bust around the neck.

"It's a good balance between the other styles." She gestured to the other dresses that hung on the bed.

"Blue, blue, or... blue?" Liana shook her head and laughed to herself. "What do you think?" Liana asked as she turned her attention to Arietta.

Arietta gulped as if Liana was signing her death sentence and after a moment of staring at the dresses, she replied, "They are all very beautiful."

Liana rolled her eyes and turned back to the dresses. She eyed them as the cheerful woman hung each.

Darkness

"Which one do you think he'd like the least?" Liana asked herself playfully out loud as she studied each.

"Definitely this one," Arietta said under her breath, standing in front of the sky-blue dress.

"If you're wondering so that you may avoid disappointing him, I'd suggest going with his favorite." Cheerful tones in the other woman's voice echoed from the right of Liana.

Liana stood for a moment and eyed the dresses that lay before her. She loathed the fact that it mattered. Frustrated, she picked up the lighter of the blue dresses and eyed it for another moment before her mind was set.

"Alrighty, let's get to it then," the woman said as she cheerfully picked up the other gowns and took them back across the room.

Wasting no time, the ladies helped Liana adorn the simple gown. They meticulously primped and adjusted every detail, from each hair on her head to each fold of fabric in the dress. The cheerful woman braided Liana's hair and pinned it in place like a halo around her head.

Liana's eyes remained fixed on her hands that lay folded in front of her. She wondered how Arietta had gotten here, and if the others were also here. The chill sting of the familiar jewels brought Liana back to reality as Arietta placed them around her neck. After only a matter of minutes, the ladies backed away from Liana and admired their work.

"You are so beautiful!" The cheerful woman clasped her hands together under her chin as she admired Liana.

"Very beautiful." Arietta nodded in agreement.

"Thank you, uh..." Liana paused.

The Light Within

"W, my Queen, and this is A," the cheerful woman spoke as she gestured to herself, then Arietta. "We are your advisors."

"Advisors?" Liana let out a short laugh.

"Did I say something funny?" W asked curiously.

"Um, no I apologize. I'm confused why *The King* would," she paused for a moment, "*grant* me advisors."

"Oh, don't be silly! He insisted." W spoke happily as she moved to stand behind Liana and adjusted her dress slightly in the mirror while she looked over Liana's shoulder. "Well, it may have been my idea, but who can be sure?"

Liana caught her gaze and could've sworn she winked at her, but she quickly continued.

"Anyway, a Queen needs someone to help them, and I simply pointed out The King surely cannot be with you at every moment. So, that's what we're here for!" She cheerfully left Liana's side and headed toward the door that led out into the castle.

"Okay, I guess. W? Is that really your name?"

"Well, the law has ordered us all under new names. So, I am W, and she is A," she insisted.

"Casimir isn't here. You can just tell me your name," Liana persisted and turned to look at W from across the room.

"Law is law," she said with a permanent smile on her face just as a knock sounded.

"Of course," Liana agreed reluctantly just as guards pushed open the large doors with an intrusive bang.

W gave a half chuckle and moved toward Liana. With no further words, she placed a stern hand on the back of Liana's dress and ushered her forward. As they walked, the guards gradually followed behind them. Liana

Darkness

tried to listen as W and A spoke enthusiastically beside her. They offered their words of direction and encouragement, but her mind darted elsewhere and allowed for limited focus.

Gradually they stopped in a dim room that stretched narrowly into the distance. An ornate ceiling hung lower than most of the other rooms. The bare walls were scarcely lit by dripping candles that hung around the room.

"Wait here," W instructed Liana before she turned from her to walk off into the distant shadows of the furthest side of the room.

Liana looked around as W left her side, unsure where she was within the castle. The guards split; half stood near the door they entered, and the others followed W. Though the room was vastly unoccupied, the deafening roar of voices echoed loudly throughout as Liana slowly moved about the open room.

"What's that?" Liana asked A as her eye caught an unguarded hall that branched off from the room they stood in.

She followed Liana's gaze down a narrow hallway, the end of which a faint glow emitted from the frames of a door. It looked simple enough, though it had no handles to open it. Liana slowly walked toward it as if a force from behind it drew her in. A gentle hand on her shoulder broke her concentration and pulled her back to the moment.

"Come on." A smiled at her and motioned for her to follow. "That door leads to The Veil," she whispered in a low voice as they walked toward W, "it also holds the daggers of the banished."

Liana thought back to the dagger Casimir had used on her, but as A led her closer to W, she shook the thought from her head. W traced a smile across her face with both of her index fingers as a real smile appeared and she nodded to Liana. Liana instantly straightened her posture and adorned the same bright and shining smile Casimir required.

W nodded to a nearby guard, who opened the door and gestured for Liana to enter. Liana drew in a long, calculated breath as she stepped through the doorway into an open and airy throne room. The clear quartz walls and floors were decorated in dark blue and silver drapes of heavy velvet that fell from the ceiling randomly about, into dark pools of carpet adorned with plush pillows.

Casimir stood in the center of the room with a man holding a small box. As Liana approached them, the man snapped the box shut and Casimir motioned for him to leave. Once the man left, Casimir examined Liana with a smile and waved for her to approach.

"Remarkable," he said quietly as his eyes rested on her form.

She exhaled the breath of fear, held captive by the constant dread that he would read the truth in her eyes. An earnest smile of relief rested over her face as her eyes turned toward the floor and she knew she was safe, for now at least.

"What?" Casimir asked playfully.

"I just forget how fortunate I am sometimes." Liana let out a small chuckle at her statement.

As she closed the distance between them, she shifted her thoughts from herself to Casimir. He held out his hand and without hesitation she took it. His expression suddenly changed as he glanced behind her to W and then to A who waited at the door for Liana. Without missing a beat, Liana lifted herself slightly on her toes and placed a small kiss on Casimir's cheek. He turned to her again, slightly surprised, and smiled.

"Good to see your mood has improved," he said quietly as he placed his hand on her back and led her toward the other side of the room.

Casimir led her through a high vaulted hallway with crystal pillars that seemed lit from above. Roaring and thunderous voices echoed all around them and pressed in uncomfortably on Liana. The doors lay open and as they neared the end of the hall, Liana could see a large crowd gathered before them. Casimir stopped at the top of a set of large wide steps.

Liana no longer saw billows of ash and smoke blotting the buildings out. Only the occasional building rose here and there amongst the ruined ones. The air was still laced with the foul odor of decay and smoldering ruins, yet it was breathable.

The restless crowd before them yelled and argued amongst themselves. Their clothing looked to be made from mere scraps compared to those on the inside of the castle walls. They lined the courtyard of the castle and stretched out into the streets beyond. She looked over the faces, sullen and tired. Remorse spread inside her as she felt their despair was her sole responsibility.

Casimir raised his hand and a hush fell across the crowd. "A new age has been brought to The Kingdom. An age of wealth and abundance; prosperity brought from the shadows of war. It is time to unify and thrive together as one. I am proud to re-introduce your Queen." He gestured to Liana and bowed slightly.

On the other side of Liana walked up the man whom Casimir spoke with previously. Spectators in the crowd whispered amongst themselves as he held out the small square box to Casimir. Casimir opened it and revealed a sparkling tiara. He carefully removed a frail, white-gold band from the box and placed it on Liana's head. The deep sapphire jewels sparkled on her pale skin and came to a point in the middle of her forehead.

He stepped back, took her hand in his, and held it up as a small amount of applause sounded through the crowd. Still holding Casimir's hand, Liana stepped forward slightly.

"A new era has been presented to us. We must embrace it."

An unintended sharpness in her words cut through the crowd and visibly rippled outward. The spectators, first unsure, slowly began to roar with cheers and applause.

She smiled triumphantly at the approval as her thoughts centered, *There's still a spark left! Now, if they can stay alive long enough.*

Casimir's grip tightened painfully on hers. With a stiff smile, he turned and roughly steered Liana back into the castle. The large doors pulled shut behind them and with his gaze on his feet, Casimir motioned for the men around to leave. Liana looked around confused. As the last of the guards disappeared down the hall, Casimir turned toward her.

He spat his words angrily in her face, "What do you think you're doing?"

"Wha..? I..." Words failed her as fear rose again and she backed away from him. He gripped her shoulder and moved in close to her. She found herself against the wall.

"I have worked far too hard for you to screw this all up now." His voice, though lowered, cut cruelly

Darkness

through the air. "No rallying the troops." He gestured to the closed doors before them. "No snooping around, plotting, *lying*." His voice escalated as he spoke and struck deeper with each word. "You just be a good…little…Queen." His hand smacked the side of her neck sternly with each word. "Understand?"

Liana stood utterly still and though she tried, she couldn't speak. *What did he want me to say,* she thought to herself, *yes master?*

"Perfect," he said to her before he turned and walked away.

She stood with her mouth slightly open and questioned herself on what just transpired. He looked over his shoulder at her briefly as he walked in the distance before he turned a corner. His footsteps echoed into the void and before long, it was silent again.

Liana stood in the stillness, utterly confused as she turned about the empty room. Slowly, her footsteps carried her on as she lost herself deep in thought; her head bowed the more she contemplated.

Wouldn't he, she wondered to herself, *want their approval? Did he not want them to celebrate?*

Lost, searching eyes, darted about the room just as quickly as her thoughts, seeing what was before her but unable to truly focus. If only she could unlock the secret of what it would take to please him, maybe then she could find a way to survive.

A glow emanated suddenly in the dark. It caught Liana's wandering eyes, holding their attention, and with it, silenced her misled thoughts. A peaceful warmth washed over her and drew her in. As she moved closer, a faint whisper danced playfully in the air and welcomed her.

The Light Within

"Stop!" A voice boomed from behind her.

Immediately, Liana turned from the light to find several guards at her side. Countless hands gripped her arms, waist, and neck. They hauled her from the corridor and the Light that called out to her.

Unaware of what was happening, or even where she was, Liana instinctively yielded to the group. Like countless times before, her head dropped as she retreated within herself. They heaved her back into the darkened chamber she was in just moments ago and threw her to the ground.

With a groan, she lifted herself to a kneeling position just as heavy boots approached her. She followed the black, high ankle, leather boots up to the dark, decorated uniform jacket of Casimir's most prestigious Commander. Her eyes instantly fell back to his boots just as he instructed her to do countless nights before. She wasn't sure his name, or rather assigned letter, for he demanded she call him Darkness.

Liana retreated further inside herself as he reached for her. His massive hand wrapped around her throat and raised her to her feet. The burning grip released her and permitted her to breathe as she stood on her own. His hand wrapped around the back of her head and wrenched a fistful of hair that he used to pull her into his furious face.

"Never go in there!" Enraged shouts washed over her unresponsive face. "Do you hear me? It's dangerous!"

Liana slowly nodded but her lack of response to the moment seemed to infuriate him further.

"Take her," he growled.

His words shook her as he shoved her into the hands of the numerous guards that surrounded them. A

Darkness

sadistic grin radiated through the shadows of his face as he watched them forcefully drag Liana off.

o　　　o　　　o

Raspy, uneven breaths echoed in her ears through the darkness. The slightest movement, even to draw in life-giving air, spread debilitating pain through every fiber of her being. Liana gradually opened her eyes to find the vaulted ceiling of the King's Chambers glaring back from above. Her achy laugh cut through the air as she rolled to her side.

She whispered aloud to the light within, wondering if it was even listening, "Why can't you let me die?"

The welcomed silence around her was interrupted again as she laughed to herself and shook her head in disbelief. Pain and confusion swirled in her mind as she pulled herself to sit against the wall.

Though she spoke in hopes of gaining clarity on the swirling questions in her mind, her words made no sense as she uttered them, "What did I do? Why is he so angry with me?"

Liana stiffened; eyes wide as a rush of air swept across her from the heavy wood that crashed open and slammed directly beside her, against the wall. She drew her knees to her chest and clung to her gown as Casimir marched into the room. He took a few strides inside before he turned around and set eyes on Liana.

Instantly, a look of disgust spanned his face and accented his words, "What are you doing? Get up!"

The icy clutches of fear gripped her yet again; it froze her muscles and forbid the slightest movement. He crossed the room quicker than she could comprehend. Confusion and panic muddied her thoughts as he gripped her arms and yanked her to her feet.

The Light Within

"Disgusting," he hissed furiously.

He shoved her against the wall before he released her and let his trembling hands linger in the air near her head. They remained there, in that moment of fear and uncertainty as his hands fought against his thoughts.

"Why do you make me *do that!*" As his words boiled over, his hand tightened to a fist and drove against the wall next to her head.

She released a long, quiet breath as her eyes connected with Casimir and she saw the pain concealed deep within his eyes. Immediately, he turned from her, shook his bloody hand, and threw the other in the air.

"I swear!" A laugh traced his heightened words before cutting off abruptly. Casimir stopped in the middle of the room, took a deep breath, then turned back to Liana and continued with a harsh tone, "It's like you have no *idea* how to be a Queen! Sitting on the filthy floor like an animal." He gestured to her disheveled state.

She looked down at her dress and suddenly noticed the streaks of dust and blood that tainted that pale blue, worn, and snagged silk that hung carelessly on her form. Liana ran her hands along her waist and adjusted her sleeves as Casimir turned from her and continued.

He bowed his head and rubbed his temples as he whispered loudly to himself, "It's like you want these people to suffer."

Liana jerked her head up and glared at the back of his head. "I-"

"See? There you go again!" He crossed the room as he spoke and gradually closed the ground between them. "Interrupting me! Speaking over me. You always have to have the last word," he continued at a rapid pace, shouted circles around her, and threw his hands up as he spoke.

Darkness

"Have to one-up me! You're insane!" He laughed and shook his head. "No wonder the Kingdom fell with *you* as its leader."

Her mouth remained open; words silenced but everything inside her ached to retort as her eyes fell to the ground in contemplation. Fear and doubt waged a war inside, threatening mass atrocities should she refuse to intervene. Attempting to survive the attack, her attention shifted internally, and her face painted the scene for him to see.

He grinned as he observed her and backed away while he gestured for someone in the hall to enter. Alluring aromas carried by a shining silver cart moved past Liana and caught her attention. The knots in her stomach immediately relaxed and let out an eager growl of approval. Jumping at the sudden noise, she reached for her stomach as if she could silence it. She glanced up nervously as the echo reached across the room to Casimir, who grinned at her from the sofa where the cart now rested.

"Hungry?" he asked with an air of concern as he chuckled and patted the cushion next to him for her to join.

I would rather starve, she thought to herself through narrowed eyes as her stomach cried back in protest.

Eyes locked on hers, Casimir reached out and lifted the cover from the tray. Scents of chocolate and peanut butter pancakes raced across the room assaulting her senses.

A defeated sigh released Liana from the wall. She broke her gaze with Casimir and returned her attention to the floor. As she reluctantly crossed the room and sat next to him, he held a small plate out to her. She reached for it and took the plate slowly, but his grip remained. He searched for her evading eyes and spoke very slowly.

"We both agree we want what's best for The Kingdom, right?" He searched again for her eyes as he spoke and as she listened, she turned her attention to him and nodded.

"Then I think it's best you let me do the speaking for now."

Her brow furrowed as he spoke, for she couldn't understand the harm in her speaking.

He raised the palm of his free hand at her defensively and a gentle reassurance washed through his words as he spoke, "Just for now. I'm just saying. Everything is very tense. It would be best if you were that *silent* presence and let me do the speaking." His voice elevated slightly in response to her raised eyebrows of protest. "So that we appear unified, to unite the Kingdom."

Her eyes narrowed again as she released the plate. His words made sense, but at the same moment were senseless. She retreated to her thoughts as he angrily slammed the rejected plate back onto the tray and sent shards of ceramic across onto the floor.

"Fine!" He stood suddenly and slammed the lid over the tray before he gestured for the servant to remove it.

Liana looked up as the servant wheeled the tray away. The lingering scents cruelly intensified her stomach's distressed state. Casimir crossed the room and stood in the doorway, his back to Liana.

"I can see you need a bit more time to think about things." He flicked his hand with a sudden jerk and the

Darkness

doors slammed shut behind him. The loud bang reverberated across the room and shook Liana.

Obedience, she questioned herself, *in exchange for food?* She laughed in disbelief as she fell sideways on the couch, exhausted.

Time slipped by in distorted fragments. The silence weighed over her and allowed the light to slip from the room without her notice as she stared insistently at the wooden door. Her mind and stomach took turns reminding her of her current diminished state. They wore on her and kept her from drifting into the relieving isolation of sleep.

After quite some time, Liana pushed herself from the couch to sit up. She took a deep breath and looked around as she realized almost utter darkness surrounded her.

When she glanced about, she could see nothing but as she focused on the objects in the dark, her vision adjusted, and it was as if she were walking in the light. In a state of disbelief, Liana got to her feet. Concentrating as she moved; she walked about the room with ease in the darkness.

With a renewed sense of excitement, she crossed the room to the wooden door and grasped the heavy ornate handles. Pausing for a moment, she leaned her ear to the wood and listened carefully. After several rhythmic pulls of her own breath being the only sound to meet her ears, she quickly yanked at the door.

Locked.

She pulled again; yanking and shaking the handle with all her strength, only for the door to hold fast. Growling out in frustration, she pounded her fist into the wood over her head. As her flesh connected with the

The Light Within

wood, she heard a deep breath, quietly draw from the other side of the door. She snapped her head to the side and listened carefully. Another long pull of air, barely audible through the door, softly and gradually filled the being across from her.

Liana silently dropped to her knees and pressed her temple to the cold, stone floor. She squinted as she tried to see through the small sliver of an opening between the floor and wood of the door. Leather boots stood incredibly still with their heels against the door. She swallowed the large knot in her throat and stood.

"Darkness," she whispered through the wood to him, calling him as he desired. She felt him stir on the other side, confirming her suspicion.

"Open the door," she said boldly as she took a few steps back and her heart raced on uncontrollably.

Silence ticked on tauntingly and she worried he wouldn't take the bait. A click of the handle echoed across the room suddenly and caused her heart to skip. The door creaked open slightly, leaving a small gap but not advancing any further. She stood there a moment before she rushed over to it. Peering through the gap, she immediately locked eyes with him.

"What?" His growl of a question crawled across the short distance between them over Liana's skin and sent a shiver down her spine.

"Please," as her timid whisper visibly excited him, she swallowed uncomfortably but continued, "I'm hungry." With her last words his expression, barely visible in the shadows, went to its uniformed coldness.

"Will you be accepting your King's reasonable request?" He asked through the door with an almost rehearsed air to his words.

Darkness

Caught off guard by his question, Liana let a short laugh escape her before she responded, "I won't be silent."

"I was hoping you'd say that." A low snarl of a laugh rose from his chest as he forcibly shoved open the door.

Startled, Liana jumped back as his form filled the frame of the door. In a state of panic, she looked around for something to defend herself, but it was too late. He caught the door before it could hit the wall, immediately threw it shut, and closed the distance to her in one large stride. His massive hand swung, clenching under her jaw, and lifted her into the air to meet his eyes.

"Can't we…" she gasped as his grip tightened, "work… something out?"

"You have no *idea*," he snarled in her face, "what you're up against, little light."

Unflinching, she choked her words out in between gasps, "Clearly, you… don't either."

As her nails dug into his hands, her legs kicked out in a pointless protest while a low growl rose in him. He pulled her in closer, his face now beside hers, and opened his mouth slightly, drawing a long and unsettling breath.

"This disobedience *must* be corrected." His haunting whispers left a cloud of fear as they settled over her.

The shadowy darkness that constantly resided over him, began to creep down the sun-worn skin of his arms towards Liana. Instantly, his eyes locked with hers and held her captive.

For the first time, she could see his face, unclouded by the unceasing shadow around him. His bright green eyes longed for her to understand. His elongated, tanned face entertained a thick, black beard that curled up as he smiled to show his rows of pointed and blood-stained teeth.

"You will submit," he whispered sternly as he set her on her feet and released her.

Her eyes remained locked on him as he backed away from her. Long locks of dark curls fell over his substantially defined shoulders. With each step he took from her, an uneasy feeling grew within her and the grip around her throat persisted. As a sinister look flitted past his stare, she grabbed for her throat and her eyes instantly widened.

An icy, tar-like substance wrapped around her throat where his hand rested moments before. As she pulled at it, the dark substance, almost a liquid, yet a smoke-like shadow, spread to her hand and crept up her arm.

Alarmed, she looked to the Commander and searched in vain for his help. His eyes remained fixed on her, excitement stirring in him as he watched her struggle. He lingered in the doorway as the horror spread over her face. With one final grin, he quietly pulled the door shut between them.

The shadows stretched across her flesh and seeped into her pores. She brushed at her hands and arms, desperate to dislodge the substance. Horrific, dark tendrils slithered across her skin and tightened their grip the harder she pulled at them. Disturbed screams escaped the pits of her stomach as she frantically dug and clawed at her flesh, pleading it to resist. The more she struggled, the faster it consumed her until her voice cut off, stifled by the darkness that overtook her.

Instantly the room went black, and an eerie silence resonated around her. Liana jerked her head up and

Darkness

looked around in vain. She pulled in several shallow breaths as she closed her eyes and pulled her knees to her chest. Before long she took a deep breath and laid her weary head forward on her legs.

"Weeeeeak..." a faint whisper echoed around the room before it settled over her.

Liana jumped as the words hit her and lifted her head to look around. Seeing only the darkness, she let out a heavy sigh that was quickly swallowed up by the silence. Questioning if she had even heard anything, Liana laid her head back down on her arms.

"...sssstupid girl."

Another whisper cut by her ear with a hiss and sent Liana instantly upright. Her eyes went wide with fear as she clutched her knees tighter to her chest like a statue. Liana held her breath as she listened intently. Long, raspy breaths rumbled behind her and edged closer to her with each slow pull until she could feel the creature lingering over her shoulder. Her stare remained fixed on the darkness in front of her, for fear of what the creature would do, should it gain her attention.

Twisted whispers gurgled from the creature; they churned around Liana and echoed through her mind, "Not so different... you and I."

"I am *n-nothing* like you," Liana stumbled over her angry whispers as she turned her head toward the creature.

"Liar!" A piercing shriek emitted from every direction in the surrounding darkness.

Liana flinched and covered her ears as she desperately tried to block out the deafening noise that sent pain shooting through her body. The creature wailed on incessantly as she struggled to block the clamor from her mind. Long, bony fingers slid along Liana's arms towards her hands as she struggled to shake them off. As the grips of the creature reached her wrists, it yanked her hands from her head and shoved her face-first to the ground.

Immediately, countless voices around her shouted, "Listen…listen…listen!"

"No!" she cried back in protest and struggled in vain beneath the creature as it pinned her wrists to her back.

Laughter from countless dark beings sounded all around her, laced by whispers from several creatures that lurked beyond her unseeing eyes, "Weak… stupid girl… LISTEN."

The sinister creature that held her in place, growled from above as it forcibly turned her head and whispered in her ear, "Everyone around you dies…"

Instantly, the legion of voices went into an uproar of screams around her, "Dangerous girl… unstable…" She could hear their talons and claws while they jumped and danced about her and created a whirlwind of commotion that confused and disoriented Liana. "Must be locked away… contained… dangerous!"

"Liar!" she shouted back desperately.

"Am I?" The creature laughed with its words, released Liana's arms as it sat on her back, and depressed her weak form into the cold stone floor.

Liana struggled under the creature's weight as she tried to catch her breath in short gasps. She wiggled desperately as she felt the beast drag its long, bony digits over her skin and up to her face. The commotion around her continued to grow until she felt the creature dig its nails into her temples and all went silent.

Darkness

Gradually her vision returned, though she remained paralyzed in place. Liana looked around her and realized it wasn't the King's Chambers where she stood. Before her, stood a vast field of wildflowers and trees, all in full bloom. She took a deep breath and relaxed as the sweet scents of the blossoms filled the air.

She questioned herself as she looked around, and as she looked down to her hands, found she held a muffin. Further confused, Liana shook her head, dropped the muffin to the ground, and looked up.

"Nicolai!" she shouted excitedly at Nicolai who stood before her.

"What?" he asked playfully and smiled at her.

"I… you…" She shook her head and stared at him in disbelief.

His reassuring smile drew her in and held her momentarily captive. Her mind raced on in confusion as she stared on in disbelief.

"Was that all a nightmare?" She asked as she stepped closer to him, "Is it really you?"

She reached for him as she closed the distance between them. The closer she came, the more tense she grew. As he reached out for her, she saw his dirt and blood-stained hands.

"You…" She stopped in her tracks and suddenly realized what was occurring. "You… can't be here."

He laughed again and smiled at her as he spoke, "Don't be stupid. I'm right here." He opened his arms wider, and insisted she embrace him.

"Liar! It's a trick!" she shouted, turned around, and squeezed her eyes shut as hard as she could.

Nicolai's voice was instantly in her ears, whispering softly; his breath crawled down her neck with each unsettling word, "*You* killed me... it's *your* fault we all died!"

"No!" she shouted and reached for her ears, but the creature held her in place.

She opened her eyes, only to be met with utter darkness again. Struggling, she kicked and squirmed against the foul beast that pressed her into the ground. The more she moved, the angrier and more desperate the creatures around her grew. Every fiber in her being screamed out for her to resist as she struggled on. Though exhaustion quickly set in as her weakened form made no progress against her captor's restraint.

The legion relentlessly swarmed around her and shouted, "Dangerous girl! Unworthy!"

The sinister creature lingered over her shoulder and whispered into her ear, "Casimir is protecting these people from *you*..."

She could feel the dark wisps of black smoke dripping from its fangs, down onto her flesh as it seeped its lies into her pores. Like a feeble insect caught in a vast web that it could never hope to escape, she persisted. It drew closer and closer; its gurgling, stale breath blew in nauseating gasps. It lingered and allowed its massive fangs to scrape against her cheek.

"You must obey your King," it hissed back threateningly.

Liana squeezed her eyes shut and searched herself for any fragment of hope as she silently pleaded for the creature to halt its attacks. The roar around her gradually subsided to a low growl as the voices faded into each other. In time, they were mere whispers of wind that howled in the distance.

Darkness

The creature slowly lifted its weight from her and pulled the darkness around into one monstrous being that lingered over Liana. Fearing she'd rouse the beast again by even the slightest glance, Liana forced her eyes shut even harder. Careful to avoid the cold wisps of lingering darkness as she moved, she raised herself from the cold stone floor to a sitting position.

She found the less she focused on the snarling beast that rose above her, the quieter its threats became. Liana focused on her own breath; long, calculated pulls of the cool air filled her mind and body. An almost silent creaking of the door behind her implored her for attention. As she shook it from her concentration, she saw a faint image growing in her mind.

Swirling about her hazy sight was Casimir, only he didn't seem like the Casimir she'd seen. The harder she focused, the more the scene revealed. He laughed and spoke merrily with her as they walked over white and blue marbled streets.

Casimir paused frequently and shook the hands of countless individuals as they approached him. The scene before her quickly faded to that of a massive celebration where Casimir enthusiastically toasted to a massive crowd. She saw herself before Casimir, blushing and bowing to him before they danced happily about.

A warmth surrounded Liana as she watched from a distance and quietly contemplated what she was being shown. She yearned for the scene to become reality; what she wouldn't give to see everyone happy and safe.

You have, a whisper echoed in her mind and focused her attention, *the power to make this reality.*

"Please help," she whispered aloud and pleaded for the power inside her to intervene.

The Light Within

Her attention focused on the scene that danced in her head and the edges blurred as she slipped back to the darkness of her closed eyelids. As she raced to recall the details, confusion distorted her memory. She suddenly found it impossible to envision herself and Casimir ever laughing together, even when she thought back to their least complicated times.

Liana wrenched her eyes open. Her gaze immediately met none other than the cold green eyes of Darkness. She didn't flinch, but remained nose to nose with him, unblinking. They both remained motionless, each unwilling to concede to the other. Slow, calculated breaths of air charged Liana as she implored her overly energetic heart to return to a safer rhythm.

He growled, without breaking focus on her, "Will you reconsider?"

Fuck no, the words leaped in her head angrily as she dared her lips to comply.

Liana held his gaze, unmoving for several moments until he shifted uncomfortably in front of her. Slowly, she dropped her eyes to the floor and nodded once, willing to accept whatever was presented before her if it meant sparing her even an ounce of further suffering.

A short, almost disappointed, grumble left his chest as he stood and yanked her to her feet. She remained as still as a statue as he ripped her gown from her form and displayed her pale curves for him to inspect. He threw the shreds of fabric to the floor in a heap at her feet and walked around her with a triumphant smile.

Eyes fixed on the ground, Liana stood, arms crossed in front of herself, terrified of the suffering he could inflict on her in an instant, should he desire. He

Darkness

came to a rest behind her and snapped his fingers before he walked to the entrance of the room.

As he crossed the room, she heard the footsteps of another approach. Once closer, the individual let out a quiet, concerned gasp. Unmoving, Liana kept her eyes on the ground as the shuffling of feet echoed from behind her. The familiar dark brown ringlets of hair caught Liana's attention as W stooped in front of her. She held open a navy-blue gown right above the floor and waited for Liana to step in.

Slowly, she raised her aching leg and carefully stepped into the opening in the gown. She twisted to lift her other leg and the room spun about her. Instantly, she reached out and caught W's shoulder for support. W looked up to her with a reassuring smile but as her eyes settled on Liana, a troubled look grew on her face. She cleared her throat and focused her attention back on the gown at Liana's feet.

Quickly and carefully, W pulled the heavy gown up Liana's form and let the strapless, corset bodice rest on her hips as she secured the lace back. The gown pinched and dug into Liana's skin with every movement and stole her breath as W finished lacing it. She slowly clasped her hands in front of her waist and waited patiently as W meticulously adjusted the beading and folds of fabric.

Periodically W stepped away from Liana and stared at her while deep in thought, like an artist applying the finishing touches to their canvas. Chin in hand, W nodded to herself and strode with purpose across the room towards the shower.

Liana curiously looked up from the floor as W disappeared around the corner. Her eyes, free from their previously secured position, slowly traced the details around the room. Warm hues of orange and pink light broke through the drawn balcony curtains and cut through the darkness of the room.

She followed the small beams of light as they illuminated the small dancing forms of dust that lingered in the air. Her eyes followed to the floor where the last of the beams' light faintly shone. She closed her eyes and took a deep breath as a warmth spread over her face.

She felt W back at her side as she gently dabbed around her head with a warm cloth. Liana remained, eyes closed, as W lifted her chin and cleaned the stains from her skin.

"What did they do to you?" she whispered under her breath.

Though Liana assumed W wasn't searching for a response, the question lingered uncomfortably in the air. Her cheeks flushed as embarrassment took hold. She tucked her chin down and returned her wide-eyed, distant gaze to the floor.

Without batting an eye, W elevated Liana's chin again and finished up with the cloth before she let go. Liana's gaze remained fixed upward as W worked until she heard the distant impatient growls of Darkness echo from the doorway.

A glance over her shoulder confirmed his presence and she wondered if he had even left. Liana gulped uneasily as W pulled the pins from Liana's hair, loosened the braids, and let her wavy locks fall over her shoulders. With haste, she ran her fingers through Liana's hair, secured a portion of the top, and allowed the rest to flow over her exposed shoulders. The blanket of hair wrapped a comforting barrier over her unpleasant situation and brought a timid smile to her.

Darkness

"Let's go," the barking command boomed through the air as Darkness approached her.

She quickly slid on the shoes W placed before her and as she turned, caught the reassuring smile of W before her eyes returned to the ground. Liana shifted unflinching, around Darkness, who had moved to stand directly behind her. Through the taps of her heels against the stone floor, Liana heard as Darkness commanded W to remain behind. Taking a deep breath, Liana raised her chin slightly, eyes fixed on the floor, and walked into the dark corridor.

Only a few steps into the hall and he was right beside her. His massive arm swept behind Liana and motioned for the guards, stationed just outside, to remain behind. The Commander moved his arm around Liana and clamped his hand just above her elbow. He yanked her into his solid torso as they walked.

His deep voice echoed around them and grew in intensity as they walked down the low stone passageway, "He will be pleased you finally decided to join us."

As they walked along the gently sloping path, the air around them grew warmer with hints of alluring aromas of delectable food and floral perfumes. They walked on for quite some time before they rounded another corner, and a black curtained entryway came into view. It looked like nothing special, except that it was heavily guarded. Liana hesitated as Darkness steered her toward it. His hand slowly slid from her arm to her back and shifted her focus as he shoved her through the curtain.

Immediately Liana jerked her head up; her wide eyes and rosy cheeks met the gaze of nearly everyone seated in silence before her. Her eyes moved along the faces, painted, and decorated to a glittering perfection; all seated around a far-reaching, black, and gold marbled table.

They all froze at her sudden entrance and remained unmoving; eyes fixed on Liana. Mouths hung open mid-sentence and lavish goblets frozen mid-drink. She followed each of their faces along the table until her eyes rested directly in front of her.

At the head, across the far-reaching, food-strewn table, leaned an unaware Casimir. His bored gaze, partially obstructed by his tousled hair, lingered on the sparsely clad ladies that sat near him.

Liana raised her chin slightly as she watched him in his oblivious state. He leaned to the side of his massive chair with one leg kicked up on the arm of it. His elbow propped against the table with his chin in palm while he swirled his drink in his other hand. As the silence permeated the room, he sat up on his throne and followed the faces around him to Liana.

Candlelight around the dim room glinted and reflected off the crystal beading of her gown, through the dark blue tulle that crossed over her chest before it glimmered across her open neckline. The light created a captivating glow about her and held his gaze.

He slowly lifted his hand and motioned for her. As his hand dropped, she shifted, and the room fell from her trance. Hushed whispers and clinking dinnerware instantly filled the room around her.

The cold clutch of Darkness urged her forward as he pushed through the heavy curtains behind her. With his touch, her face instinctively went flat. As her eyes made their way to the floor, the defeating, smug grin from Casimir burned in her mind.

Darkness

Grateful for the grandeur of the table, Liana fought to ignore the many whispers. The gown fought back while she tried to breathe and caged her from the relief a deep breath could bring; stabbing at her if she dared to seek it.

She looked up from her internal struggle to find she now stood before Casimir, who motioned for her to sit. Head slightly lowered, she glanced up to meet his gaze and was instantly captivated.

He smiled at her as she absently lowered herself; mesmerized by his dark eyes that now swirled with deep red and flecks of gold. He leaned deeper in his high-backed chair and took a long drink before his words finally cut through the room.

He scoffed into the cup that lingered near his mouth, "I take it we've reached an agreement?"

As he spoke, the icy hands of the Commander brushed along her open neckline and arranged her hair behind her back. Her attention remained fixed on Casimir as Darkness moved the chair beneath her and pushed her closer to him, into the table.

Her heart practically thumped from her chest, yet she held Casimir's gaze and elevated her chin slightly. Just when she thought he might explode, she nodded once. Eyes still fixed on his, she reached for the glass before her and raised it to him.

Triumphantly revitalized, Casimir sat straight up and lifted his goblet out to Liana before he turned to the table. His silent guests stared on, hanging on his every move, and held their glasses out to him.

"Your Queen."

His foreboding voice was drowned out by the cheers of the guests around, who, with great enthusiasm, clinked their glasses and sang out to the Queen.

Chapter 3
Late Night Stroll

"My Queen." The man knelt before her addressed her briefly before he rose to his feet.

Liana nodded to him as he shuffled backward a short distance. Guards appeared at his side and turned him before they escorted him from the open throne room. She looked over the countless faces that stood, lined before the throne. They stretched off into the distance in an infinite line of desperate souls. Each varied drastically from the last but all pleaded the same request, for any help that could be spared.

Liana watched silently, as previously instructed, and nodded as she was addressed, one by one. Yet another worn individual shuffled to the base of the steps and rested at the foot of the throne before dropping to his knees. His tears cleaned the dust and dirt from his face as they raced down his sunken cheeks.

"Please, your highness, my family. Please, your Majesty, we have no food. The fires consumed all the crops. My family," his shaking hand gestured behind him as he continued, "the people, we are all starving." He kept his eyes on the ground as he slowly choked his words out through the tears.

A short sigh of irritation burst from Casimir and caught Liana's attention. She glared sideways as Casimir rolled his eyes and waved his hand, indicating for the man to stand. When the man did not budge, for his eyes remained on the ground, Casimir gestured to the guards, who yanked the distraught man to his feet.

Late Night Stroll

"We will add your grievance to our list of citizen concerns for consideration during the deliberation to formulate a plan to stabilize the Kingdom. Someone will reach out to you and your family as soon as we have a solution." Casimir wore a smile of reassurance as he nodded to the man.

"Thank you so much, your highness!" The man nodded and bowed several times before he turned to Liana and bowed again. "My Queen. Your presence lifts our spirits." The man raised his head and smiled at Liana before he bowed to Casimir. The guards half-drug, half-carried him from the throne room.

The small, reassuring smile that remained fixed on Liana's face wavered as she watched the scene play before her. Frustration mounted as the oblivious citizens shuffled through Casimir's charade, completely unaware of his true intentions. Yet another person knelt before her as she nodded absentmindedly.

"Your highness," the stern voice reverberated through the throne room and drew Liana's attention to the thin, short in stature individual that knelt before her.

The Commander boomed from the opposite side of Casimir as he unsheathed the sword that hung from his hip, "How dare you not address your King!"

Alarmed by the sudden outburst, Liana jerked her head and glared at Casimir. With a growl of frustration, he sat up on his throne. He rolled his eyes at her, then waved his hand dismissively to the Commander, who sheathed his blade with an angry fervor.

Liana nodded to the bold individual before her, as Casimir's glare burned into the side of her head. The individual shook the grasps of the several guards that swarmed during the Commander's outburst from their frame and stood boldly.

"Your highness," they bowed slightly to Casimir but kept their sights on Liana as they spoke. "Please, we need help. There are still thousands out there," the individual's dark, boney arms gestured behind them as they spoke. "All wounded and dying as we speak. We need supplies, your Majesty, and support." As their words finished, they dropped their closely shaven head, and waited patiently for a response.

Casimir nodded to the individual as he shifted in his throne and after a moment of silence, voiced his rehearsed line, "We will add your grievance to our list-"

Fierce eyes of deep brown remained fixed on the stairs at the feet of the throne as they spoke clearly, yet with haste, "With all due respect, your Highness, this isn't something that can wait for your committee to deliberate away, assuming the issue will resolve itself. People are dying. We need immediate support."

Casimir furiously stood and lifted his hand for the guards to take the individual. As the guards took the brave one, their eyes locked with Liana's pleadingly. Liana stood suddenly next to Casimir and raised her hand to the guards.

"Wai-" She cut herself short as Casimir snapped his head in her direction and fixed his eyes on hers.

As his glare burned into her, she slowly closed her mouth and lowered her hand. A myriad of thoughts swarmed her mind as she lowered her gaze to the floor and sluggishly sunk back into the throne next to Casimir.

"To the dungeons with this one," Casimir waved dismissively. "That's enough."

Late Night Stroll

Casimir nodded to the guards at the doors who led the disgruntled crowd from the throne room. As the grumbles of the crowd gradually ebbed, Liana stood and looked about the room for W or A, who usually arrived shortly after to escort her to her next task.

"Wait," Casimir spoke over his shoulder to Liana as she stood.

He lifted a hand slightly behind him, extended it in front of her, and blocked her from moving forward. Her jaw clenched at the command, though her eyes remained flat. As his outstretched hand came in contact with her stomach, she flinched backward away from his touch. Casimir threw a quick glance at her before he dropped his hand into a fist at his side.

While she stood perfectly still, she watched as the last of the individuals were escorted from the massive throne room. The murmurs faded away and left her with the hushed, intense words from the discussion that took place near her. Liana listened intently; her eyes fixed on a distant pillar as though she admired its detail.

The Commander questioned eagerly, "...and what of the tiny, defiant one?"

"All yours," Casimir spoke with an air of delight as he opened his arms up to his Commander.

When his final orders were given, he turned to Liana and his demeanor immediately shifted to that of an exhausted warden. Liana swallowed the lump in her throat as she turned toward Casimir. Her blank eyes remained fixed downward, focused on his hands as he stood silent before her. Terrible thoughts swirled in her mind of the horrors that Darkness had planned for this innocent, brave soul.

The Light Within

He won't listen to me, she thought to herself and stood quietly while the survivor inside her waged war against the protector. *He only listens to Darkness.*

Her eyes opened wider with realization. Instantly, her attention was drawn to Darkness, who smiled proudly over Casimir's shoulder at her.

"Please," she swallowed nervously again and bowed her head as she continued, "my King, please consider leaving that insignificant soul to waste away in the dungeons. Why waste more time and...resources?" As she spoke, she lifted her head and nodded to the Commander before she turned her gaze to Casimir. "Surely the message has been sent and his energy can be directed elsewhere?"

Casimir's expression changed from one of irritation to contemplation, as she spoke. His focus shifted over her shoulder as the three stood in silence. Liana glanced up to Darkness who stood firmly behind Casimir, eyes narrowed suspiciously and locked on her.

"After all," she continued as she stared daringly back at Darkness, "was it not *my* command that led to this individual's boldness?"

Casimir tilted his head at her final words and cut in, "Fine." He raised his hand to silence her and blocked Darkness from her view as he spoke, "Let the tiny one rot away and leave us."

He flicked his wrist, dismissing his Commander. As his hand fell, Darkness lunged over Casimir. He reached for Liana, grabbed her arm, and yanked her toward himself while he raised his fist in the air above her.

Casimir's voice boomed through the vast throne room, "Release her!"

Late Night Stroll

Instantly Darkness opened his grasp and released her, but let his open hand linger in the air.

As Liana moved away, Casimir closed in on Darkness and growled threateningly, "They'll be countless souls for you once it's done. Compose yourself!"

She rubbed her arm as she strained to listen to Casimir's orders. As he turned and walked toward Liana, she caught the threatening gaze of Darkness that loomed over his shoulder. Casimir quickly put an arm around her, turned her, and steered her away from the throne room, and his Commander.

Several twists and turns later, Casimir's strides finally slowed to that of a casual stroll. Liana looked up from her thoughts at the unusual pace to find they were in an open courtyard within the castle. Pillars lined the perimeter of the room and held a narrow section of marbled roof that gave way to grey skies at the center of the courtyard.

"Liana," Casimir began as he released the grip around her arm and continued to walk toward the center of the courtyard, "my unique… gem." He turned to her with a smile before he continued, "I know all this is a lot to adjust to."

As he reached the center of the room, he lowered himself to one of the many stone benches that were meticulously placed about. Casimir looked up to Liana, who still stood at the entrance, and quickly patted the stone next to him. Liana sighed and lowered her head with an eye roll as she approached Casimir. Slowly, she lowered herself to the cold stone and ensured enough space between them to draw his attention. As he began to speak again, she tilted her head and looked out to the shifting skies.

The Light Within

"Understand, it is important to hear the citizens' complaints. They must feel their voice is being heard enough that they are satisfied, but we simply cannot accommodate every silly request that comes to the throne." He laughed, slightly amused at the notion. When she didn't laugh with him, he looked over at her and followed her gaze upward.

She wondered to herself, *Every silly request? Starving... dying. What does he even consider serious then?* After a moment longer of contemplation her thoughts settled, *nothing that comes from them surely...*

Minutes of silence crept by before Casimir continued, "I-"

"But Casimir, I ju-" Feeling him stiffen next to her, she cut her sentence short.

"Go ahead," he spoke slowly through a clenched jaw as he turned his attention across the room.

"Forgive me for interrupting you, my King..." She lowered her head for a moment before she continued, "I just have a few concerns." Her voice lowered to that of a timid child and drew his attention.

Raised eyebrows of curiosity adorned a now smiling face as he turned and lifted her chin to meet his gaze. He let his hand fall to the gown on her leg and replied, "You have no need to worry."

"It's just the Comman-"

His laugh cut her words short, and after a moment, he tapped her leg and assured her, "Don't mind him. He is under my control. Think of him more of puppy being trained. Now, anything else I could put your mind at ease on?"

Late Night Stroll

"My love…" She let the words linger in the air while his smile grew before she continued, "if I may ask, what *really* happens next?"

Casimir chuckled lightly with his reply, "Of course! Each complaint is compiled to a list, which is brought to my council. Once we meet, we will consider each issue and what action should be taken against it. When that is settled, I hand select someone to execute each decision."

She nodded and intently listened as he spoke. *And by then the people will have all died,* she thought behind her flat stare that concealed the anger that burned within.

"Anyway," he said as he stood and looked about the room.

His gaze landed on A as she entered the courtyard. He watched her as she stood silent in the entrance, until she turned her back to them.

Casimir turned his attention back to Liana and continued, "I ensure all of those details are taken care of. Nothing to give another thought to."

She stood and nodded to him. He smiled down at her and gripped her arm for a moment in an awkward embrace before he turned and walked away.

Liana silently gulped before she spoke up again, "Cas-My love? Do you think I could… perhaps… I could see one of *those* too?"

Casimir froze in his steps and allowed the stillness of the air around them to resonate heavily. He turned to her and revealed a suspecting face that quickly gave way to one of internal humor as he spoke. "Oh, my dear gem, those are so stale and boring. I wouldn't want to weigh your pretty little head down with all of that nonsense."

"Oh," she chuckled as she spoke and nodded to him with a smile, "I understand."

The Light Within

He nodded back at her before he turned again to walk toward the door.

"I just-"

He paused, mid-step, without turning and waited for her to speak.

"I just enjoy watching you take charge. I have so much to learn." Liana watched from behind him with a smile of victory as his head lifted with her words.

After a moment, without turning, Casimir spoke, "Perhaps I could arrange something. If you *insist*. I *am* the King after all."

She took a deep breath and composed herself before she spoke quietly, "Only if you think it's best."

Casimir nodded, adjusted his clothing, and stood up taller before he walked off. His gaze lingered on A, whose stare remained fixed on the ground. As he approached, she stepped aside for him to pass. They remained still while his steady strides echoed in the distance. When they could hear no more, they both let out a massive breath of air. With the safety of the stillness in the air resting around her, Liana lowered herself to the nearby stone bench and heaved a massive sigh.

A gradually made her way across the room. Her eyes rested on the pillars around them as she sat next to Liana. A peaceful silence resounded around the pair, occasionally interrupted by a breeze that drifted from the open ceiling. A closed her eyes and took a deep breath while Liana stared off across the room.

"You know," Liana took a long breath before she continued, "these long purple vines once scaled those pillars and hung down all over this room." She paused briefly and traced the room with her eyes. "They had these

Late Night Stroll

unbelievable silver flowers that would bloom all over them in the winter."

A small measure of peace grew within her as she closed her eyes. She remembered walking through the vines and could almost feel them as she reached out with her hand. Sizeable, fluffy puffs of snow glided down from the open roof. When they connected with the vines, copious tiny, silver flowers opened and refracted the bright light around them.

As she replayed her fonder memories of the castle, a figure moved on the other side of the vines. The smile that dared grace her face quickly retreated as the familiar laughter of her true King raced through her memory. She opened her eyes at once, unable to bear the sight of him.

"Sounds beautiful," A said as she looked about the room. "Much better than the blank canvas it is now." Her focus turned upward, and for several moments, she stared out at the pale, overcast sky above them.

"Heh-yea…" Liana dropped her face into her hands as her elbows hit her knees. "Arietta…I…" She shook her head to herself while a war waged internally. As she weighed the danger her speech could subject A to, a murmur of her stifling thoughts slipped out, "If I had been paying attention… hadn't let them speak… I don't know!" She sat up straight and gripped the fabric of the gown at her knees in her frustrated fists.

A shook her head as Liana spoke. "It's best not to waste thought on all of that. You can't control what every person will say or do; when they will do it, how they will do it, how others react. Even if you could, you shouldn't."

Liana nodded as she stared upward with A and spoke again, "Now the people are worse off out there."

"They may be worse off for now but it was nec-"

The Light Within

"Their tiny warrior, the only one who was fighting for them, locked away… somewhere; probably in the Commander's bedroom!" Her face went sour as she spoke and was quickly replaced by horror with her last words. An image of the brave individual, surrounded by the legion of Darkness, tormented Liana's mind.

A sighed heavily as she stood. "Liana, I'll take care of it."

"What? Really?" Liana questioned and looked up with a spark of hope.

"Yes. I'll make sure they're taken care of. Now, please." She gestured toward the doorway and continued, "Please, don't waste any more energy on those thoughts…"

Liana stood with a nod before she followed A from the room.

o o o

Darkness surrounded her like the edge of an abyss that reached infinitely in every direction. Liana looked around, baffled. She had no clue how she had ended up where she was and further puzzled about the where aspect. Looking down, she noticed a perfect circle of light illuminated where she stood. She followed the shaft of light that radiated around her to the source above and could see nothing but a blinding brightness.

The commotion around her grew increasingly frightening and caused her heart to bounce frantically against her chest. Through the darkness surrounding her, Liana heard as the indistinct roaring winds broke into countless disturbing sounds. Sinister laughter gave way to growls of countless unseen beasts. A myriad of voices called out to her and suggested terrifying plans for her should the safety of her light cease.

Late Night Stroll

Liana trembled as she stood frozen in place and lifted her attention to the light overhead. When she concentrated, she could hear roars of excitement and applause coming from above. Liana took a deep breath and tried to calm herself from the madness that churned around her. As the air filled her lungs, she looked on in horror to the light above. The once perfect circle of light that emitted above her slowly waned and as it did, the chaos around her intensified.

Wake up, a whisper echoed urgently across her mind.

Of course, she thought as she realized this all had to be a dream.

She looked around in the dark and hoped to catch a glimpse of anything meaningful about this moment, should this be more than just a dream. The last of the circle above her suddenly cut off. As every fragment of light was removed from the room, countless hands reached for her, and fear instantly consumed her mind. They grabbed and tore at her flesh. Her screams only intensified their hunger. She dropped all her weight to a crouch just as something massive moved over her head. It narrowly missed her but collided with several of the beings around her and effectively loosened their hold on her.

Wake up, she thought insistently to herself and pulled her hands over her face, *come on!*

Liana looked up to find she remained in the nightmare. A mixture of fear and curiosity filled her eyes. The once dark abyss that surrounded her was now fully visible and revealed an elaborate decrepit chamber. As she concentrated around her, she could focus through the dark on the scene that played out. Still crouched and forgotten amidst the sudden attack, she shuffled quickly and silently to a nearby corner.

Wake up, the voice echoed stronger in her mind now.

She found safety in her unseen state and wanted to see more, so she dismissed it.

"Finally."

Liana heard the frightening growl rise from behind her and immediately recognized it. As she turned, she found the wall she thought was to her back was nonexistent. A massive hand reached from the shadows for her and gripped her entire throat in a suppressive hold. As her feet lifted from the floor, she kicked out, desperate to free herself. She wrenched and clawed at the fist that held her but could not escape their grip. He raised her slowly from the ground until her face was level with his.

"Just a dream!" she shouted and forced her eyes shut just before they met his.

Liana jerked into a sitting position and reached for her neck while she gasped for air. The sinister laughter from Darkness resonated around her and echoed off the walls of the King's Chambers. She shook her head, but she couldn't shake his presence. After several crippling minutes of trying to convince herself, she let out a short breath of a laugh.

Just a dream, she thought to herself and tried to recall the details.

Suddenly her eyes opened wide. She looked around the pitch-black room, able to see everything. She jerked her head to the side and, to her excitement, found Casimir fast asleep. Her gaze remained on his face for a moment, fascinated at the peacefulness that rested with him in his distant slumber.

Late Night Stroll

A small smile crept across her face as she studied him. It lingered only a moment, until her mind brought the large list of atrocities to attention, all committed by or in his name. Her eyes narrowed as she reexamined him in his defenseless state.

It would be so easy, the thoughts swirled around her mind, *just as he did to your King.*

She shook her head angrily and slid from the bed. Standing quietly at the edge, she watched him a moment longer before she turned. With the utmost silence, Liana yanked a heavy robe from the wall. She pulled it on and tied it as she crept across the room.

Liana paused, hand on the door, deep in thought, *Arietta said that room had the daggers in it...*

She glanced over her shoulder to the slumbering Casimir and heaved the door open. When he didn't stir, she poked her head out into the hall. She focused intently on the shadows that blacked out the way before her. Gradually she could make out the stone floors and pillared room before her.

Soft snores from the attending guards at the end of the hall brought a sense of excitement as Liana slipped from the room. Noiselessly, she crept down the hallway and took care to hold her breath as she edged by the oblivious guards. Once in the open corridor, she looked about, suddenly unsure which direction to go. She never stumbled on the room in her previous time here and wasn't exactly paying attention to how she'd ended up there in her recent encounters.

Her face lit up as she recalled they were near the throne room each instance. She paused only for a moment to listen for the distant snores before she turned and headed toward the front of the castle. Thick shadows

The Light Within

permeated every corner, in every area she passed through. Even the moon and stars hid in the night. They concealed Liana in opportune, absolute darkness.

Without interruption, she reached the throne room in a matter of minutes. Liana lingered on the edge of the massive hall and focused on the large marble throne that boorishly protruded from the smooth quartz floors. It had a golden glow about it that held her attention as she concentrated through the darkness. She stared on, wondering why everyone fought so hard for this seat.

Liana reached out and slid her hand along the smooth, cold arm of the throne. The sting of the chilled marble sent a shiver through her entire being. It caused her to jerk her hand away, slightly offended by the stone's assault. She turned immediately from the throne and pulled her icy hand into her chest defensively. Glancing up, she traced where she had entered the massive room, to her current position, unsure how she had crossed the distance so quickly.

Looking up from herself, Liana stared out over the massive throne room. The significance of the great hall appeared magnified from her current position. Overwhelmed by the weight of her thoughts as they swirled, she collapsed into the seat of the throne, deep in deliberation. The notion of removing Casimir seemed silly to her now. She had no clue how she could possibly help everyone on her own.

Look what happened, the thought surfaced in her mind, *last time you were left in charge.*

Liana shook her head and leaned forward on the throne. She dropped her face to her knees and pulled her arms over her head. She knew she had to do something;

she couldn't carry the weight much longer. With tears of frustration clouding her vision, she jerked her head up.

He must be stopped, she thought with more certainty now than ever.

As she stood, she envisioned the many faces of her people as though they stood before her; looking to her for any help she could spare. Several lengthy breaths filled her lungs as her mind swarmed with the endless possible implications of her choice.

No, she thought to herself, *I can't kill him… then I AM him.* She shook the idea from her head as she lowered it in thought and walked from the throne. *There must be another way.*

Countless plans formulated and immediately dissolved as her feet, now numb to the icy grasp of the stone floors, carried her through the dim castle. Strange scents lingered in the air. They dared to distract her from the deepest despairs her mind could whip up, should her retaliation fail or even the idea of it escape. Liana looked up from her spiraling thoughts and fanned herself from the warmth that rose in the air around her.

Her nose crinkled as a lingering stench registered with her. She lifted the sleeve of her robe and covered her face as she continued to walk on. With a glance behind her as she fanned herself, she wondered where she had wandered off to now. A crunch beneath her foot blocked out her sigh of annoyance. As she jerked up the base of her robe, she reached down and peeled a tiny orange leaf from her foot. When she dropped her robe to the floor, several leaves fluttered from her down the hall.

Eyes narrowed; Liana's head quickly pivoted in all directions. Unsure if she was sleeping or awake, she raised the delicate leaf in her hand out in front of her face. The

The Light Within

tiny stem tickled her fingertips as she twirled it back and forth. As the leaf swirled and danced in front of her, a black shimmer against the many oranges caught her attention. She quickly stopped the leaf and saw the small surface of orange was periodically broken up by tiny black veins that stretched from the stem.

Liana quickly dropped the leaf and looked up to the corridor before her. Countless leaves lay scattered through the darkness of the infinitely stretching, snug hall. Curiosity rose and pushed her to move quickly yet delicately over the crunching foliage. Only a few strides in and her inquisitively excited demeanor immediately halted. Mouth open, she froze in awe as she admired the massive tree that towered over her in the open passageway. While examining the branches above, Liana moved from the narrow hallway into the spacious foyer before her that housed the great tree.

New additions to the castle walls now reached far above the tree, closing the Kingdom off to the glory of its far-reaching boughs. Though it remained cut off from the elements, a furious wind still howled. It raced through the white and golden branches, as though it were trying to outrun something sinister. The winds ebbed and flowed as they rushed against her but the howling never ceased.

The branches jostled and clashed above her and sounded of a far-off battle that waged on. Only it wasn't far off; it was right before her. Her carelessness had brought the war right into her own home and it was destroying everything.

Liana dropped her head and fell to her knees at the base of the tree. The rotten, disgusting odor was inescapably present even more now. With a heavy cough, Liana looked up to see that the same dark substance that

Late Night Stroll

lingered on the leaf, also saturated the roots and base of the tree. It slithered up the tree's trunk, twisting like a dark, poisonous serpent that reached from the ground and threatened to pull under the tree.

As she focused through the darkness, she could make out a faint golden aura that wrapped around the tree. Slowly, she stood and reached for the tree. The closer she moved, the bright the glow shone. Cautiously, her fingers intertwined with the golden radiance and as they did, a warm and peaceful comfort enveloped her. As she relaxed, Liana took a deep breath, only to choke out several coughs at the stench that filled her lungs.

She pulled her sleeve over her face as she continued to cough. Amidst trying to catch her breath, Liana lurched forward and tripped over the clutter around her feet at the base of the tree. As she toppled toward the tree, she reached out and tried to slow her fall.

A scream of horror sprang from Liana as her exposed skin came in contact with the trunk of the tree. She immediately released it and let herself fall to the hard floor. In an instant, she felt the pain and suffering of thousands of souls as they cried out. Gasping and terrified by the images that burned in her mind, Liana hurriedly scooted away. Eyes wide for fear of what she may see should she close them, Liana sat for several moments trying to calm herself.

As her heart returned to a more desirable rhythm, she heard the faint sound of footsteps as they quickly approached. She got to her feet and turned toward the intruder. As she attempted to see them through the darkness, something heavy collided with her. Entwined in a jumble of limbs, Liana and the other slid across the open foyer. They came to a crushing stop against the solid wall as she desperately tried to free herself.

Her peeved whisper cut through the air as she fought harder to pull herself from the tangle, "Seriously?"

"Liana?" He called out to her over the roaring winds from the tree.

"Khius!" she exclaimed in an excited relief.

Though she wasn't thrilled about the situation with Khius, she'd much rather run into him than some of the others that lurked about. He groped awkwardly in the darkness for her and eventually grabbed her arm and pulled her to her feet. As they brushed themselves off, she examined him through the cover of the night's darkness.

"You," she growled as her skin flushed red.

"Wait, Liana please!" Khius held his hands up and turned blindly as he pleaded.

"How dare you," she shouted through the roar of the wind around them.

Through the seclusion of the shadows, she watched as Khius dropped to his knees, bowed his head, and spoke, "My Queen... I'm truly sorry."

A chill crept through the heat in the air as she crossed the short distance between them. She stood in front of him in silence and examined him through narrowed eyes. A strange sensation stirred within her in seeing Khius knelt before her as he did. Slowly, she approached and slid her hand around his neck. As her skin connected, a thousand memories flooded her mind and raced by her eyes in distorted fragments.

Blurry images of Liana at a distance in a sea of women in white faded to that of an angry crowd. As she pushed through the memory, she heard the voice of Khius emanate from her own body. She looked down to see his

Late Night Stroll

hands were hers and as she looked up again, she saw her own bloodied self, knelt before an angry council. Desperate shouts poured from her in Khius' tongue but only fell on an unhearing crowd. She watched, from his memory, as her banishment faded to a smiling face at the gym.

Tears filled her eyes as each memory flitted by and caught her in an ever-changing whirlwind of emotion. Her brow furrowed as she watched Khius' hands grip a steering wheel. A churning nausea twisted her stomach as she glanced over her shoulder. To her horror, she saw her incapacitated self on the floor of a cargo van, in between several hooded individuals. She felt the van lurch to a stop and Khius' voice boom from within as he stood.

As he reached out, the memory faded to his nervous grip on a machine. She watched as he looked up to Casimir who stood under blinding surgical lights. Fighting the urge to take the quartz blade from him and do it herself, she heaved a sigh just as Khius did.

The memories unfurled one by one and her once delicate touch against Khius' neck gradually tightened. She watched on as Khius slipped from the booming house party into the darkness of the trees to whisper something into the shadows.

Heart pounding, her fingernails dug into the flesh of the surrendering Khius as she watched his previous self willfully succumb to attackers in the woods while he stood over her. Looking behind, she saw through his memory, the horror on her own face as a gunshot fired in unison to her own debilitating scream. Not able to withstand a second more and suddenly aware of her hold on Khius, she quickly released him.

The Light Within

"You were working for the enemy the whole time!" she shouted through the tears and shakily backed away.

He spoke in a hurried hush; his voice barely carrying over the howling of the winds, "I was never working for the enemy."

Liana stared down at him in disbelief and shook her head with her reply, "You lie! I saw it all for myself! Tell me the truth!"

In one swift movement, she snatched Khius' wrist, still outstretched from pleading, and a deafening zap pulsed from her. His free hand reached in front of him for the ground as he collapsed.

In that instant, she heard as his warning echoed across their connection, *Casimir is here with us, be careful what you say!*

Liana tightened her grip, pushed a larger electrical pulse, and just before she released her grip, advised him, *Don't caution me, I don't care what he hears! Tell me the truth!*

Khius collapsed, face to the cold floor. He laid for several minutes and caught his breath before he responded, "I am working *with* him *for* the Kingdom."

"Here you go twisting words again! You helped the very one who killed your brother!" With her shout, she threw her hands in the air, turned from Khius, and paced with her swirling thoughts while she choked back tears.

Khius sighed, dropped his head, and spoke softly, "I owed it to him to get you back to your rightful place, at any cost. You're here, aren't you? That was my plan; get you here. I knew Nicolai would fuck it up, so I made sure you'd get here either way." As he spoke, Khius pulled himself to a sitting position.

"What?" she asked in disbelief.

Late Night Stroll

He lowered his head and shook it as he spoke, "You had to come back; I didn't care who brought you back. I thought I could control the situation."

Liana turned, crossed the room toward him, and questioned, "You ever think if you would've helped Nicolai instead, maybe all of this wouldn't have been fucked up?"

"Yea, I thought about that, and Nicolai still would've messed it up. Casimir wanted you here more than Nicolai did." He paused and allowed time for absorption before he cautiously continued, "Nicolai just wanted to *be* with you. Casimir had more motivation to get you *here*."

As Liana approached Khius, she glanced up to see that Casimir watched intently from across the room. She smiled slightly and looked down to Khius, quite sure she still held the secret of her new sight. She reached out, grabbed Khius' hand, and pulled him to his feet.

"How do I know I can trust you?" She let a few small sparks pass to Khius and spoke through their connection, *Yea, great job. Get me here to be held prisoner and tortured!*

He yelled out dramatically and dropped to a knee in front of her. After a moment of exaggerated breathing, through clenched teeth, he said, "Don't trust me."

Woah, a little overkill, she thought through her connection to Khius.

Well why, he concentrated on their connection, *do you have to keep shocking me? And yea, the situation isn't ideal.*

She stared at his unseeing gaze in disbelief, *Not ideal?*

He dropped his head and concentrated on his thoughts to Liana, *we all have our trials to endure.*

The Light Within

Before she could react, he yanked his hand from hers and sat back on his heels.

She dropped her hand to her side and examined him as she spoke, "How can I keep you around if I can't trust you?"

"Do you trust Darkness?" He paused and let his words linger in the air as she shifted uncomfortably in her silence. "Don't you keep him around?"

Liana rested her hand on his shoulder as she spoke, "Fine." She paused and took a deep breath before continuing sternly, "Don't make me regret this moment."

She let a trailing electrical current linger as she lifted her hand and before her connection with Khius was severed, she left him with her final thoughts, *you think you can work with the enemy, but you'll end up working for them if you aren't careful.*

Her hand lingered over Khius as her thoughts echoed in her own mind; their meaning resonated within and sent a shudder through her being. She pulled her robe tighter around herself and walked from the room. As she left the foyer and stepped into the hall, the roaring winds around the tree instantly ceased, as if suddenly unable to reach her ears. She paused momentarily at the sudden silence. With a slow swallow, she passed cautiously by Casimir, careful to hide her awareness of his presence.

As her distance from him grew, the silence around her assured her of her solitary state. With the stench of the tree far behind, she could breathe a little easier and moved quickly through the shadows. As she reached the corridor leading to the King's Chambers, she paused and held her breath while she peered around the corner.

No guards.

Late Night Stroll

Strange, the thought rose in her mind as she pulled her head back around the corner and pressed herself against the wall.

Maybe, she tried to convince herself as she stared blankly in the darkness around her, *they know I'm missing. Maybe they went to look for me. I'll go back to bed, tell them I've been there the whole time, and just deal with Casimir later.*

She nodded several times but failed to calm her nerves. Turning the corner, she cautiously made her way through the darkness. After a few steps, she shook her head and smiled as she looked up. With little effort, she concentrated on the shadows and willed them to recede. As the cover of darkness shifted, so did her fears.

Standing before her, blocking the passageway to the King's Chambers, towered the arms crossed, wide grinned, Darkness. A wrenching sickness in the pit of her stomach drove her quickly from the room. He did not pursue her right away but lingered for several moments. This was a game for him after all and he cherished the chase. His booming laughter reached her first; it taunted her and forced her further into the castle.

Turn after turn through the endless hallways, Liana quickly lost her bearings and found herself at the end of a hall with nowhere to go. A quick glance around the corridor yielded no possibility of a weapon. His laughter materialized around her again and moved her instantly to the nearest door. Without hesitation, she slid into the room and quietly closed the door.

A thick air of perfume instantly assaulted Liana's senses and encased her in a cloud of lavender and rose. She pulled the sleeve of her robe over her face and desperately fought back the urge to cough and rid her lungs of the smothering aromas. Still as a statue, Liana

The Light Within

remained, back against the wall, and listened intently for Darkness' pursuit. As his steps echoed further and further up the hall, she relaxed and allowed herself to breathe again.

Liana immediately regretted her decision and fought back the desperate scratches in her throat that begged for relief. She pulled both of her sleeves in her hands, cupped them over her mouth, and quietly coughed. The distant steps behind her came to an immediate halt and sent a jolt of fear through her.

Concentrating on the floor before her, she silently tiptoed across the open space. Just as she neared the other side, she heard the soft thuds of the door behind her as it opened and shortly after, closed. As her senses grew accustomed to the perfume around her and the silence persisted, she took another deep breath.

"Liana," his yearning growl crept across the room to her, "well, well, why have you lured me *here* tonight?"

Her brow furrowed at his question. She gradually turned, faced Darkness, and allowed herself to view the chamber in its entirety. Nothing but distance stood between them but to her left lay a sizable room, the center of which was hidden by a wall of curtains that dangled from the vaulted ceiling.

The room seemed innocent enough, but Liana knew the reality. Her fists shook as she recalled the many nights spent beyond those curtains, hopelessly pleading for dawn to break. The scents of blood and drips of sweat, all vividly haunted her and made her stomach reel the longer she gave them thought.

A whisper echoed in her mind until it was the only thing she could hear, *focus.*

Late Night Stroll

Liana glanced around the room again before she set her sights on the slowly approaching Darkness. She laughed as she lifted her hand to her forehead and concealed her concern while she rubbed her temples.

"Lure you?" she questioned.

"You brought me here, did you not?" He touched his palms to his broad chest before he opened his arms up and looked around.

The rhythmic clunk of boots on the solid floor followed as Darkness edged towards her. Her arms folded over her chest while she held the distance between them and stepped in unison to each of his. She shifted to her left with each step. Her eyes darted from the curtains, almost behind her now, to her only exit that lay quite a distance away, but no longer blocked by Darkness.

"I distinctly remember t-trying to go to bed." Her voice struggled to remain casual as she turned her attention back to Darkness.

With the blink of her eye, he was instantly within reach of her. An amused smile traced his lips as she stiffened in response to his sudden proximity. He raised his hand near her face and watched her every movement as he did. Just as his palm was to embrace her cheek, she jerked her head to the side.

Entertained laughter spilled from Darkness. "Ahh, so you *can* see me!"

"I-" Instantly, she looked to her feet and withdrew within herself.

"Much better." His tone softened as he lifted his hand again and caressed her unflinching cheek. "Now, why were you out in the first place?"

Focus; the word echoed again in her mind and shifted her concentration.

The Light Within

"Just a nightmare," she replied and as she took a step back, the soft fibers of the curtains brushed against her hands.

His intrigued groan traced over her skin and left her hair on end. He leaned over her, placed his face in her hair, and drew in a long, unsettling breath.

As his lips caressed her forehead, he continued in a whisper, "Was I there?"

"You always are," she whispered.

He drew another deep breath in before he jerked her head back and locked her in a suffocating kiss. She pulled his massive figure in closer to her as she took another step back. In one swift motion, she gripped the curtains behind her, flung them over his shoulder, and caught them in her other hand. His eyes locked with hers as she twisted, kicked off his solid chest, and pulled the curtains with her entire weight away from where they hung.

Her heart threatened to jump from her chest as she dug her heels against the smooth floor and leaned all her weight into the curtain. Thankful for the sturdiness of their fibers at this moment, she glared at his purpling face as she pulled harder.

He dropped to his knee and gripped the curtain out in front of him with a grin as his eyes met hers. In an instant, he yanked the curtain and dragged her directly into his arms. He gripped her into a crushing embrace as he stood. The harder she struggled, the more he pressed himself into her.

"Just the way I like it."

His words crawled down her spine, sent a shudder to her core, and woke a growing nausea in the pit of her stomach. Unable to move in the slightest against his iron

Late Night Stroll

hold, she immediately ceased her struggle. Liana remained silent and still even as his snaking tongue slithered up her neck. Concentrating on the wall in the distance, she fought to hide the grin from her face as the air of his disappointed sigh rushed welcomingly over her ear.

He released her and dropped his hands to his side behind her. Liana returned her gaze to the ground and tried to view him in her peripheral. She swallowed uneasily as they both remained motionless. The soft clunk of his boots brought the heat of his being against her again.

Tutting as he lifted his hands, he gripped the sides of her arms and moved the sleeves of her robe up and down as he whispered her name, "Liana... Liana."

She braced herself for his next assault, waiting and praying she could escape whatever sinister plan he formulated. He grabbed the back of her robe and shoved her through the wall of curtains. The force against her back sent her falling over the numerous floor pillows strewn about and to the ground where she lay gasping.

Eyes fixed, he watched her intently while he made his way over. Liana glanced up to the table she had nearly been tossed into, to see several sinister-looking blades strapped underneath. Quickly, her eyes darted to Darkness who lifted her to her feet and yanked her robe from her. He tossed it to the floor behind him as he shoved her against the table.

"Stop!" She cried out desperately as she kicked him.

Pushing her body against the table, she shoved the palms of her hands into his chest with as much force as she could. Her hands lingered in the air as fresh red stains caught her attention. The taunting laughter of Darkness reverberated around her as she glanced at the corresponding stains on the floor. She knew it wouldn't be long before she met the same fate as this room's previous tenant.

"You always were my favorite."

He threw her to the table and slid himself between her legs. She stared blankly past his dark knots of flowing hair as he moved closer. He reached up and wrapped her neck in his massive fist. She knew he wanted her to fight him, he enjoyed her misery, and she would rather die than give it to him. She smiled at the thought, distant from her body as he slammed her against the table.

Her eyes locked with his as the idea materialized and in an instant, she reached under the table, gripped the handle of one of the many blades, and wrenched it free. In one swift motion, she dragged the tiny blade across his chest, then gripped her wrist. Using all her strength, she drove her elbow down on his and broke his hold.

Staggering back quite a distance, his hands clutched at his bloodied chest and brought Liana to the desired moment. She tucked to the side, rolled from the table, and collapsed to the solid ground. The sting of the harsh landing radiated through the arches of her feet and begged for her to pause. A rush of adrenaline quickly silenced any lingering anguish and intensified the closer she came to the door.

"Enough!" He howled furiously as he turned to pursue her.

Throwing the door open, she propelled herself up the hall, not daring to look behind as the commotion from his desperate hunt painted the picture well enough. Her eyes remained focused on the floor before her. Though she had reached the end of her plan, she focused on the final stage; run.

Late Night Stroll

Cardio never was her strongest feature. She became increasingly aware of the issue as she leaned against the icy wall and attempted to catch her breath. His relentless pursuit echoed distantly behind her and churned the anxious whispers in her mind that begged for a strategy. Her eyes darted around and searched for any hint, only to return the same cluelessness to her hopeless situation.

She pushed herself from the wall, unwilling to let him have an easy win, and continued up the corridor. As the echoes of his boots drew nearer, her quiet creeping led her to another door. A glance inside put a fluttering to her step before she silently shut the door behind her.

With as little noise as possible, she hurried across the empty throne room. She didn't stop when she heard the click behind her or bother with the silence that followed. Her eyes fixed on the doors across the vast distance and kept her unreceptive to his taunts while her numb feet instinctively carried her forward.

"Enough. You're wasting my time." His knuckles cracked as they curled into a fist, itching to correct this disobedience.

As she neared the doors, she reached out, and he instantly appeared in front of her. She froze mid-step, eyes staring unblinking into his chest. He moved under her outstretched arm and lifted her onto his shoulder in one gut wrenching-movement.

So close, her head spun with the thought. She stretched for the door and kicked against his chest.

"Wait! Casimir is that w-" As the words left her lips, regret consumed her.

She immediately ceased her struggle and retreated within to assure her eyes would reflect the blank subservience that could save her. With the sound of the name, Darkness stopped in his tracks and dropped Liana from his shoulder. Her eyes fell to his boots as he set her to her feet. He gripped her arms and pinned them to her sides as he shook her.

"Look at me," he spat.

Her head snapped up at his command. The glow of the nearby throne, through the darkness of the night, rested over his face. It reflected in his glaring green eyes and held her captive.

"How do you know where he is?" His deep, precise words echoed individually around the expansive hall.

"I-" She cut herself short and pressed her lips together firmly. *Just shut up,* she thought as she desperately tried to formulate a plan, *before you make things worse.*

"Well?" His eyebrows raised questioningly as he leaned closer to her.

Silence resonated around them as her attention slowly fell to her feet.

"Fine!" He shouted and smashed her arms in at her sides. He leaned his head back, chest heaving as he took a massive breath of air and released it in a massive sigh before he turned his attention back to her and continued in a whisper, "We will find out eventually."

Her head snapped up with his final words and confirmed her fears. She watched, with horror, as his snaking darkness made its way down his arms toward her.

"No!" Screams of dread bolted uncontrollably from her.

As she pulled and twisted with all her strength, he clamped tighter and almost squeezed the breath from her.

Late Night Stroll

Great, her frustrated thoughts echoed in her mind, *way to make things worse!* She ceased her struggle and watched the shadowy wisps creep closer to her.

"Liana," he spoke through his own amused laughter.

Hands now fists at her sides, she glared daringly back at Darkness as she shouted, "No!"

Tiny sparks erupted along her skin. They were barely visible and provided a mere tingle as they connected with Darkness. His entertained laughter echoed distantly as the room swirled. Blinking several times, she forced herself to focus. He released her arms and allowed her to breathe freely again. A sudden shiver brought with it the awareness of the slimy shadows that slithered up her arm and raced to consume her.

Out of plans, Liana mustered the last bit of her strength and cried out, "Casimir!"

"Ah, ah," his head shook with disapproval as his words continued, "Allow it and I will make it less painful."

"No," she whimpered disappointedly to herself as her body impulsively knelt before him.

I can't, the thought resonated within, *fight anymore.*

"Please," her whispered prayers reached to the Light within, "help."

She turned her head to the side; her eyes rested on the throne as its golden glow reached to her through the darkness. Suddenly her sight failed and left strange whispers that churned around her. Liana focused, trying desperately to see in the utter darkness. The room slowly materialized before her and revealed the massive tree.

The Light Within

"No," she whispered while she watched through the shadows from across the room, as Khius dropped to his knees. His head bowed, followed by muffled speech.

"Please help," she whispered as she fought to escape her memory.

"Quiet." His warning lingered over her shoulder and met her wide eyes that watched on in horror as her delicate memory was dissected.

She watched as the memory of herself approached a kneeling Khius and examined him through narrowed eyes. She slid her hand around his neck and instantly tears filled her eyes.

"What's happening," Darkness whispered in her ear as they watched the scene unravel.

Liana watched on, unable to speak as she watched Khius slowly being strangled by her own hand before she finally released him. Incoherent shouting rippled across the room from her previous self as she backed away and stared down at him.

Darkness growled in her ear, "What did you say?"

When she didn't answer, his shadowy talons dug into her collarbone and demanded her attention.

"I don't remember! Okay?" Her words flew from her in an irate, whispered rush and she promptly dropped her sights to the floor.

"*Try* to remember!"

His nails dug into her cheeks as his hand gripped her chin and turned her face back to the memory. He forced her to watch as it played out before them. Tears filled her eyes as she watched the distant Liana grab Khius' wrist and release a deafening zap. His free hand reached in front of him for the ground as he collapsed while she issued a second pulse and released him.

Late Night Stroll

Khius crumpled to the floor. She watched for several minutes as he panted before he finally spoke, though the words came out a garbled mess. She watched herself, as she paced near him, shouting indistinctly, and throwing her hands in the air. As the memory of herself turned, Liana could see the clear confusion and fear swirling over her face as she paced deep in thought.

"Focus," Darkness whispered as his grip on her tightened.

Khius pulled himself to a sitting position across the room as he spoke, "You're here, aren't you? That was my plan; get you here."

"What?" the memory of Liana asked in disbelief.

"You had to come back; I didn't care who brought you back. I thought I could control the situation." Khius lowered his head and shook it.

Liana watched as the memory of herself turned and crossed the room toward Khius, "You ever think if you would've helped Nicolai, instead of the enemy, all this wouldn't have fucked up?"

No, she thought as she concentrated on her resistance.

She closed her eyes and desperately struggled against Darkness. Liana struggled to pull herself from the memory as he pressed on. Long, indiscernible reverberations of Khius' voice swirled tauntingly in the air about them. Khius paused for a moment before he continued, and the muffled melodies gained distance.

"Focus!" Darkness demanded.

Startled, she opened her eyes just as the memory of herself approached Khius. When she reached him, she glanced up across the room. As her sight rested on Casimir, Darkness released her, and the room slipped from her sight. The relief of his overwhelming power as it receded, brought her to her knees before the throne.

"Liana?" A distant voice echoed around her and only reached her awareness after they stood in front of her.

With a cautious glance, she found Darkness was no longer at her side, yet someone towered over her. She snapped out of her fog-filled, weary state and reached out thankfully.

As her eyes settled on his face, her words burst with relief from her chest, "Oh Casimir!"

"Liana?" He examined her reassured face as he helped her to her feet. "What are you doing? Are you okay?"

"I, uh..."

Pain raced through every fiber in her body as he helped her up. Liana clung to his arm for balance while she skimmed the room. Her eyes landed briefly on Darkness, who skulked unseen in the outlying shadows as he watched them. Quickly, she looked around the rest of the room before turning back to Casimir.

"I-I'm sorry." Speaking through shivers, she pulled her arms around herself, suddenly aware of the chill in the air, and continued, "Must've been a nightmare... or something."

Dipping his head, Casimir lifted her chin and searched her eyes for understanding. "A nightmare? Then, how did you end up here?"

"I remember waking up and I was just so... terrified that I couldn't go back to sleep. I thought if I took a walk, it would help, and," Liana looked around the throne room again before she turned her attention back to Casimir. "I ended up here I guess."

Late Night Stroll

"Come on." He wrapped his arm around her as he spoke, pulled her shivering form into his, and led her from the throne room.

Though his touch would have normally repulsed her, she clung tight to his torso, comforted by the fleeting protection he offered. The warmth from his flesh radiated across her icy skin and eased her frightful shaking. As they made their way, she clung to the brief moments of peace.

Casimir's voice cut through the silent stillness around them as he suddenly asked, "What was it about?"

Lost in her own thoughts, Liana absently responded, "Hmm?"

"The nightmare, what was it about?"

"Oh..." Liana stood up a little straighter as she tried to recall the details, "There was this light above me and..." She paused for a moment, confused by her inability to recall any of the details now. After a few calculated breaths she continued, "I'm not sure... but then it was really dark..." Swallowing the knot in her throat, she carried on in a whisper, "Darkness was there."

Condescending laughter belted from Casimir. He quickly stifled it and continued with confident intensity, "My dear gem." He squeezed her in closer to his side and rubbed her arm as he spoke, "Don't let the Commander trouble your thoughts like that. He is within my control. In time, I'm sure you'll find you have more in common than you know."

Lips sealed for fear of the retaliation that any words may bring, she walked on with him in silence. She yearned for the endless corridors to cease and bring her to the King's Chamber where she could rest.

The Light Within

He let the silence linger in short fragments as he dissected her responses, before he pried further, "This nightmare, it was so... terrifying?"

"Yes," she answered obediently, trying desperately to mask her irritation at his insistent probing.

"Still you can't recall any of the details?"

"I-" She dropped her head with a frustrated sigh before she continued, "I know it's strange. I can't remember much, just the feeling."

"So," with the word, he stopped in his tracks and dropped his arm from her side. He took a deep breath, crossed his arms over his chest, and continued, "*Feeling* completely terrified, you decided to leave the comfort of our bed and walk about this dark place?"

Thoughts obscured by exhaustion, Liana's gaze found the floor as she combed for the words, "I... I- I'm sorry. I should've woken you."

"Yes. Yes, you should've. Yet, you chose to wake Khius instead?"

"I," as the word left her lips, her timid state instantaneously conceded to the gnawing urge to defend herself against his misplaced accusations. She lifted her head and countered, "What? I did no such thing!"

In an instant, he gripped her shoulders and shoved her against the nearest wall. "Then I suppose you two just ran into each other in the dead of night?"

Brow furrowed, Liana shook her head and let out a short laugh. "Well, yea actually." She waved her hand back and forth between their faces as she spoke, "It's pretty dark."

Unamused, he instantly snatched her waving hand and shoved it down to her side while he spat at her in a

Late Night Stroll

feverish whisper, "Don't play with me. I know the darkness doesn't cloud your vision like the others."

With a sudden intensity, the words broke through the barrier that her exhausted state could no longer maintain, "Maybe I *can* see sometimes, but I didn't go searching for Khius! I swear!"

Like a regretful tidal wave, they flooded from her. Her words crashed over Casimir and along with them, all the emotions she had tried desperately to cage.

"I'm sorry!" Tears streamed down her face as she fought to choke the words out. "I ju-" Liana buried her face in Casimir's chest, muffling her words and cries as she tried to regain her composure.

A look of bewilderment consumed Casimir as she sobbed uncontrollably into his loose-hanging nightshirt. His arms lingered in the air awkwardly, still outstretched from his attempts to restrain her. After several moments passed and her anguished cries only intensifying, he cleared his throat.

"I-I'm s-sorry," her muffled speech broke in between sobs as she fought to calm herself. "This is all just so much. I don't want to be…" Liana paused and took several deep breaths before she peeled herself from Casimir. She took a step back, and with her eyes fixed on the floor, she continued in a slow, steady voice, "I'm sorry. I don't want to upset you, it's just all so much. I just wish it could all go back to the way it was when we first met."

"Oh, Liana." As he spoke, he raised his hand and wiped the tears from her cheek before he continued, "We were nothing back then. Look at all we are now." He gestured around to the castle floors and walls.

As she looked around, a half-smile crossed her face, accompanied by a short sigh of disbelief. "Of course," she whispered, barely audible, as her head shook with the words, "what was I thinking?"

"See?" He rubbed the sleeves of her nightgown as he spoke, "I know things are a little overwhelming, but the sooner you surrender yourself to me, the sooner it'll get better." He dipped his head and tried to meet her gaze.

Her blank stare remained on the floor as she nodded.

"Alright then." With his final words, his arm wrapped around her back, gripped her shoulder once more, and ushered her down the corridor in silence.

Chapter 4
The Veil

Golden rays from the morning sun cascaded from the countless windows perched at the peak of the vaulted ceiling. High above the individuals seated at the table below, tiny particles of dust swirled and twirled in the shafts of light; their hidden dance illuminated briefly in the spotlight of the rising sun.

Liana rolled her hand over on the table where it rested and opened her palm in the light. As the bright beam washed over her skin, its tingling warmth radiated through her and kept the constant chill in the air temporarily at bay. Her eyes, heavy from the night's proceedings, skimmed lazily about the room.

As she traced over Casimir's face, Liana stiffened in her chair. It was as though someone cranked the volume on a muted show and suddenly, she became fully aware of her surroundings. Silverware against ceramic, glasses clinked against each other, and numerous murmurs, clashed in a whirlwind of commotion that screamed out for her immediate awareness after being previously ignored by her sleepy state. The lingering heat of the sun on her hand attracted her attention again and dismissed the anxiety-inducing crowd around her. Her eyes lingered on the light as she gradually drew in the cool morning air.

She picked up the intricate silver fork and pushed the food around on the plate before her. A soft sigh left her lips and breathed annoyance across the strange food that lingered in front of her face. Liana swallowed slowly as her stomach turned, yet again, and dismissed the slightest notion of nourishment.

The Light Within

She glanced up at Casimir again as her fork returned to her plate, curious about the individual who held his attention. Her eyes traced his face for only a second before they returned to her plate. She prodded the food before her as her brow furrowed in thought. His slender, pale face, devoid of any emotion and framed in long silver locks of hair, held a certain familiarity to it that Liana couldn't quite identify.

"I see you didn't inform him of our little," the Commander interrupted his low grumble and cleared his throat in his seat next to Liana. He lifted his fork and crudely ripped the meat from it before he continued, "*dance* last night?"

While she strained to decipher his barely audible remarks, Liana reached for her glass and raised it to her lips. "It hasn't come up," she said subtly to the glass. Slowly she tipped it back and sipped the bubbly, orange drink before she finished, "yet."

Feeling his tension as he shifted in his chair, Liana fought to restrain any trace of excitement from her face. *Dance*, the thought amused her, *he assumes our dance is over, yet we waltz.*

His hand waved in the air dismissively at the words, "Maybe it doesn't, and neither will your sight."

With an amused short laugh, she retorted instantly, "Oh that?"

With her words, Casimir looked up from his conversation and, as he stared at her, lifted a hand to silence the individual to his right. Instantly, Liana locked eyes with him and let a small, genuine smile grace her face. Casimir blinked a few times before he leaned in his high-backed seat slightly and nodded to her with a half-smile. After a moment, he snapped his head back to the man

The Veil

sitting at his side and, as he dropped his hand, they continued their conversation.

The smile lingered on her face as she shifted her focus to the light above them and continued with a quiet composure, "Go ahead. Though he despises his time being wasted."

The Commander lowered his fork to his plate and clenched his napkin. He held it hostage in an angered grip against the table. The moment lingered in an unsettling stillness as the room carried on around them. Liana's unwavering silence persisted as she waited in anticipation for his next move.

"Perhaps I could forgive the whole incident with my tiny one, should you," he paused for only a moment to clear his throat before he continued, "remember last night as merely a dream." He lifted his head and stared off into the distance. His posture relaxed as he recalled their night fondly.

Liana tilted her glass to her lips again, cleared her throat, and immediately snapped the Commander out of his dream-like state. She merely wanted to interrupt his twisted thoughts, but in doing so, drew unwelcome attention. As Casimir thoughtlessly lectured on, Liana met the gaze of his silver-haired subject from across the table.

His glowing, golden eyes held her focus until his slight smirk caught her attention. Not wanting him to misinterpret the moment, she immediately turned her disregarding stare and looked a distance down the table. Her eyes wandered over face after face, all seated in a heated conversation with each other at the infinitely stretching table.

As she fixed her sights on a face in the distance, her lips grazed the edge of the raised cup with each careful

The Light Within

word, "Fair enough and since it was merely a dream, there should be no need for further inquiries."

While he reached for his drink, the Commander followed Liana's gaze to the end of the table where Khius laughed with several others. The Commander dropped his head and shook it with a grin. After a moment, he leaned his head against the high-backed chair, lifted the large goblet to his mouth, and sipped it as he stared at the ceiling. Liana sat unwavering; her gaze fixed on the plate before her as their dance came to its final moments.

Lowering his goblet, the Commander shifted in his seat and looked down to the liquid as it sloshed. "Fair enough."

A powerful sigh escaped his enormous form as he stared down at the liquid. Finally, he tilted the goblet back and downed the rest of the contents in one large gulp. With one pull of his massive arm, he wiped away the dribbles of red liquid that escaped his lips into his beard. As he slammed the heavy chalice on the table before him, he stood and bowed slightly to Casimir, then Liana. With a rush of air, he turned and marched off.

She didn't bother to cage the small, triumphant smile that rested on her face as she leaned back in her chair and twirled the drink before her. She sipped happily, lost in her reminiscent thoughts. The shifting sunbeams washed over her and wrapped her in their warmth again as she waited for the area to clear.

I miss sweatpants, she thought to herself as she adjusted her gown to cross her legs, *and silent breakfasts.*

She glanced up at the increasingly obnoxious group that roused her serene state. The crowd gradually shifted around Khius at the furthest side of the open dining hall. They grew louder with each comment he made.

Must be nice, she lamented on the thought with an extended sigh as she glared at them, *to be so fucking happy during all this.*

With a jolt, she sat upright as Casimir cleared his throat. As she turned her attention to him, she noticed his focus remained on his conversation, though he lifted his hand dismissively at the rowdy group. Immediately, the room began to clear, and as her focus lingered on Casimir, he took notice and glanced up at her. She nodded with a thankful smile and quickly turned her attention to the exiting individuals.

As she leaned back in her chair again, she questioned within, *what is so important that it takes all morning to talk about? Who is that guy anyway?*

Her brow furrowed as she tried to recall the details of the face of the man that held all of Casimir's attention and wondered where she had seen him before. Her train of thought quickly derailed as her eyes landed on the scowling face of Khius. He shuffled along at the back of the large crowd; glare fixed on Liana.

She glared back, annoyed but wondered if he was trying to tell her something. He quickly broke her gaze and filtered through the door with the others. Liana rolled her eyes with a sigh before she turned her attention back to Casimir. She glanced over their faces again before she returned her attention to the glass at her lips. Though the clamor of the room had died down significantly, she was unable to decipher their conversation. The fragments she caught were merely indiscernible whispers of a language she couldn't interpret.

The Light Within

Assuming it could be ages if she waited for a moment alone with him, Liana sat up in her chair, eyes fixed on Casimir, and cleared her throat. Without even a glance, Casimir waved a dismissive hand to Liana. She scowled at him and slowly rose to her feet.

As she turned to leave, her eyes landed on W who waited for her in the doorway. Her sincere smile beamed at Liana from across the room. Liana took a deep breath as she turned to Casimir, raised her chin, and cleared her throat again. His hand lifted to dismiss her.

Before her nerves could consume her, she quickly muttered, "May I speak with you, please?"

Casimir stopped mid-sentence and turned his attention to Liana. He quickly flipped his lingering dismissive hand, palm up to her as he hastily spoke, "What is it you need?"

Her eyes immediately darted to Casimir's conversation companion, who gradually sat back in his chair as he stared at her. She swallowed slowly and turned her attention back to Casimir as she spoke, "To speak with you, alone for a moment, please."

A disbelieving grin spread across his irritated face as he turned his attention back to his closely seated companion, whose focus remained fixed on Liana. Casimir leaned his elbow into the arm of his highbacked chair, pressed his fingertips into his temple, and lingered there momentarily before he turned his attention back to Liana.

"The Elder and I have a lot to attend to. If you wanted a private moment, you should've waited for one. Yet, you chose this one." His words, though deliberate at first, quickly took off in a flurry of irritation until he paused, took a deep breath, and continued slowly, "Now, what is it you need?"

The Veil

Taken aback by the reaction to such a simple request, Liana glanced away from Casimir over his shoulder, to W who waited patiently in the doorway. She nodded to Liana and gestured for her to breathe. Liana quickly turned her attention to the matter and searched desperately for the thoroughly rehearsed lines while she lifted her posture.

As her gaze turned back to Casimir, her eyes lingered over the Elder. His examining stare pierced intrusively and held her attention as he tucked a section of his long silver hair behind a pointed ear. Liana blinked and glanced a second time at him before she turned her focus back to Casimir. She stared helplessly at him as he watched her, his patience thinning the longer she lingered in silence in a desperate search for the words.

How do I, she thought frantically, *tell you you're holding me hostage...killing me?* The too familiar, expressionless stare set over Liana's face as she searched her thoughts, *wasn't it something about being his pet or being caged... no, why would he care...*

"Well? Speak," Casimir ordered as his fist drove down onto the table before him.

"I," she paused as a whisper of the word, *breathe*, entered her mind. She let her chest fill with air before she continued, "I cannot rest with all these nightmares." She shifted her sights uncomfortably to her feet as she continued, "I need out." She lifted her head to look at Casimir but as her eyes rested on his clenched jaw and furious stare, the gripping fear of his impending reaction stifled her thought. She pushed on and tried to choke out her viewpoints before she could speak no more, "Like some space t-"

"Out?" Casimir interrupted harshly.

The Light Within

He shoved the massive table before him and scooted him in his chair a sizable distance from it. His words cut through the silent hall as he stood.

"Space?"

Liana was to her feet, unwavering, as he moved with a few heavy strides to stand directly in front of her. She stared into his chest, frozen and wide-eyed, as he lifted his hand to her chin. His embrace lingered, caressing her cheek for a moment before his grip suddenly tightened around her chin and tilted it so she met his stare.

"I-I don't mean like that," she stumbled through her words as her thoughts contradicted them. *Well, of course*, she thought, *my freedom would be a good start.*

"This conversation was over nights ago!" He squeezed her chin painfully and yelled angrily in her face, "After all I've done, all *everyone* has done? Everyone around here has worked tirelessly to get you this!" He shoved her face aside, backed away, and gestured around as he continued on his angry rampage, "It's a fucking castle! How much *space* could you want?"

Through glaring eyes her thoughts retorted where her words failed, *any space beside the King's Chambers would be a great start.* She let out a short laugh at the absurdity of the conversation. Her head shook with disbelief as she rubbed her temples.

Throwing his hands up in the air, Casimir turned from her and strode across the room. He tossed and kicked every chair that neared his path as he exited the great hall. Liana stared on in amazement as the commotion from his tantrum gradually dwindled into the distance.

It wasn't until the Elder cleared his throat, that she noticed he stood beside her. Liana watched him suspiciously, confused by his sudden proximity. His eyes traced her up and down, reading her response for a moment, and remained on her as he tucked his arm to his stomach and bowed. She nodded slowly to him and watched his every movement as he silently exited the room.

The moment the massive double doors clicked behind the Elder, Liana collapsed in her chair. With a defeated sigh, she laid her head sideways on the table. As the soft steps of W drew nearer, she lifted her arms over her head to block the light from her face.

W placed her hand on Liana's back and with an airy hopefulness, tried to make light of the situation, "Well, that might not have been the best word choice."

"Yeaaa," Liana said as she sat up and laughed at the moment as it replayed in her head. "Not *quite* what I was going for."

With a regretful sigh, Liana stood to her feet and welcomed the embrace of W as she escorted her from the breakfast hall.

o   o   o

Liana leaned her forehead against the solid glass panel. It blocked her from a taunting breeze that swirled through the branches just beyond her reach. As she shifted, she brushed tiny fragments of stone from her skin, back to the floor; remnants of the balcony's banister that was so hastily removed during more of Casimir's 'modifications' to 'ensure her safety'. She rolled her eyes as she recalled yet another conversation that ended poorly.

Clutching her knees to her chest, she leaned again and exhaled a curtain of fog across the glass. As the haze quickly receded, her eyes landed on a tiny blackbird. A slight smile emerged at the sight of the tiny bird as it chirped merrily and hopped along the swaying branch in front of her. The morning light reflected off its wings as it moved about and illuminated an array of color across its feathers.

"Good morning beautiful bird," Liana peeped back at the bird as it danced along the branch.

Two sharp knocks echoed unexpectedly across the room. Her eyes narrowed at the door and when no one entered, she looked back to the window. To her disappointment, the little bird had disappeared. Annoyed by the interruption to her agenda of doing nothing for the day, Liana grumpily got to her feet.

She took her time to cross the room while she adjusted and tightened the robe around her. After a momentary pause with the door's handle in her grasp, Liana took a deep breath and pulled the heavy door open a crack. To her surprise, the Elder stood in the hallway before her.

Liana kept her eyes fixed on him and spoke through the small opening in the doorway that she allowed, "Oh, Good Morning Elder. I apologize, but the King is not here."

An amused half-smile traced his face as his sights lingered uncomfortably on Liana, "I know."

Great, Liana stiffened as her mind raced, *another here to do as they please behind his back.*

The Elder studied her as he let his words carefully flow, "In speaking with The King, we have decided it would be best if you walk the grounds periodically."

Instantly, her head snapped up. In her excitement, she released the door and allowed it to open; her request *was* heard. She looked at his face and her enthusiasm settled as she contemplated, *I'm sure this will cost me.*

"Of course, there are conditions."

The Veil

Their eyes locked for several moments and as Liana's lips parted to inquire what he wanted in return, he stepped aside. Behind him waited another, close in Liana's height, clad entirely in black wraps. A simple mask concealed anything below his eyes and drew attention to their glowing green hue. He bowed briefly as their eyes met. Instantly, her attention was drawn to his pointed ears that stood out prominently against his short and spiky, red hair.

Elves, she thought to herself amused, *long-ago Liana would've loved this!*

She knew of them all too well now. With her powers returning, came countless memories of her time here before. She remembered the stories she was told about the elves that were so consumed in manipulating their power to fulfill their own selfish pleasures. They squandered their gift of immortality and created the Kingdom of darkness that she battled to this day.

They must be, Liana's gaze lingered over them curiously, *some of the last of the light.*

"For your safety, one of my personal bodyguards will escort you and *must* remain with you at all times," the Elder instructed calmly.

With his words, her focus immediately returned to the guard before her. Her eyes narrowed as her thoughts swarmed, so *I'm to be walked, like a dog?* Instantly, she shook her head and her eyes turned to the floor as she struggled to realign her thoughts, *this is what I asked for. Well, at least it's a start.*

"Of course, if you'd rather remain here," his voice trailed off as he looked down his nose to the shadowed room behind her.

The Light Within

Her heart jolted as he turned to leave and without thought, she reached for him. "No, wait!" As he turned back to her, she straightened herself and with a nod continued gratefully, "Thank you."

A fleeting smile warmed his frozen face and with a swallow was quickly subdued. Folding his arm to his chest, the Elder bowed before her. He lingered only a moment before he turned and noiselessly proceeded down the hall. Once out of sight, Liana turned her attention to the guard with an appreciative smile.

"Thank you." When he didn't speak or even blink in response, she cleared her throat and continued, "Okay... please give me just a moment."

He remained, still as a statue, as she gradually shut the door between them. Ear pressed to the door; Liana listened for a moment for any movement. Silence persisted and met her pessimistic ear as she lingered at the door. After a few seconds, she shifted her attention and moved with haste around the room. She pulled on one of the many gowns left by W and adjusted her hair. In a matter of minutes, Liana was catching her breath back at the door as she yanked it open.

The morning's light flowed from behind Liana into the darkened corridor before her and stretched the shadows into endless ribbons of darkness at her feet. Her gaze lingered momentarily on the back of the guard's head before she turned to pull the heavy door shut.

"Okay then," she said as she passed the silent elf and made her way from the room.

He moved noiselessly along with her, slightly behind her, yet just out of sight. The usual stone glare set over Liana as she retreated internally. She wasn't sure why she was concerned with where he chose to walk. Perhaps it was her preconceived notion that he would walk alongside her as everyone else had before. Yet she wondered if it wasn't her desperate need for interaction, even in the slightest, that riled her temper over something so simple. Liana sighed and looked up from her thoughts as she walked.

"What's your name?" she asked as she glanced behind herself at the trailing guard.

Her gaze lingered momentarily on the guard while she searched for a response. After a brief moment of silence, Liana turned away from the guard and focused her attention on the path she aimlessly wandered.

"Very interesting. Might be quite difficult to call out in a moment of need..." Liana trailed off as her hand connected with the stone wall nearest her.

Fingertips traced each subtle groove in the stone from the chisel that previously shaped it. She admired the beauty in the detail while she walked. Even after Casimir stripped the whole castle bare, the raw magnificence and simplicity were breathtaking. Unsure if it was the morning's light or the castle brought to its current conditions, Liana looked on in amazement as if seeing a whole new fortress.

As she walked on, warmth radiated from the stone at her fingertips. Liana absently shook her hand and placed it back on the stone as she passed doorways and branching corridors. Her skin connected with the hard material again but this time a significant warmth caught her attention. She stopped and looked down to her hand, then up at the wall before her. As she placed her hand on the stone again, she felt a warm pull and turned to follow the wall around a narrow, darkened passage.

The Light Within

When she turned, the guard moved instantly in front of her and blocked her path. She scowled at him and attempted to go around, but he shifted each time, in perfect step with her. Liana met his glowing eyes with a questioning glare. He lifted his arm and gestured for her to continue down their previous path.

Arms crossed in front of her, Liana stared unblinking as she muttered, "I thought you were here to escort me, not tell me where I could go?"

The guard shifted nervously in front of her while he held his position. His eyes darted around them for a moment before he suddenly stepped aside. She shuffled around him in the narrow space and continued. As soon as she touched the wall again, the sphere of warmth in the stone met her hand. She followed the growing heat it emitted along the wall at a quicker pace.

As soon as the hall opened to a larger corridor, the guard was instantly at her side in stride with her. Her curiosity ignited a little flicker of excitement to her step as her eyes fixed on the stone at her fingertips. At first, she assumed the warmth was the perimeter of some random shower room or kitchen. It was clear to her now that the source of the growing warmth wasn't isolated to a specific room. As Liana walked on at an increasing speed, she realized it didn't seem to radiate through the stone either, but rather was something resting over the stone that drew her along.

She glanced up from her hand to the path before her and stopped in her steps. Mouth agape and eyes wide, Liana stood before the glowing door she searched many nights for. She glanced around and found the guard was no longer at her side. Quickly, Liana looked about her and with no one in sight, stepped into the narrow hallway.

The Veil

A warm, sweet breeze swept over her entire being and met a growing warmth inside her core. Her steps turned light as air as she silently glided toward the door. A curious peace surrounded her and calmed her racing heart while her open hand reached for the door. She paused as she examined the door and pulled her hand away just before it could connect. The door blended perfectly against the wall, dark against a slim glowing doorframe with no handle.

Faint whispering danced playfully on the other side; it welcomed her and invited her closer. Liana stepped back and raised her palms slowly to the whispering calls. She stood there for a moment before her embarrassment led her to drop her hands to her side. She sighed, clenched her fists, and took several slow breaths as she edged closer to the doorway. Slowly, she moved her ear to the door and when she leaned in, she stumbled through the doorway as though no door existed at all.

Liana cried out and grabbed at her eyes from the blinding light she was met with. At her voice, the winds instantly whipped around her and stirred the whispers to an encircling loud hum. She clenched her mouth shut but the loud humming remained. Liana squinted through her hands around the room.

Massive bright walls stretched on infinitely into the light from each side of Liana and created a massive hallway before her. The walls appeared almost liquid; like flowing curtains of golden light that continuously billowed in the unfelt breeze of the millions of whispers that lay beyond. She looked above her as she turned around. Her jaw dropped at the sight of the walls that appeared to extend endlessly upward into a bright golden mist, dotted with multi-colored stars.

The Light Within

As she looked around, she searched for the door she had come through. She found it now matched the walls around her. She raised her hand and pressed, expecting to reach through. Instead, she met a solid surface. Liana swallowed slowly; she realized there was no going back.

Once her flesh connected with the veil in front of her, the loud humming of voices instantly reduced to whispers. Liana withdrew her hand and held it to her chest as strange shadows started to form on the other side. She stepped back cautiously; her unblinking gaze fixed on the shadows as they moved. Some gradually formed into a human-like shape. The strange shadow before her lifted its arm; its long stretching fingers reached for her as it approached the wall.

Liana jumped back, hand clutched to her chest, and continued her backward movement while she kept her startled gaze on the shadows. A warmth rose in her core again and called her away. She turned from the creature without another thought. Her shoulders relaxed and slowly, she dropped her hands to her side as she stared at the bright, infinite hall before her. Without hesitation, she walked along as a peaceful humming rose around her again.

After only a short distance, Liana noticed a small curve in the wall as it moved around a waist-high pillar. Her heart leaped when her eyes fixed on the empty, quartz-like blade that stood on the pillar before her. She approached it as her thoughts swirled.

What would you, the thought arose in her mind, *do with it?*

She lifted her hand and as her eyes narrowed, so did her thoughts, *Casimir.* Instantly she froze, her outstretched fingers lingered over the blade as her thoughts countered themselves, *what could be done with it in the wrong hands?*

Instantly, she retracted her hand, stepped away from the blade, and confirmed within, *it's enough that there's already one out there.*

Liana turned back to the path and continued with confident haste. She squinted in the light as it seemed to glow even brighter and before she knew it, she had to shield her eyes again. After only a moment, she was able to move her hand and with a look of amazement, she realized she was no longer in the strange bright hall. With a short laugh, Liana sat on the stone bench near her and looked up to the familiar opening in the courtyard.

Isn't the same, she thought to herself as she looked around fondly, *without those purple vines.*

In the distance she heard the labored breathing of someone as they approached. She sat back on the bench calmly and enjoyed the moment of peace while she could. Liana looked up just as the guard who was escorting her stepped through one of the many pillars into the open courtyard.

He approached her in an angered fury and reached for her as his voice cut through the air, "Where were you?"

She avoided his grasp and quickly stood to turn to him. Through squinting eyes and over crossed arms, she countered, "Oh, so you *can* speak?"

He froze and with a glare, stammered over his words, "I-I...What?" He took a deep breath, crossed his arms, then continued slowly, "Where have you been?"

"What are you talking about? I've been right here." Liana lifted her hands as she looked around the room before she continued, "Where have you been?"

The Light Within

He glanced around the room suspiciously as she spoke before he tried to recall his steps as if unsure, "I..."

"Wouldn't want to let the Elder know you left my side." She dropped her head and shook it with a mock disappointment as she spoke, "and on the first assignment."

He dropped his head back with a sigh, then cocked it to the side, his eyes on hers as he countered, "Indeed, you speak truth. Would be a tragedy to lose your little chances of 'freedom'."

She took a deep breath as she crossed the few steps and as she came face to face with the guard spoke with composure, "Listen carefully please, because I'm only going to say it once. I have had about enough of everyone telling me what I can and cannot do around here as if I am not The Queen!"

Unflinching, the guard stood, eyes locked with Liana. For a brief, tense moment, she held his attention with her furious, unheard stare. He swallowed slowly, and with one minuscule nod, broke her gaze.

Liana turned from him, took a deep breath, and adjusted her gown. She raised an open hand slightly to the hall nearest her. With a nod, he opened his hand to the path and walked alongside her as she turned to leave.

She held her pace while her inquisitive stare secured on his face as she spoke, "Since you *can* speak, what is your name? Please don't ignore me this time."

The guard's rushed pace came to an abrupt halt. He immediately turned to her, his eyes rolled as they landed on her and he spoke in a hurried hush, "There is no *letter* in *his* language for my name. Therefore, I have no name."

The Veil

As sorrow filled her face, the guard turned from her and resumed his pace. She shook her head and followed closely behind while her mind raced along.

Nameless, she wondered, *how many shared the title?*

o   o   o

An enchanting melody circled Liana and encased her in an alluring, warm bubble. Slowly, she filled her lungs with the sweet and vibrant air that surrounded her. As she gradually opened her eyes, her jaw dropped at the scene before her.

Her heavily jeweled wrist dangled carelessly over Casimir's decorated shoulder. She traced over the magnificent royal garments that accented his frame perfectly and found she was blushing. Suddenly repulsed at herself, she turned her attention to the room around them.

Several lavishly clothed figures danced and twirled about them in a vast ballroom. A shadowy mist lingered over the room; it blocked the faces of several dancers that surrounded her and cast others in complete darkness. The room slowly began to dissolve as Liana tried desperately to cling to the dream.

With a sigh, she turned her attention back to Casimir. His distant mutters remained drowned out by the beautiful music. Liana absently smiled while she examined his face. He smiled back. She was instantly lost in his gorgeous cheekbones. Her brow furrowed as her misleading feelings caused her to shake her head.

When she returned her sights to Casimir, his eyes locked with hers and drew her into their deep, dark pools; only this time it wasn't infatuation that held her attention. She stared back, eyes wide with fear as an unseen suffocating grip crushed her chest and held her in place.

The Light Within

His words echoed indistinctly in an anxiety-inducing whirlwind around her.

Liana gulped and as she attempted to control her breathing, reminded herself, *A dream, it's just a dream.*

His head tipped back with an exaggerated laugh that echoed tauntingly around her. He shoved her hand from his shoulder, stepped aside, and dissolved into the shadows as Liana's wide-eyed gaze fixed horrifically in front of her.

"No," she whispered in disbelief.

Unsettling whispers hissed spitefully around her, "*You* did thisss."

She shook her head, but she couldn't look from the horrific image before her. Across the vast ballroom of oblivious dancers stood a gasping Arietta. Her hands gripped desperately at a massive gash across her neck that spewed dark liquid down her front, into a pool at her feet.

"No!" Liana screamed as she reached out frantically for Arietta.

When she lunged, something stopped her abruptly. Liana looked to her wrists to find the familiar bangles were now shackles that bound her by chains to the cold floor. She looked up to Arietta and realized her vision was no longer obscured by the dancers. An icy air crept across her skin as the room around them grew eerily quiet.

Suddenly, the horrible choking and gurgling of Arietta's struggle surrounded Liana. It tormented her as she stared on and fought in vain to help. Like a dark wall of fog, the shadows slowly edged around her. She dropped her head; she refused to give in to their torment and tried to focus on anything other than Arietta.

The Veil

Voices reached from the shadows; they threatened to devour her and stirred into an increasingly vicious whirlwind at her lack of attentiveness, "*You* did thisss."

She closed her eyes and with a slight smile, whispered back, "Just a nightmare."

Within a few seconds, Liana opened her eyes. Her smile persisted as the familiar ceiling of the King's Chambers came into focus. A relieved breath of air filled her lungs; yet was temporarily held captive as soft whispers met her ears. As a heavy sigh reached across the room, Liana released her restrained exhale and let her breathing resume.

"But can I trust him?" Casimir's haunting tone bled into indistinct mutterings that churned from him at an alarming speed.

Liana rolled to her side and kicked at the blankets that fought her as she pulled them over her head. She squeezed her eyes shut and tried to ignore his ramblings to drift back to sleep. It wouldn't be long before she'd be unable and eventually forced to function in such a state.

"and what to do with *her*?" Groans traced his words and sent chills down her spine.

Her eyes shot open as she listened intently.

"What does she want? How can I-"

Strange whispers interrupted his train of thought, then trailed off and left the room in an eerie silence. After hearing nothing for quite some time, Liana shifted slightly to peek over the fluffy comforter at Casimir.

His face, concealed behind a raised arm, was pressed against the thick glass wall at the balcony. He rested his nearly bare figure against the glass in an exhausted stance. The moonlight washed over his lean form and illuminated every subtle detail. His breath came in shallow, unsteady, and jolting gasps.

Liana pulled the covers from her face and slowly sat up as she watched him. She could barely hear his soft cries from where she sat, but the pain she saw was undeniable. Her heart ached as she watched, unsure of how, or even if, to help.

How could I, she deliberated as she fought the strange pangs of compassion, *care for such a monster?*

A tickle on her cheek drew her immediate attention and as she reached to wipe it away, she realized it was a tear. Without another thought, she pulled herself from the bed and quickly crossed the room to him. As she neared him, his hands formed into fists and drove against the glass.

She froze in her steps, hands drawn into her chest at his frightening display. She stood in the shadows, just behind him yet unseen in his current state. He let out a frustrated growl, pulled his head back, and rammed it into the glass in front of him.

Liana lurched forward and grabbed his shoulder as she cried out, "Please stop!"

Instantly, he turned, pulled her grasp from his shoulder, and lifted his fist high above her to strike. As his eyes landed on her tear-drenched face, he immediately released her.

"L-Liana... I-"

Dread filled his face and cut off his voice as he examined his own hands. Casimir shook his head with a confused look. As he turned from her, he rubbed his forehead.

"I didn't mean to startle you... I ju-" Liana cleared her throat and collected her courage before she continued,

The Veil

"Is everything... Are you okay?" A look of genuine concern filled her face as she wiped her tears away and stood beside him.

A quick breath of condescending air escaped his chest in a half laugh, half sigh of frustration. "You don't have to pretend to ca-"

"Look," she interrupted and ignored his side scowl as she stared back. "We certainly have disagreements, but your battles are my battles now."

He turned his gaze from her and stared into the gardens far below them. She watched his reflection in silence. His brow furrowed as the internal war she knew all too well waged on.

"It all affects me too, doesn't it?" Liana questioned as she leaned her shoulder against the glass next to Casimir.

Finally, his distant stares broke with a sideways glance at Liana. His shoulders lifted with a deep breath and after a small moment of silence, he slowly began, "Where I come from, people submit to their King. They," he gestured his open palm to the unseen citizens behind him, "would let me kill every... single... one of them, rather than submit!" As he spoke, the back of his hand struck his open palm. "What good is a Kingdom with no citizens?"

With the shake of his head, he turned his inquisitive stare to Liana and waited for the answer he wasn't able to find on his own. As he looked to her, their eyes connected and they both froze, each held captive by the pain and fire that churned within the other.

If I can help him, she thought, *I could save the others from his wrath.*

The Light Within

"Maybe," she broke the silence and tried desperately to seize the opportunity, "they still don't see *you* as *their* King?"

A dismissive scowl instantly consumed his expression and he turned from her to stare over the gardens again. She reached for his arm to reassure him and as her skin met with his, he immediately looked down at her hand.

Maybe, she sincerely hoped, *I can show him a better way.*

Her hand lingered on his arm and after a moment she quietly continued, "Maybe there's a way we can show the-"

He suddenly shoved her hand away, turned from her, and threw his hands in the air as his words took flight, "I swear your kind are so stubborn! Just give in and let me rule over your lives. Things will be so much better!" He let an exaggerated sigh interrupt his rant before he continued, emphasizing each word with his booming anger, "Yet, they fight me, just as you do!"

"I- Wha-" The perplexed look she wore was soon replaced with one of frustration as she pushed back, desperate for a shift in the situation, "Let me help!"

"The Kingdom is *different* now L-i-a-n-a." He drew her name out like a child desperate to torment as he paced the room. "We had to rebuild the mess you left the Kingdom in! Two completely different Kingdoms coming together as one. You think that just happens? It isn't easy! Laws *have* to change. You *must* embrace it!" Amidst his pacing, he rounded on her and moved closer as he spoke, "The Kingdom needs to see *true* strength, not this compromise bullshit you've been trying. They *need*, no," he leaned his face into hers and forced her against the glass wall behind her, "*crave* someone who can exert true strength!"

As he turned from her, she rubbed her temples, exhausted by his hardened heart, and muttered, "You have no *idea* what *true* strength even is."

He moved across the room, oblivious to her words, and continued on his rant, "Went through this whole fucking ordeal to get you back here for these idiots to bow down and yet the war rages on. Useless!"

With a nervous swallow, Liana slowly moved back to the bed. It was clear to her now that she was reaching the end of her rope with Casimir. Her eyes widened as she drew the covers over her head and wondered what it meant for her now that she was *useless*.

o   o   o

The compounding scarcity of sleep and disturbing events from the previous night forced a sleepy yawn from Liana. She hurriedly hid it behind her hand, not wanting to offend W, who carried on enthusiastically next to her. As they gradually made their way to the breakfast hall, she tried halfheartedly to focus on the conversation. Her mind wandered as fast as her eyes; they flitted around without focusing on much of anything.

"Liana?" A prodded Liana's side and gained her immediate attention.

As W and A burst into laughter, Liana realized she must've been in another one of her daydreaming states. A pink hue rose in her cheeks and with a half-laugh, she rubbed the back of her neck awkwardly.

"Okay, I wasn't paying attention." She shook her head as they continued up the hall.

The Light Within

"W was simply advising you to do... the opposite of what you were just doing." A smiled at her reassuringly.

With a light airy laugh, W chimed in, "Simply trying to avoid another... incident."

They exploded with laughter and rounded yet another corner.

"Ahh, good morning, ladies."

His voice echoed from the distance and as it reached them, their laughter immediately ceased. The sudden silence brought a cruel smile to his face and instantly stopped them in their steps. Casimir stood a distance away, arms behind his back, while his Commander loomed dauntingly behind him.

"Please," he began again as he leisurely made his way to them. "Don't stop on my behalf. Come," he gestured to W, "let's hear the joke."

Gulps sounded from beside her. As W opened her mouth to respond, Liana cleared her throat and interrupted her.

"Nonsense, just silly ladies' talk." With an innocent smile, she waved her hand at W, who immediately sealed her lips with a favorable smile and nodded.

Casimir stopped before the group and examined Liana. She stared back; her sleepy smile unwavering to his prying stare. The moment lingered on uncomfortably and she sensed her companions stiffen under the weight of tension in the air.

He turned his sights on the others and as his eyes met theirs, he suddenly spat in angry fury, "What are you looking at?"

W and A immediately turned their attention to the floor while they each mumbled an indistinct apology.

The Veil

Liana's eyes narrowed to a scowl as she crossed her arms in front of her chest.

"Don't talk to them like that." Her soft, yet stern words caught Casimir off guard and held him in an open-mouthed stupor for a brief, yet glorious moment.

Casimir quickly snapped out of his stunned state and closed his eyes. He took a deep breath before his voice boomed through the walkways, "Leave us."

He looked to Liana and gestured dismissively to the ladies at her side. As they turned to leave, her gaze fell to the floor. As soon as their backs turned, Casimir reached for her, grabbed the back of her neck in a stern grip, and steered her down the corridor.

She stiffened at his touch and instantly her lifeless stare fixed on the open palms of her interlaced fingers that hung carefully in front of her waist. As the alluring scents of the breakfast hall wafted in the warm air, Liana closed her eyes. Instantly, the memory of Casimir in her earlier dream raced across her eyelids. She immediately opened her eyes as the color rose in her cheeks, all the while the confused feelings swirled in her mind.

Liana shook her head slightly and attempted to shift her thoughts to a more desirable topic. As the aromas called for her attention again, she thankfully contemplated the decadent food that was sure to be served. She twisted her head to the side as Casimir's grip tightened uncomfortably around the back of her neck.

As he pulled her by the passageway that led to the breakfast hall, several of the lingering individuals that conversed just outside the hall's doorway, caught sight of them and began to whisper. Casimir shifted his grip to Liana's hand and pulled it around his bicep. He squeezed it in a crushing grip to hold it in place as he smiled and nodded to the others.

She turned to them and nodded but as her eyes landed on Khius, she quickly turned her attention back to where Casimir led her. Her head soon dropped as she realized he led her away from the breakfast hall.

"Oh." He looked to her concerned face and with a short, condescending scoff, turned his sights down the hallway and uttered his dismissive words, "You're skipping that today." After a momentary pause, he muttered, "Your gowns have been looking a little snug, after all."

She rolled her eyes and tried to ignore his sad attempt at a wound as she fixed her gaze on the hall before them.

"Besides," he paused and let out a massive sigh before he continued, "we have more important things to discuss."

He lifted his hand and gestured for her to proceed. She looked up to find the Commander at a small silver door before them. As she approached, he pushed it open. She stepped inside and instantly drew a sharp inward breath.

Liana held her breath until they moved into the room behind her and closed the door. The small, scarcely lit space before her was occupied by a young woman. The woman jumped as they entered, which caused the shackles at her wrists and feet to clang violently against the stone floor.

Liana's hand covered her mouth as she examined the young woman's disheveled state. Her beautiful gown of black and white was stained and torn in several places, yet it scarcely compared to the state the woman was in.

The Veil

Liana looked away to the dark corners of the room and gagged as the smell of sulfur assaulted her nostrils.

"I require just a simple task, then we can get on with our day," Casimir spoke quietly as he approached Liana.

Liana shook her head and stared on in disbelief as he shushed her.

"*Convince* her that she would very much like to… *embrace* the Commander." With a smile, he turned and gestured openly to Darkness.

Her chin tucked to her chest as her posture straightened and she questioned him, "Embrace?" She looked away from him, shook her head as she rubbed her temple, and questioned again, "Wait, convince? What do you mean convince her?"

She immediately turned toward the woman. With a laugh she spoke, "Ma'am, would you like to *embrace* the Commander?"

The woman stared back at Liana; brow furrowed in confusion. She pulled her arms into her chest and unsteadily shook her head 'no'.

Liana shrugged and as she turned back to Casimir, began again, "I guess she doesn-"

Her sarcastic defiance was immediately interrupted as the shadows around her struck her down. She spun slightly and reached out just in time to stop her face before it connected with the floor. As she blinked back the darkness that crept up in her line of vision, she reached for the side of her face. Casimir's steps thudded menacingly as he moved to stand in front of her. He crouched suddenly and as he cautioned her, she saw a red flicker in his eyes.

The Light Within

"Don't play stupid with me girl. I know you have the power to," he pulled her hand from her face and waved it before her, "*persuade* people."

Her mind instantly flitted to the previous night and how he withdrew from her touch.

"Yeaaa, that!" he shouted in her face before he shoved her hand into her chest.

That's what he thinks that was, she contemplated in her confusion, *instead of how my heart actually broke for him?*

Her brow furrowed while she shook her head as she insisted, "I wasn't try-"

He held his finger up and called for her silence, "Shh, shh. Let me see what you can do, that's all. Then we go to breakfast and move on from," he gestured from Liana to the young lady, "all of this. What do you say?" Casimir stood to his feet. He towered over Liana as he crossed his arms and waited.

When she didn't budge, he pressed further, "You want to help the Kingdom, don't you? Then show me you'll use your power for *me*."

Liana glared up at Casimir briefly before she pulled herself to her feet. She brushed herself off and with a sigh, crossed her arms in front of her chest. "I'm not going to force someone to do something against their will. If she doesn't wa-"

"It's MY will!" he shouted furiously in her face as his hand hit his chest. His attention shifted behind Liana momentarily before he continued with an unconvincingly calm tone, "It is *my* Kingdom, so it is *my* will. You *both* will obey."

Liana swallowed slowly and shivered as she became aware of the chilling presence of Darkness that loomed behind her. Her eyes connected with Casimir again, though momentarily, for as they flickered red, she sighed and turned from him.

She approached the young girl, who raised her arms and cowered. Liana reached out, snatched the girl's wrist in her fist, and stared intently at the young woman as she thought to her, *is this worth us both losing our lives over?*

The young woman's eyes opened wide when she heard Liana. She looked to the connection at her wrist, then to Casimir. Casimir's footsteps echoed as he crossed the floor. Gaze never leaving her, he watched Liana curiously and perked up as the girl looked at him with horror. The fear she wore spread over her whole being as she looked to the approaching Commander.

Liana smiled slightly, seeing it all perfectly through the young woman's eyes. An icy tingle of air crawled up her spine, sent a shiver through her core, and reminded her of the daunting task at hand.

Focus, she insisted to the young woman who immediately turned her gaze back to Liana.

As her eyes connected with Liana's, she relaxed and gradually Liana saw dozens of images play out before her own eyes. Tears welled up as she felt the powerful emotional connection between this young woman and the One she showed Liana.

Turning her head from the woman, she blinked back tears rapidly and tried to focus on the room around her. She swayed as the connection overwhelmed her and released the young woman's wrist. Liana stood for a moment, hands on her hips, while she stared up at the ceiling. She blinked several times as she slowly regained her focus and debated within. Casimir's sigh of irritation cut through the air.

The Light Within

He called out from a short distance behind her, "Well?"

She shot back instantly, "I can't."

A formidable laugh echoed from Darkness as his boots clunked closer.

"Wait," Casimir said.

Liana turned to see Casimir's hand lifted towards Darkness. Darkness stopped in his steps, raised his chin, and eyed Liana suspiciously. She turned her attention to Casimir who approached her. Slowly, he circled around her while he studied her. Liana turned her focus to the floor and braced for whatever spectacle he plotted. She held her breath as he stopped in front of her and reached for her hand. He smacked the top of her hand playfully, which caused the bangles at her wrist to jingle.

With a short laugh, he finally spoke, "We cannot punish her if she cannot get it the first time. You need practice is all."

He released her, moved his hand to her chin, and tilted it to meet his gaze. She stared blankly at his unseeing eyes and caused him to shift uncomfortably.

"Come, you must rest," he said as his hand slid around the back of her neck and steered her from the room.

Chapter 5
Still Fight Left

Liana jolted upright in bed with her covers clutched tight to her chest. Her wide eyes examined the King's Chambers around her and as she found she was alone, her breathing gradually slowed. Her mind, however, raced on uncontrollably and tried to recall the details of how she ended up here.

With a sigh, she hauled herself from the bed. She rubbed her head while she sluggishly crossed the room to mindlessly wash and dress. Liana jumped suddenly at the familiar knock of the guard as it sounded at the door. Without hesitation, she quickly crossed the room and yanked open the massive doors. The elven guard, dressed in his usual dark wraps, jumped as the light flooded the darkened corridor.

"My Queen! You're up and about?" he asked with an elevated air of excitement to his words.

She eyed him in confusion at his question and retorted, "Yes, of course I am. Why wouldn't I?"

"It's... it's been weeks. I meant no offense," he replied as he tucked his hand to his chest and bowed slightly.

Weeks, she questioned herself internally, *there's no way!*

He turned toward the hall and gestured for her to lead. She shook the look of shock from her face and proceeded up the narrow passageway. Her mind, clouded in a strange fog, withheld her most recent memories as she struggled to recall even the slightest detail. With her arms crossed over her chest, she walked on deep in thought.

"No questions today?" he asked curiously.

The Light Within

She jumped slightly at his inquiry; she had nearly forgotten he was there with her as she quietly replied, "I'd rather be the silent one who doesn't answer this time."

With a short laugh, he conceded, "Fair enough."

The small break in her spiraling thoughts allowed her the chance to direct her attention elsewhere. As they walked on, she recalled the brief days in her past when she would walk with her King. She closed her eyes and hugged her arms to her chest as she clung to the small fragments of memory from her time with him.

She recalled the radiant, calming warmth that surrounded him and how his words themselves brought about an air of peace. As she remembered, she was convinced the air surrounding her was warming up. Her chest filled with a deep breath and finally, she relaxed. She opened her eyes while she walked on and suddenly heard a distant whisper. Her heart leaped as she instantly recognized his voice.

Impossible, her thoughts fought for her to be rational.

Brow furrowed; she shook her head. A short burst of wind blew past her cheek and with it, another whisper, in an exhilarating breeze that visibly shook her.

"Did you hear that?" she asked as she turned to the guard for confirmation.

"Hear what? I thought you weren-"

"Shh."

She held her hand up and almost touched his mask as she listened intently. The whisper, more distinct now than before, echoed down the corridor from their position as she tried to point it out.

"That. Did you hear that?"

"We should retu-"

Still Fight Left

With a glare, she scoffed at him, turned, and jogged after the elusive call.

"Not again." He sighed as he ran after her and shouted, "My Queen, please!"

As they rounded the corner, their eyes landed on the mysterious door of light at the end of the darkened, narrow corridor. He reached for her just as she lunged and gripped her wrist in a delicate, yet unbreakable grasp.

She caught the brief look on his face once his eyes connected with the mysterious door and turned to him, searching for answers, "You know what that place is?"

"I...It's beyond your understanding. You should not play in there. It is dangerous." He pulled her closer as he spoke; his vibrant, emerald eyes urged her to comply.

"Yea, so they say," she said through narrowed eyes and with one swift motion, turned, pulled his arm over her shoulder, and broke his grasp on her.

Liana moved swiftly around him and ran for the darkened hall. The illusive voice called to her through the whispers around her just as she entered and caused her footsteps to halt. Instantly, the guard seized her around the waist with one arm. He braced himself against the frame of the entryway, held onto the wall with one arm, and reached into the darkness with his other.

He yanked her from the shadowed hall and held her against his chest while he pleaded with her, "Please! It *is* dangerous!"

She dug and clawed at his arm that secured her against his solid torso but was unable to break his grasp. Frustrated, Liana grabbed his arm with both of her hands and shouted, "Let go!"

The Light Within

As her words flew, so did numerous tiny sparks. The guard immediately released her. They both stood, open-mouthed, and stared at Liana's hands.

I assumed you left me, she thought to the power within as hope flickered inside her.

Their heads lifted in unison and as their eyes met, he reached for her and implored, "My Queen, please!"

"No!" she shouted and raised her hand to meet his neck.

As her palm connected with his flesh, a large zap sounded around them and sent the guard sliding across the stone floor. She cringed but her eyes never left his limp form. Drawing her hands to her mouth in horror, she waited for any sign of life.

His back rose suddenly as he drew in a trivial breath and Liana expelled hers in a pained whisper, "Sorry."

With a quick glance around the corridor to confirm it remained unoccupied, she turned from the guard and ran up the shadowy hall towards the door. As she reached the peculiar frame of light, her steps halted. The warm glow that illuminated from the other side, radiated over Liana, and comforted her restless heart. She froze only a moment longer until the oddly familiar whisper that drew her there, called to her again.

"My King!" she exclaimed as she excitedly pushed herself through the solid-looking curtain of shadows.

Her hand instinctively covered her eyes, though the previously blinding light that met her on the other side of the door didn't seem as harsh this time. As the swirling whispers ebbed to a low hum around her, her vision focused, and she realized she stood alone.

Still Fight Left

"So stupid," she cried aloud to herself. "Of course, it isn't you!" she exclaimed angrily. Liana fell to her knees and covered her face with her hands while she whispered to herself, "I'm losing it."

As the weight of her lost words swirled viciously over her, she desperately tried to stop the tears. Her mind continued to spiral and compiled the list of atrocities that could arbitrarily link to her bloodied hands in even the slightest manner. Tears continued to pour as she reached out and steadied herself against the fluid walls of the bright room.

Through her gasps for air and stifled cries, she called out, "M-My King...I'm so s-sorry. I let your Kingdom fall to ruins... I...I let the darkness in. Please... forgive me."

With her last words, she closed her eyes and let her head rest against the wall. Slowly but surely, her breathing returned to normal, and her shoulders relaxed. As she calmed, so did the commotion around her; the loud hum of chaotic noise gradually faded to distant whispers.

"Liana," a murmur reached through the others and caught her attention.

Her eyes shot open immediately as she felt something move across the palm of her hand that rested against the curtain-like wall. She lifted her head, immediately pushed herself from the wall, and clutched her knees to her chest. On the other side of the flowing wall, a shadowy figure rose from its previously crouched position.

As its height increased dauntingly over Liana, she quietly pulled herself to her feet. She stood frozen in place, a cautious distance from the wall as she studied the shadow. It paced slowly in front of her for only a moment before it stopped and tapped the wall with a slender finger.

Countless whispers swirled around her, yet her focus remained on the wall before her as she heard it call to her again, "Liana."

"I'm here," she called out nervously.

The shadow before her perked up instantly and significantly grew in height as it called to her, "Don't let your pain shift your focus."

Her brow furrowed as the words whirled around her. She edged closer to the wall and narrowed her eyes as she tried in vain to focus through the foggy curtain of the wall before her.

"There is power in restraint. Be wary of how you use it," it called to her again.

Instantly, her memories stirred and drew her thoughts to the stench of a decrepit room as his words reverberated tauntingly in her mind, *convince her...you have the power to persuade.* As the remarks stirred in her mind, so did the restless spirits near her.

The winds whipped violently around her and blocked the shadowy figure's voice as it called out through the veil to her, "...not of the light... Casimir... never use... lose... consuming darkness."

"What?" Liana shouted frantically through the roaring winds.

Steadily, she pulled herself through the forceful air currents that fought to keep her from the wall. As she reached the wall, she looked up to see a looming darkness rise behind the shadowy figure that called to her.

"Look out!" she called, desperate to warn the shadow.

Still Fight Left

The winds lashed harder and stifled her warning. They pulled at her and almost knocked her from her feet. In one last attempt, she reached for the wall and placed her palms on the silky, solid curtain.

As she connected with the palms of the shadowy figure on the other side, she screamed, "Behind you!"

With her words, released a massive pulse of energy and the room quickly faded from her. She gasped out for air and desperately searched around her until she realized she was no longer in the mysterious room of light. Liana pulled herself to her feet as she brushed the dust and dirt from her dark blue gown. When she looked up from herself, her eyes traced over two ornately decorated, green doors in the distance before her.

"The garden!" she whispered excitedly to herself as she set off towards the doors.

Her hope increased with every step that brought her closer. Liana tiptoed over the stone floors, careful not to send the echo of her escape to the wrong ears. She glanced around constantly as she made her way down the extensive corridor. Just as she thought she was in the clear, she heard the terrifying clunk from the boots of the Commander echo distantly behind her.

Without a second glance, she turned towards the doors and ran. Though she was quick, he was right behind her. As she entered the branching hallway that led to the doors, her foot hit a rug, and just as he grabbed hold of her, she slipped. They went down in a jumble of arms and shouts. She kicked and struck at him while she struggled to get to her feet.

"Why do you keep fighting me?" Casimir asked through gritted teeth.

The Light Within

Liana glanced fearfully as the Commander approached, then looked back to Casimir. Casimir held his hand up to stop the Commander before he turned his attention back to Liana. He grabbed her wrists and pinned them against the rough rug as he pulled himself over her. He struggled against her, pulled her wrists together in his crushing grip and moved his free hand to hold her face still.

"Can't you see?" His angry words spit through his teeth, "You are nothing without me."

In one swift movement, she pulled her knees between them and kicked as hard as she could. He slid with the rug, over the floor from her. She turned over and pulled herself across the floor as she climbed to her feet. Liana bolted for the end of the hall where the doors to the garden lay.

When she stopped to struggle with the large, hooped handles of the doors, Casimir slammed his form into hers. They crashed through the doors and landed on the gravel of the garden's walkways. She screamed out in agony from the sting of the stones as they buried themselves into her skin. Casimir stood, grabbed a fistful of her hair, and hauled her over the stones.

She reached for her hair and cried out before she buried an elbow in his thigh. He dropped to his knee with an angry growl as she stood. Liana snatched his hair and pulled Casimir's face into her knee. As he crumpled to the ground, Liana turned and ran. She darted through the flowers and shrubs of the elegant garden. Once she reached an iron gate, she wrenched it open, and immediately stopped in her steps. The sight before her made her entirely forget the desperate battle that lay behind.

Still Fight Left

Beyond the gates lay a ruin of smoldering stone. Her hand found her open mouth and she slowly stepped out of the garden as she took in the chaotic scene before her. Lifeless bodies, stacked on each other, lined the streets that led to the lower levels of the city. Soldiers and citizens clashed all around her as children ran from their homes screaming.

"Stop!" she shouted as she saw a guard raise its blade to a young child.

Immediately, she ran over, dipped under the blade, and took the child into her arms. The guard staggered, then turned toward her and lifted the sword again.

"Wait," a stern voice called out over the commotion from behind the guard.

The guard turned, bowed slightly, and backed away to continue in the battle that surrounded them. The commotion whipped around her as she clung to the child in her lap. Casimir took his time to approach her. Once he reached her, he stood and silently watched her for a moment.

"Is this really what you want? This rebellion?" His arms opened wide as he gestured around to the death at her feet. "This is because of you after all. They fight in your name."

She cradled the small child in her trembling arms while the tears cascaded down her cheeks. "Make them stop," she whispered into the child's hair.

"What was that?" he questioned spitefully.

"Make them stop!" she shouted and turned her sights on him.

He looked at the guards nearby and jerked his head in Liana's direction. The elven guard, accompanied by another close by, wrenched the child from Liana's arms and sternly yanked her to her feet.

"Wait..." She looked behind her and cried out again, "Wait! What about all of this?"

"Come now," the elven guard muttered as he harshly pulled her from the scene.

o   o   o

Deep pools of walnut swirled with golden light and gazed back with a cry no ear could hear. Liana's eyes shot open, yet the child's eyes stared back in the dark of the room. With a sigh, she rolled to her back and stared hopelessly at the canopy above her. As she shifted, her arm caught a draft of air. She looked down to the drawn-back bedspread and realized Casimir was nowhere in sight. Gradually, she sat up and looked about the room for any sign of him.

Nothing, her eyes narrowed as her suspicious thoughts emerged, *so where exactly is he then?* With a deep breath, Liana slowly laid back in bed and tried to redirect her thoughts. *Who cares? Maybe he's off dying somewhere.*

Liana closed her eyes and immediately reopened them when she was, yet again, met with the child's eyes. A growl of frustration emerged deep from within her as she slammed her fists down to her sides, into the comforter.

"Those are my children!" she screamed aloud.

With a sudden kick at the restraining blanket, Liana jumped from the bed and paced about the room. Tears poured down her face as she agonized over the fate of the child and the countless faces she may never know.

"The dagger," she whispered to herself as she dashed to Casimir's side of the bed.

She ripped open the drawers beneath the bed and carefully felt around. Swiftly, yet silently, she went through drawer after drawer. With a sigh, and empty-handed, she stood and lifted the bedding. Sighing again, Liana dropped the bedding in defeat and plopped down on the edge.

I can't let him take what power is left, she thought as she focused on her search. *He wouldn't keep that around here.*

She glanced at the door, then back to her tapping fingertips in her lap. Without another thought, she strode across the room and reached for the handle. As her fingertips brushed the metal, she paused, her mouth crooked to the side as she contemplated the repercussions. She shook her head, grabbed the handle, and carefully pulled the door open.

Liana peeked through the stifling darkness. To her surprise, she could see only one guard pacing in the distance. She watched quietly in the shadows as they shuffled past her hall and further down the corridor.

Instantly, Liana slipped from her room and shut the door behind her with a soft click. She flinched and moved quickly to the wall. A sharp inward breath was quickly stifled when she heard the slide of the guard's boot on the stone as they turned around.

She stared on, wide-eyed and waiting as the guard appeared at the end of the hall. With a relieved smile, she watched as the guard shuffled on in their patrol. As they passed her hallway and continued, Liana crept further. She listened with anticipation as the guard turned and made their way back. Liana swayed near the edge of the hall. She stopped and braced herself against the wall; her breath held captive in her chest as the guard moved by.

The guard slowed suddenly and straightened; their hand moved to the blade at their side as they glanced down her hallway. Liana closed her eyes and prayed they didn't turn too far. The soft squeak of a boot signaled the guard's resumed pace and brought a smile to her face. She opened her eyes and watched as they slowly shuffled along.

With a cringe, she stepped into the hall, moved quickly up the corridor, and rounded into the next hallway. In silence, she ran on and with each step, the sting of the cold stone became more apparent. She looked down to her feet and slowed her pace as she shrugged regretfully at herself for not remembering even a robe.

Liana made her way through the darkness, across the castle. Her hand found her chin as she eyed a door that stood open across a lofty, open room. It was dark beyond, not even a flicker of candlelight shone through the crack. Steps echoed near her and immediately sent her flat against the wall. She listened as they crossed the open room and when the steps grew distant, she peeked around the wall to find another guard on patrol.

She watched as the guard marched off into the shadows of the night. Once the hall was silent again, she ran for the open door. Noiselessly she slid through the slim opening and pressed herself against the wall. Through the darkness, she concentrated and made out a narrow, infinitely stretching, hallway full of doors.

In search of a distant muttering that echoed indiscernibly, she paused and leaned her ear near one of the doors. Liana waited as the guard shuffled past the open hall she had come from. Once they moved by, she quietly tiptoed along the wall of doors. She crept by door after door until she heard the undeniably cheerful tones of W rise through the eerie silence.

Liana immediately stopped and crouched against the wall. Slowly, she peered around the frame of the door and through the small crack of its slightly ajar position.

Still Fight Left

Her eyes widened as she watched W and A kneel at the feet of Casimir. He paced back and forth, his head in his hand, while he muttered to himself.

"Your highness, I can assure you this is not necessary," W spoke softly as the clunk of the Commander's boots reverberated around the tiny room.

"Silence!" Casimir yelled out and he threw his fists to his side.

Liana's heart threatened to leap from her chest as she watched on in silence from the hallway. Casimir gestured for his Commander, who slowly moved between W and A. As Casimir lifted his palm, Darkness placed his hands on the back of each of their necks.

I have to do something, Liana agonized internally as she watched the horrific scene before her, *but what? They'd just kill me...* the thought trailed off as she watched the wispy shadows rush from Darkness and wrap around the necks of the ladies next to him.

"Now, I'll ask again." Casimir took a deep breath before he continued, "What have you done with the tiny one?"

Laughter boomed from Darkness as he released W and turned toward A.

"What have you found?" Casimir questioned as he paced closer to his Commander.

"Sir," A started slowly at the urging of Darkness. "The Queen mentioned her concern for the being. I told her it was best not to think of those things."

Darkness laughed again, then squeezed her neck as he growled over her, "You told her you'd take care of them."

A laughed mockingly and turned her attention to the Commander as she replied, "Yea take care of them, like a bullet to the brain. I'm not sloshin soup from the kitchen, all the way down those stairs, on and on, then to the left and shit."

"Alright, alright," Casimir rolled his eyes and gestured to the Commander to drop her.

"Wait," Darkness urged, "there's more."

Liana gulped as Casimir urged the Commander to continue. He turned toward A and lifted her in a crushing grip until she was at his eye level. Slowly, his dark sludge crawled over her as she screamed out until her cries suddenly cut off. Her body went limp, and a smile grew over the face of Darkness.

"Liana called her by name," he growled before a puzzled expression manifested on his face, and he closed his eyes.

"And how does she know her name?" Casimir asked as his pacing slowed and he rounded on the two. After a moment of no reply and only indistinct grumbling from Darkness, he spoke again, "Well?"

Darkness growled and shook A before he barked back irritated, "I can't say. There's something hidden."

"Release her." Casimir waved his hand.

Instantly, the Commander pulled the tarlike shadows from A and dropped her to the floor. The Commander and Casimir huddled a short distance from the ladies and conversed in hushed tones, inaudible to Liana. She watched as A lay gasping for air and eventually W moved to help her to her feet. A took several deep breaths as the two of them turned back to Casimir and bowed their heads.

"Fine," Casimir said as he raised his hand to the Commander. "She's yours then, find out what you can."

Still Fight Left

"No!" A screamed in horror as Darkness rounded on her.

Liana clamped her hands over her mouth and stifled her cries while tears streamed over her fingers. Darkness grabbed A's hair in his fist and in one swift movement, drug her toward the door. Liana moved to the next room and silently shut the door just before the Commander burst through the door she had previously been crouched at.

Casimir's voice echoed from the next room, "Let this be a lesson to you."

Liana pressed her ear to the cold stone wall as W's voice echoed softly, "Yessir."

Breath held captive in her chest Liana listened attentively for the soft steps of Casimir and W as they proceeded from the room and up the hall. When she could hear them no longer, Liana slid down the stone wall to the floor. Tears spilled from her into her hands that now hid her face.

One small slip up, Liana thought as her mind began to spiral, *so stupid! When he finds out she was in the house with me...*

Liana shook her head and pulled herself to her feet. She pulled her nightgown to her face and dried her drenched skin. Slowly, she drew a massive breath of air, held it for a moment, and slowly released it.

Arietta is strong, Liana confirmed within, *please help her resist him.*

As she lifted her hand to open the door, a small white light appeared at her fingertips. She turned her hand over as the light traced down to the center of her palm before it pulled away from her. As it left her flesh, she swayed and caught herself against the wall. The tiny wisp of silvery, white light bounced playfully in front of her for a split second before it shot through the door.

Unsure of what she just witnessed, Liana stood for a moment before she jerked the door open. She stepped into the hall just in time to see the small ball of light shoot into the distance. Brow furrowed in confusion, Liana stood near the rows of doors for several moments.

"Okay...cool," she whispered aloud to herself as she looked down to her hand.

Suddenly, footsteps echoed near her. Liana shoved herself against the wall as the shadow of a guard passed by a branching corridor. Once they sounded far enough into the distance, she bolted up the hallway. As she silently walked through the castle, her thoughts held her attention and blocked the urgency of her return from her mind.

She questioned herself as she replayed the encounter in her mind in disbelief, *Would she really kill them? Arietta said she took care of them... A bullet to the brain, and now they're missing.*

She shook her head as she assured herself, *No, she wouldn't. She had to have said that to throw them off. Wouldn't Darkness sense that?*

Liana rubbed the temple of her forehead with her fingertips as she tried to unravel the puzzle.

Arietta's voice echoed in her mind as she recalled the details, *'kitchen, all the way down those stairs, on and on, then to the left'.*

Liana perked up instantly as she realized, *that must be how to get to the dungeons! Maybe that's where they'll take her. Tomorrow night,* she nodded to herself, *we have to get out of here.*

"Hey! What are you doing out?" The guard's voice startled Liana and brought her back to reality.

Still Fight Left

She looked up from her thoughts to find herself in the hall leading to the King's Chambers. With an eye roll, she held up her hand as the patrolling guard neared her. Taken aback, they paused and watched her as she walked up the hallway towards the room. As she pushed the doors to the chamber open, her sights fell on Casimir, who paced at the balcony glass. She cringed and turned to close the doors.

I can't handle him right now, she thought, irritated. *Poor Arietta, I'm sure Darkness isn't being easy on you.*

She shuddered at the thought. As she turned around and saw his gaze fixed on her, she dropped her sights to the floor.

"Where have you been?" he asked calmly.

She adorned the familiar blank stare as she searched for a decent response, to no avail.

Words laced with irritation, he spoke again, "I asked you a question."

He turned, fully facing her now, and slowly walked to her. As he turned, the moon glinted off something secured at his side. Her eyes lingered only a moment as her heart leaped with excitement.

The blade, she thought with a determined exhilaration.

"Out to see Khius again?" he questioned her with a suspicious glare.

Her eyes locked with his and as she shook her head with disappointment at his accusation, she countered, "Where have you been?"

"You don't need to concern yourself with that," he said with a dismissive wave at her and as he stopped in his steps, he pulled his shirt off and tossed it carelessly onto the nearby sofa.

The Light Within

She pushed herself from the door and made her way to the balcony window as she pressed further, "I think I do."

He heaved a sigh and ran his hands through his messy hair. "Liana please, I need your full cooperation. Just tell m-"

As he spoke her fingertips reached for her temples. She couldn't take another of his hateful spirals and before she knew it, she shouted through gritted teeth, "Oh, shut up!"

Before her hands even reached her head, her eyes widened with the realization that her lips spoke the words her mind normally caged. The room remained silent, and she didn't dare turn to confirm his feelings on the matter. She stiffened when his breath crawled across her neck.

Is this it? She asked herself as she took in the garden below, *will I be able to fight him off this time?*

He gently moved her hair to the side, "You have a lot of nerve."

She rolled her eyes and scoffed at his words.

"What? What else would you like to say?" he questioned with an air of curiosity in his words.

Before she could stop herself, the words spewed from her in a tidal wave that her exhausted state could no longer contain, "*I* have a lot of nerve? You have some nerve dragging me back to fix the mess YOU started. Then you flip out when it isn't *instantly* resolved."

"I don't *need*," he said with a clenched jaw and instantly wrapped his arm around her neck. He pulled her close to his body and slowly lifted her from the ground. She clawed at his arm and tried to pull it from her neck as his whispers continued, "you to *fix* anything! I can do it all without you."

Still Fight Left

The moonlight reflected their image in the glass before them; it glinted off the blade again. Liana kept her eyes fixed on the stars as she fought for air.

Her vision blurred as she heard a tiny voice plead within, *give in. Just submit.*

"No," she squeaked out and with the last of her strength, she raised her legs and kicked against the glass before her.

The force sent them to the ground and as she landed on top of Casimir, she knocked the air from him. He released her instantly and she rolled off of him to the floor. Gasping and desperate to fill her lungs, Liana held her throat and slowly pulled herself away from him. She hauled herself to her knees and crawled towards the glass.

Casimir was to his feet and followed tauntingly behind her, "Why do you insist on fighting? Just do what I say already." He stooped and grabbed a fistful of her hair, then whispered threateningly into her face, "Don't you understand I'll end you?"

Eyes fixed on the glass before her, she growled and as she shouted, her elbow drove upward into his face, "Shut up!"

Liana pushed off the floor and ran at him. She threw her shoulder into his stomach and shoved him against the glass. Just as his fist drove into her ribcage, she freed the blade from the holster near her face. He thrust his elbow down onto her back and sent her to the floor again. Immediately, the shadows around her lifted her and threw her across the floor. As she slammed into his nightstand, she rolled over and slid the blade beneath the bed.

His face turned flat as he turned from her. He walked along the balcony and ran his hands through his hair as he caught his breath.

The Light Within

"Why do you make me do this?" he questioned with a sigh and peered out to the gardens.

A determined glare burned in her eyes as she got to her feet.

"The Commander was right when he said you liked things rough," he taunted with a sadistic laugh.

"You're a monster!" she shouted and lunged at him.

He turned just as she reached him and allowed her arm to land across his neck. Her eyes burned with rage as she shoved against him with all her weight into the glass.

"Do it," he urged her with a smile as his face turned red.

Confusion flickered across her face at his response as her thoughts swirled, *he's distracting you. Kill him!* She shook her head and pressed harder.

"Yes, kill me," he choked out and gasped. "Do it!"

She glared and suddenly grabbed his neck in her hand. When she closed her eyes, the familiar pulse of energy never came. His laughter reverberated around her. She opened her eyes and found not even the tiniest of sparks. Liana opened her hand and slowly backed away from him.

The room slowly tilted and spun around her. She reached out, caught herself against the sofa, and lowered herself to sit as she tried to regain her energy. His laugh grew behind her as he neared her.

"Oh Liana," he said as his laughter finally dwindled. "You act like you're the one in control and you may have power, but," he paused and tucked her hair behind her ear to view her face. "I control when you use it. So, who has the real power?"

Still Fight Left

She rubbed her pounding head as the familiar tinkle of bangles drew her attention. A look of horror spread across her face as she lowered her arm and examined the bracelet.

His growling laughter rose in his chest as he spoke, "That's right."

She stared down at her wrists as he confirmed her fears.

His steps echoed ominously as he moved around her and spoke, "I knew it was necessary to take precautions to restrain your unruly," he paused, knelt before her, and jerked her face upward, "spirit."

A tear fell down her face and she shook with the realization that she was powerless against him. He smiled as the thought crossed her mind. Instantly, she shut her eyes and prayed within, *please protect me.*

"Stupid girl! The light can't save you from me!" he growled.

Casimir stood and lifted his hand. While her prayers formed to whispers, surrounding shadows drug her from the couch.

As the room faded from her sight, his words ripped menacingly through her mind, "We still have some work to do with you."

Chapter 6

For Peace

"Get up," Casimir urged while he nudged her shoulder with his boot.

Liana raised herself slightly to her elbow and tried to blink away the fog that blanketed her vision. The room slowly manifested before her in a darkened, surreal state.

"What? What's going on?" she asked, confused.

As she lifted her hand to rub the disorienting haze from her sleepy eyes, he gripped her elbow and yanked her to her feet. She swayed when he released her and immediately felt the soft, yet stern grip of another at her side. Once she steadied herself, they released her and moved about the room. Liana kept her eyes fixed on Casimir who studied her from the balcony window.

W appeared before her; her smiling face interrupted the pangs of frustration rising in Liana as Casimir lingered mysteriously. She gestured for Liana to lift her arms as she gently removed her ragged nightgown. Gradually, she helped Liana into a stretchy, blue, iridescent gown and adjusted the fabric. Casimir turned and peered through the glass into the distance.

"Liana." Casimir cleared his throat before he continued, "My Queen. We must hurry to a significant ceremony where I *must* have your *full* cooperation. We will announce vital changes for the Kingdom to move forward."

The dwindling glow of the evening's sun reflected warmly across his face. Yet, as he carried on, his words chilled her, and she turned her focus away. Her wandering eyes landed on the minuscule fragment of the blade that

For Peace

stuck out from under the bed and begged for her immediate attention.

Her gaze turned, and as her wide-eyed expression locked with W, her heart skipped a beat. W's brow furrowed momentarily as she watched Liana's display before she adorned the familiar fixed smile. Just as she finished adjusting Liana's hair, she gave a quick wink. If Liana hadn't been staring directly in her face, she would've missed it.

Suddenly, Casimir shoved W aside, waved her away, and set his sights on Liana. She kept her stony expression glued on his face. Not even as W nudged the blade beneath the cover of the bedframe on her way from the room did she dare look away. She swallowed regretfully and hoped she didn't just cause the torture of another innocent, like Arietta. Liana blinked back tears at the thought and chased the idea of her plans for the night from her mind just as Casimir reached for her.

He gripped her jaw in his bony clutch and hissed menacingly into her face, "Are you listening?"

"I am," she quietly answered.

"Good," he said as he released her and let his hand linger. "As I was saying. We must maintain a united front before the Kingdom. If you truly wish to end this nonsense war, then you must appear to support me, even if you don't."

He glared directly into her eyes.

"I understand," she muttered without a blink.

His scowl turned to confusion and was quickly replaced with a skeptical stare as he continued, "That means n-"

"No speaking. Smile, look pretty, and be a good little Queen."

The Light Within

Her robotic repetition of his previous threats didn't seem to amuse him as much as it did herself. She flinched as his lingering hand found the back of her neck, gripped tightly, and yanked her closer.

"I mean it." He took a massive breath and turned his head upward to expel it before he turned his attention back to her, and he continued, "And if you run, even if you escape, I will *always* find you and I will personally end you."

She gulped and stared blankly into the distance as he released her with a sickening smile that settled over his face.

"Let's go," he said while he clenched her arm in a restricting grip and steered her from the chamber.

As they neared the throne room, Casimir secured Liana's arm around his bicep in a crushing hold. They stood before the doors of the throne room alone and silent for a moment before Casimir stiffened, cleared his throat, and looked to Liana. She rolled her lifeless eyes with a sigh then turned a properly smiling face to Casimir.

"Beautiful," he said and matched her smile.

He turned from her as the doors before them opened. Her perfectly placed expressions hid the uncertainty that swirled within as she pondered the confusing compliment. Her thoughts didn't center on the topic long for, as the doors opened, the crowded room before them gained her undivided attention.

Liana looked over the heavily painted faces before her while they cheered and applauded with enthusiasm. As Casimir jerked her forward, she raised her hand and gave a few half-convincing waves. Casimir stopped several times when crossing the hall to shake hands with different individuals.

For Peace

Each time they stopped, numerous hands reached for her, and though her face hid it well, with each connection came the draining effects of their muddled minds. By the time they reached the massive doors leading to the Kingdom, Liana was forced to lean into Casimir for support. He turned to the crowd behind them with a huge grin while he wrapped an arm around her.

"Thank you," his voice echoed as he lifted his arm to silence the crowd. "Thank you all for your encouragement. Your unrelenting support is vital as we push to unite in this difficult time. Now, follow me into the heart of our Kingdom and embrace the exciting changes that await us!"

The crowd erupted even louder than before. Casimir turned Liana just as several guards pulled the massive doors open. He steadily guided her into the open streets of the city while his supporters followed close behind. The previously scorched streets, littered with the lifeless and torn by conflict, now appeared almost new.

The sight before her revitalized her and brought an airy spring to her step. The streets shone a bright white against the deep blue accents that swirled decoratively where scorch marks once burned. Liana gasped and waved excitedly at the citizens that lined the streets.

"Isn't it beautiful?" Casimir asked while he pulled her along. He periodically leaned into her and muttered, "See how it can be?"

As they traveled further, she nodded absently to him. She reveled in the beauty and grandeur in the buildings that branched out intricately into the distance. They paused intermittently for Casimir to shake a few hands while he briefly spoke. Gradually, the crowd following them grew until they reached a large open circle in the street at the center of the city.

Casimir opened his arms wide and welcomed all around to come closer. He stepped onto a small platform that was erected near the hole in the ground and lowered his hands as he called for silence. From the street, next to the platform, Liana glared up at him as the crowd's whispers died down. The last of the evening's light illuminated his being in a fiery orange that held her gaze captive and, as he spoke, his bewitching smile stirred the perplexing embers deep within her.

"Since the beginning, the Kingdoms of Light and Dark have been separated by countless boundaries. We have been presented with a unique age of unity if only our newly integrated Kingdom can find balance. The Queen and I," he paused and gestured to Liana.

With his break in speech, the crowd cheered enthusiastically and brought an immediate scowl to his face.

Casimir cleared his throat and when the crowd came to a hush, he continued, "We have been in discussion over the laws governing our mighty Kingdom and noted several significant differences in what each citizen is accustomed to."

He glanced down to Liana with a reassuring smile and as she warmly returned the display, she nodded for him to continue.

Casimir turned back to the crowd and raised his voice as he continued, "We realize change can be difficult to embrace. So, after considerable deliberation, we're excited to announce a compromise. Citizens," his voice boomed as he lifted his hands. "I call you to cease your fighting in the streets and stop opposing the enforcers. We will uphold the Light's laws in the light."

Several individuals in the crowd began to stir as Casimir spoke. At his last words, hateful whispers whipped around, chased by several disapproving boos. The disapproval reached across the crowd and stirred the citizens into a nearly uncontainable frenzy as the opposing views clashed.

The guards positioned around Liana and Casimir shoved the angry citizens back as they pushed closer to the two. Liana looked at each face, puzzled by the perceived issue of upholding the law. As she glanced over one angry citizen after another, there was no way to decipher who called against the Light's laws; for they varied in every conceivable way.

Casimir allowed the chaos for several moments before he waved a hand to silence the quarreling crowd and continued, "We ask all citizens please withhold all freedoms of the Dark to be released after sundown in the lower levels of the city."

Liana's eyes grew wide at the notion he proposed and slowly her stare fell to the hole in the courtyard before the platform. Murmurs of angst and excitement rippled through the crowd as Casimir stepped from his stage. While he spoke, Casimir made his way around the crowd, careful to pause at several individuals who resided within the castle, all of which nodded in agreement with his misguided vision.

"If individuals succumb to their inherent nature in this safe environment, without fear of punishment, chaos will cease for the city and the citizens who wish to live in peace."

The Light Within

In hearing the word 'peace', those opposing his proposition whispered excitedly to one another. As he began again, they listened with hopeful anticipation.

"Therefore, every night at sundown, we will seal the gates to the lower city," Casimir gestured to the gate standing slightly ajar behind the platform as he spoke, "granting chaos below to those who crave it and peace above to those who desire it. There will be no law or punishment restricting anything that transpires below the city under the cover of night."

As Casimir lifted his hands, the crowd roared its approval. All except Liana, whose clenched jaw and stony stare, secured the churning anger she fought to contain. Casimir made his way through the crowd to the platform and, as he passed Liana, she laced her fingers with his and pulled his hand close to her torso.

She looked at him while she pleaded through their connection, *Please Casimir! Giving in to these desires will only fuel them further. They can never overcome them by indulging in them. What of the people this will harm? This type of chaos cannot be contained and could prove fatal for the Kingdom!*

He yanked his hand from hers with a hateful glare. In one swift motion, he gripped her upper arm in a crushing hold and dragged her onto the platform alongside him. With his back to the crowd, he turned her to face him.

While the crowd cheered on, his sharp whispers cut across the short distance to her, "Full cooperation, or else, remember?"

With a slow gulp, she nodded to him and lowered her head.

As the roar of the crowd began to fade, with an amused smile, he added, "Plus, I saw this one time on one of those," he paused and lifted his head as he searched for the word. He snapped his fingers as joy flitted across his face and he continued, "shows! Back in that terrible realm. It was awesome!" Like a child receiving candy for the first time, he gleefully turned from her.

Are you fucking kidding me, she thought as her scowl burned into the back of his head.

He chuckled lightly and gestured to Liana as he addressed the crowd, "It appears the Queen is so excited for this important change that she's insisting on placing the last lock on the gate to the lower levels."

Liana gave a trivial smile and waved as the crowd laughed and cheered with Casimir. He jumped from the platform and gestured for the guards to assist her. They reached for her and yanked her from the platform. She walked up to a low arch behind the platform as Casimir handed her a hefty, intricate lock. The heavy iron gate screeched and scraped along the stone street while several guards jerked and pulled until it closed with a loud bang.

Liana drew in a long, defeated breath as she approached the gate. With as best a smile as she could muster, Liana looked to the crowd and clamped the lock onto the gate. As the tiny click sounded, the crowd erupted in celebration. Casimir's hand instantly reached for the back of her neck and steered her back to the platform. His hand slid from her neck, down to her arm, and pulled her into his torso. He lifted his other arm and called out to the crowd again.

"We will now allow any final participants before we seal the last entrance," Casimir's voice boomed over the crowd as he gestured to the hole in the courtyard before him. He raised both hands as he continued, "and commence the start to a new era of safety and prosperity."

The Light Within

Several individuals stepped from the crowd and as the applause reached deafening decibels, they jumped into the hole before Liana. She applauded obediently until the last of them jumped into the darkness below.

"In fact," Casimir spoke quickly over the energetic crowd, "our Queen is so supportive of this new movement that she wanted to show her enthusiasm by being involved firsthand."

Before she could react, Casimir nudged her forward and she dropped into the hole. Instantly, the deafening applause gave way to a suffocating silence. As Liana hit the soft ground below, she staggered and fell to her knee. The light cascaded over her shoulders to the floor below and reflected in small pools of water at her feet. An angry gaze stared back in a tiny puddle for a moment before she realized it was her own eyes that held her attention.

Suddenly, her sight shifted and landed on the reflection of Casimir. He lingered over the opening in the ground with a sickening smile that turned her stomach. She stood slowly and turned her head upward. She had no words for him; she merely wished him an extravagantly painful future; in case she couldn't provide it herself.

As he disappeared, the grate above slowly slid across. Liana glanced around nervously, for as the applause above gradually faded, the chaos around her grew to a startling whirlwind of commotion. She pulled her arms around herself as she stared, wide-eyed, into the darkness just beyond the waning circle of light.

What do I do? Her mind raced in hopeless circles, *what do I do?*

She swayed as the light above her dwindled, and her rapid, shallow breaths increased. Growling laughter rang around her; it forced the strangling grip over her to a paralyzing hold. She whipped her head around at each shuffle as they closed in on her.

As the last of the light was swallowed into the darkness of the sub-levels of the city, a faint voice called out from within, *breathe.*

She immediately responded and took a huge breath of air into her lungs. As she did, she heard the voice call with more certainty, *duck.*

Liana instantly dropped to a crouch and pulled her arms over her head. Instantly, she felt countless arms reach over her. Their legs pressed against her as they fought above. Each reached desperately and, as their clutches returned empty, their frenzy was fueled further.

Move, the voice called to her again.

Without hesitation, Liana opened her eyes to find the complete darkness was hers to navigate. As the others blindly swung at each other, she crawled through an opening in their legs. Effortlessly and without notice, she pulled herself from their desperate tangle and backed against a stone wall in the distance.

Suddenly, her eyes opened wide as the nightmare of this encounter replayed in her mind. She got to her feet, knowing all too well that Darkness could be upon her at any moment. Liana crossed the open cavern in a quiet jog and kept her eyes on the rowdy crowd behind her as she went. When her outstretched hand met the wall she ran toward, she paused and took in the massive cavern that contained the chaos.

Numerous buildings towered over her. They stood, intricately carved into the cavern's pale walls, and stretched out into the darkness beyond what Liana could make out. Countless screams sounded in the distance as

The Light Within

each home was disrupted. Her hand clamped over her open mouth as she shook her head in disbelief. The tears streamed down her face and her heart begged for her to intervene all while her mind demanded her own safety.

She turned from the horror and followed the wall before her. Her hand instinctively raised to the cold brick that lined the passageways, and as she followed along, it led her further from the commotion. With each step, the further she ventured, the more she swayed. She stumbled suddenly and caught herself against the wall. The noise of the chaos behind her seemed far enough off. She paused, leaned her back against the wall, and let her sight diminish.

Several deep breaths filled her shaky form and as the darkness weighed over her, she whispered to the light within, "Please, don't let this be the end. I have more to do."

She nodded to herself and pushed off the wall. Without the slightest sound, she moved along in the darkness. Thankful for the torturous training of her past; Liana lifted her hand to the wall with a smile and crept along. No longer able to hear the screams of the chaos behind her, she listened carefully to her surroundings. The sudden sound of a stone as it was kicked across the path sent Liana instantly against the wall.

Just as she concentrated on the darkness around her, a torch lit so close to her face that she feared she'd burn. She cried out and shielded her eyes from the sudden, blinding light. As soon as she raised her arms, she was instantly restrained against the wall. She turned her head and squinted against the light as she searched for the faces of her assailants.

For Peace

"Finally," the voice called out as they held the torch above Liana's head. "King Casimir sent us for you."

Liana wasn't sure if that meant well for her at this moment. She turned her attention to the woman before her and focused. Tight red curls stood out in every direction and defied gravity as though they were alive. The deep red curls on the top of her head faded to a tight crop around her pointed ears. Liana's eyebrows lifted as she studied the elf before her with curiosity. It wasn't until her sights fell on her deep green, moving lips that Liana focused.

"Well," the elf laughed as she continued, "protect you from death that is."

The elf extended a bare, yellow arm as their eyes connected and forcibly turned Liana's head to the side. When Liana's focus landed on the stares of one of the several that restrained her, she couldn't help but laugh. The elf was less amused and tapped impatiently on Liana's cheek with her bloodied razor nails. As Liana persisted, the elf sighed and covered Liana's mouth.

"Darkness warned me about you," the irritated elf muttered.

Liana's eyes narrowed at the remark. She lifted her legs, kicked out at the woman, and sent her flying against the wall. Instantly, the others around her snatched her outstretched legs and pulled at her in every direction.

"No!"

With Liana's shout, pulsed a powerful golden light that sent the others flying. Their grasps broke and sent her to the ground with a loud grunt. The room spun around her as she fought to pull herself to her hands and knees. Once she staggered to her feet and regained her balance, Liana pulled herself along the darkened corridors.

The Light Within

She rounded a corner, but the elf was quickly behind her. Liana cried out as their nails dug into her shoulder and, with a sudden motion, she turned and threw her elbow in the elf's face. When she turned to run again, a low growl emanated from the shadows in her path and immediately stopped her in her tracks. The elf was right behind her. She raised her torch over Liana's head and illuminated the snarling fangs of a large shadowy creature before them.

"Quickly! Here!" the elf yelled out and turned her attention to the group that slowly regained consciousness in the distance behind them.

Liana stared at the massive, panther-like creature that filled the hallway before them. Several dripping fangs extended past its bottom jaw and as it roared, she could see several rows of teeth lined its jaw. Claws the size of Liana's head, raked the stone ground as though it were sand. She knew this beast was not something she wanted to challenge.

As the elf's reinforcements arrived behind Liana, she heard a soft voice echo in her thoughts. As it whispered, *duck,* she immediately responded and dropped as close to the ground as she could manage.

Just as she moved, Liana felt a massive rush of wind from the creature as it passed over her. She didn't dare to turn as the shrieks of the elf were drowned out by a snarling roar and instead bolted up the hall before her. Her foot slid on the wet, spongy floor as she slid around the corner. She caught herself on the crumbling brick wall and paused to catch her breath.

The dwindling glow from the flickering torch in the distance, cast the creature's shadow against the wall. Liana held her breath and scooted further up the passageway.

For Peace

With an abrupt jerk of her head, she glanced back to the where she had come from. Her heart almost leaped from her chest as the shadow of the creature increased until a sizzle in the distance and sudden, absolute darkness, queued the torch's end.

Liana blinked several times as she willed her sight to focus. Just across the room, she could make out a massive crack near the corner of a wall. Hoping to hide from the creature, she lifted her foot and immediately froze. Laughter and voices echoed up the hall, only a short distance from her destination. As she looked to her prospective hiding spot again, a gust of warm air rushed past her arm from behind her. She turned to her left and immediately raised her hands pleadingly.

When the creature leaned its massive head into hers, she opened her palms and whispered, "Please! I'm not here to hurt anyone."

It lifted its head over Liana's as the voices echoed closer. Suddenly the creature bent low and nudged her. Liana stumbled backward as it continued to shove her until she hit the wall. With a glance behind her, she smirked and immediately ducked into the crack she previously intended to reach.

The creature roared like a thunderous lion and bounded up the hall towards the unsuspecting group. Liana flinched as their screams rang out and shifted to cover her ears. As she attempted to ignore the clamor in the distance, she looked around in the darkness. To her amazement, the small, low ceiling room was strewn in beautiful silk curtains and fully furnished.

Liana quietly shifted away from the entrance and moved across the room as she heard the shuffle of someone just outside. The massive, shadowy paws of the beast moved across the crack in the wall. It stretched out with a sleepy roar, then reached its furry paw through the opening. She pulled her knees to her chest and watched, wide-eyed as the massive beast slowly faded to a shadow of a person. They kept their back to her and watched attentively out of the opening.

As the immediate dangers of Liana's reality faded from her attention, her mind centered over her treacherous situation, *I can't believe he tossed me in that hole.* She ran her hands over her face as her mind raced, *I'm trying my best, what does he want from me? Maybe it isn't me.*

Her head shook back and forth and as she rubbed her temples, the words swirled in her mind until she whispered to herself, "He wants to destroy me."

Her attention shifted as the shapeshifter across the room nodded in agreement; their silhouette through the darkness yielded little detail but, as they nodded, their long, pointed ears caught Liana's attention. She tried momentarily to focus on them through the shadows but as the room began to spin from her exhaustion, she retreated into her web of reflection. While her mind replayed the countless dark moments orchestrated by Casimir, she wondered how she had ended up in this mess.

If only, she focused on her collapsing views, *I knew what he was when I first saw him… maybe I could've stopped him, maybe I could've saved…*

She pressed her face against her knees but just as the tidal wave of emotion crested to drown her, she heard a tiny voice reach out to her, *breathe.*

Liana sat up, tipped her head back against the wall she leaned against, and took a deep breath. As the air filled her entire being, the fog of confusion mudding her thoughts, cleared. She took another deep breath and allowed her deliberation to center.

Something's wrong with him, the thought entered her mind, and instantly something stirred within her. *His mind is twisted,* she nodded slowly in agreement with herself as she gradually stood.

"I have to get out of here," she muttered to herself and paced about the small room while she formulated a plan.

"Shouldn't be much longer," the delicate whisper lifted gracefully through the air to Liana.

She turned immediately in search of the owner. To her surprise, the only individual in the room with her remained to be the shadowed elf who sat guard at the opening in the wall. She made her way across the room and slowly sat near them.

Liana cleared her throat and whispered, "Th-thank you for... spari- for saving my life."

An amused giggle danced about the room and the elf's elegant voice rang through the air again, "You're most welcome."

As her laughter subsided, Liana curiously asked, "So, uh, how did you end up down here? Did you come to participate in-"

Liana cut her questions short as a deep growl rose from the woman next to her. She snapped her head forward and whispered, "Sorry, I didn't mean t-"

"No," the elf's gentle voice cut through her growl. "It's not you. It's... This is where I live, for now."

"Oh," Liana said and lowered her head.

"Yea." The elf let out a short laugh before she continued, "Your King forced those of us that were... too unique." She paused and shook her head, then continued

155

again, "or that wouldn't comply, from the upper levels of the city. Most left, but the forests are treacherous and no place for children, or the weak. So, the rest moved below. I stayed to protect them." She paused again and lifted her hand in the dwindling darkness to gesture to the open corridor in front of her. "From his goons that come to let out their aggressions and this sickness. I pray it doesn't consume me." Her long, wavy locks flowed back and forth as she shook her head.

Liana swallowed as she asked, "consume you?"

The elf suddenly got to her feet and peered out of the crack in the wall. Liana stood with her and watched attentively.

The moment lingered until the elf turned unexpectedly to Liana, pressed her against the wall, and whispered urgently, "You know what I speak of, The Darkness of course."

Liana nodded and tried to force herself further into the wall while the elf pushed closer. Light gradually filtered into the tunnels as the elf held Liana's gaze.

She whispered insistently, "You must resist it. Never let it corrupt your power."

The elf held her attention only a moment longer before she broke away from Liana and stepped through the crack into the passageway beyond. Liana lingered, slightly shaken from the urgency in the elf's message.

I know, her frustrations grew as her mind went in circles, *I have to resist it. No one seems to want to share how.*

Liana heaved a sigh, shifted along the wall, and peered through the opening. A dim golden glow reflected in her eyes as they grew wide in amazement. With a couple glances around, she stepped into the small room beyond. A growing radiance illuminated the extending corridor before her and reflected down the path to her left near the ceiling in a beam of light. She edged around the corner, amazed as the beam bounced from a mirror in the corner and further into the hallway beyond.

"The light rises, let's go," the whisper of the elf called from further around the corner.

Liana jumped at the sudden sound and, as the elf peeked her head around the corner, she let her relieved smile linger. She darted up the hall after her and as she turned the corner, the elf reached out and shoved her against the wall. She lifted a pale blue finger to her purple lips and urged Liana to remain still. Distracted by the beautifully blending hues across the elf's skin, Liana didn't take notice of the shuffling in the distance. The elf suddenly turned from her just as someone rounded the corner.

"W!" Liana cried out relieved as she rushed around the elf.

W jumped and shuffled along the path. Even as she was mindful to avoid each puddle, she wore an energizing grin and stopped to look at Liana as she neared. Liana stopped as W glanced up and the golden light around them danced over her mocha skin as though it were made of a million fragments of glitter.

"Oh Liana, so thankful you're okay. Let's get you out of here hun," W said quietly as she waved Liana over.

Liana nodded and joined her. "Which way?"

W and the elf chuckled. Liana turned to view them both and tilted her head to the side as she waited patiently. They continued to chuckle and turned to one another. The elf offered her arm up to W, who embraced her with a thankful spirit and jumped over another puddle.

The Light Within

W motioned for Liana to follow them as she walked right at the wall before her. Liana raised her hand to warn her but just as she did, W and the elf stepped through as though there was no wall and turned around a corner. Liana ran up to the wall, her brows stitched together in confusion, and examined it. As she lifted her hand, she realized it was a branching hall that blended with the wall. She stepped back and barely noticed the walkway.

"Huh," she said aloud to herself in amazement.

Her head turned in every direction as she wondered how many of these hidden walkways she had overlooked. Liana hopped by the wall and turned the corner to pursue the others. She pulled herself up a crumbling stone staircase and carefully closed a creaky iron gate behind her as she stepped into an open courtyard.

Liana spun quickly, wanting to catch up with W and the elf, but as she turned, she stopped in her steps. They stood, conversing in the small, enclosed courtyard. The courtyard was partially surrounded by high, dense shrubs and overlooked the majority of the city. Beautiful pink and orange hues of the rising sun filtered through the distant tree line and reached across the land. The luminous rays painted the city into a magnificent masterpiece that warmed and revitalized Liana's spirit. She turned full circle and admired the beauty of the shimmering city in a way she had never witnessed before.

Liana glanced over the two as they embraced and let her gaze linger over the elf. Her bare skin was an ocean of swirling blues and purples. The hues crashed into one another along her flesh, creating a beautiful contrasting swirl of color and markings. Yet, in some areas, the two

For Peace

hues blended so beautifully that they disappeared from their individual shade and became one. Her long, blue hair faded to green and fell to her hips; it blanketed most of her exposed form from view.

W leaned into the elf, lifted her hand to her cheek, and gently kissed her. A small smile snuck across Liana's face at the thought of love existing in a place such as this. Liana's lingering gaze immediately dropped to the ground. She was certain this moment required more privacy than her unreliable memories could manage.

Focused on the bricks that connected at her feet, Liana noticed a path of moss with tiny flowers. Her attention followed the moss back to the elf. Several flowers opened at the ground where she stood. Her gaze shifted when the two turned and approached Liana.

"I'm certain it isn't safe to know your name," Liana said and shook her head disappointedly. The elf nodded with understanding as Liana continued, "I am extremely grateful for your kindness tonight, thank you."

The elf bowed slightly and with melodic, soft words, she replied, "Anything for the good of The Kingdom."

Though her presence uplifted Liana, her words left a perplexing sting. The elf turned to embrace W again before she crossed the courtyard back to the gated entry where the lower levels of the city waited. She nodded to Liana as she closed the gate between them and left.

Liana instantly turned to W with enthusiasm. "Okay, let's get out of here."

W gestured toward some of the lower hedges a short distance from where they stood. Liana rushed over and as W approached her, she reached through the hedges. For several moments and with a look of concentration plastered over her face, W fiddled with something through the branches. After several frustrated whispers escaped her lips, a loud click sounded. The shrubs before them moved like a small door and allowed them to pass through.

Liana hurriedly ran up the narrow stairs before her and pushed open an ornate, vine-covered gate. As she stepped through the gate, her heart sank. W had led her into the gardens inside the castle walls.

"Wha- I thought..." Liana shook her head and dropped it.

So much, Liana's defeated thoughts swirled viciously, *for escaping this nightmare. How could she work for that monster? Can I even trust her?*

"No, sorry hun, I'm bringing you back," W mournfully replied and turned to secure the gate that blended perfectly with the plant wall.

"Seriously?"

"He sent his Commander after you, would you have rather me let *him* bring you back?" W questioned as she turned to face Liana.

"Well...no but I can't go back!" Liana pleaded with her.

He tried to kill me! He's insane, Liana's mind screamed constantly as her will for W's safety fought for her silence.

W lifted her arm and gestured through the garden as she spoke, "That's your throne. Who's next to you, what they did, matters not in this moment. You have to work with what you're given for the good of The Kingdom."

Liana heaved a sigh and turned from W as she spoke, "He's impossible."

For Peace

"Don't speak that over him. He just didn't trust the *previous* Liana," W said as she circled around Liana to stand in front of her. "Hasn't all this changed your perspective a bit?"

Liana nodded slowly. *Though I'm certain,* her thoughts centered, *it didn't change me the way he intended it to.* Suddenly her eyes lit up.

"So, perhaps he can learn to trust this *new* Liana." W cleared her throat and continued, "Right?"

Liana gave a short nod and followed along behind W as her mind raced. She knew very well she couldn't let her people be at the whims of Casimir.

As unqualified or unworthy as I may feel, The Kingdom isn't safe unless I take back the throne and rectify the damage. She shuddered as her mind fixed on Casimir, *and the damaged.*

Chapter 7
Nightmare Realized

"Please shift the atmosphere," Liana whispered aloud while she bowed her head. "Give me the strength to overcome him."

Her mind calmed with her words. She hadn't experienced peace like this in a long time. Liana closed her eyes and played the possibilities of Casimir's reactions to her return over and over until she was certain she had calculated them all. She no longer cared for his plans for her. She had her own; tucked in the furthest, unreachable trenches of her mind. Though it seemed like one impossible battle after another, Liana focused on winning the war.

His heavy stride thudded further up the hall; like the marching of a war party, it signaled the impending battle before her. She silently drew in a calculated breath and, as Casimir burst through the doors of the King's Chambers, Liana stood and opened her eyes.

His words, traced with hate, echoed through the room as he strode through the door, "I see you made it back just fine."

"Sorry to disappoint," she said with a laugh.

"You think this is some sort of joke?"

She lowered her head with her response, "No, my King."

He circled her slowly; his suspicious gaze fixed on her. After a moment of silence, he stopped in front of her, crossed his arms over his chest, and calmly questioned, "Is there anything you'd like to say *now*?"

Nightmare Realized

"Yes, my King." She nodded her head and met his gaze as she spoke, "I've wasted quite enough time fighting against you, and understand we need to work on a lasting solution for the Kingdom. I apologize that I've disappointed you somehow. I assumed last night's display was to help the Kingdom fully embrace these changes and if they saw we both entirely supported it, then it would have the best possibility of success."

Casimir cleared his throat, then responded, "Yes, uh-xactly and you aren't upset?"

A warm, understanding smile traced her well-intended words, "Of course not, not even harmed."

His eyes narrowed as she raised her arms out with a slight shrug and revealed her freshly washed form, clothed in a simple gown. He lifted his hand and ran it along the porcelain skin of her arm until it rested along the side of her neck.

"I just want you," he whispered between clenched teeth as his grip tightened on her neck. "to quit causing problems. Is that too much to ask?"

Her heart raced uncontrollably. She forced her attention away from him to the wall.

"Is this... disobedience finally out of your system?" She nodded.

"What of your power?" he asked.

She swallowed and urged her mind to focus on her words as she mumbled, "It is yours to use as you will."

Instantly, the young woman in the decrepit chamber appeared in her mind, then immediately dissolved. Though it was a mere flash, she was certain Casimir saw it too as his grip tightened further. His hand moved to her chin and turned her face towards his.

The Light Within

His hand slowly slid from her chin back to her neck, careful to never lose its connection to her flesh as he spoke, "Now tell me, what have you done with the blade?"

"I..."

She paused and furrowed her brow in mock confusion. Her mind wandered to the detail of the blade when she handed it over to Casimir, so long ago in the forest upon their arrival.

Her eyes shifted from him as she intently thought, *If he doesn't have it that means anyone could and could take my power whenever they please.*

His grip tightened at her thought, and she turned her gaze back to him to reply, "I'm sorry my King. I haven't done anything with it."

She shrugged slightly as the worry lingered on her face. Casimir tilted his head back and studied her.

Suddenly, his angry words spewed from him, "You think I won't end you? You think this is some game?"

She shook her head frantically and pleaded, "N-no please Casimir. I'm tell-"

"Shh shh," he hushed and placed a finger to her lips. With a small smile, he whispered, "so beautiful."

His lingering hand stroked her cheek and slowly tucked her hair behind her ear. She turned her gaze from his lifeless stare when his hand slid from her neck, down her chest. His slender fingers traced lightly over her cleavage. She felt a sudden sting and as she reached up to her chest with her hand, she backed away from him.

Something wriggled against her fingertips that clenched at the wound. She looked to Casimir and caught his inquisitive gaze just before he turned from her. Instantly, she lifted her hand and cried out in disgust. She desperately scratched and raked at her skin as a thousand tiny, black worms squirmed through the fresh cut.

"Please Casimir!" she screamed at him.

Tears streamed down her face as she looked from him back to the wound and continued to scratch hysterically. When she looked up to him again, he was instantly in front of her. He yanked her hands from her chest and held her still as he smiled down at her.

"Oh, my dear Liana, don't worry. The poison is slow. I'd much rather this be as painful as possible."

As the last of the tiny worms disappeared into her flesh, he released her.

"Poison," she whispered aloud to herself as a thought lit her face.

"Now, give me the blade, and I can call it from you. Before it's too late!" His elevated voice cut off with a burst of sinister laughter as he crossed the room and peered out of the balcony.

"I don't have it!" she screamed to his back.

Though, she knew she wouldn't give it to him; even if she knew what happened to it. She searched upon her arrival, only to come up empty-handed but was thankful for that at this moment. Liana welcomed death like an old friend, eager to meet its beautiful smiling face. As ready as she was to finally rest, the urge to keep pushing for the others drove her.

Frustrated that he couldn't hear her truth, she turned from him and rushed from the room. Her heart skipped as she neared the end of the hall and she stumbled. She reached for the wall and steadied herself for a moment. Determined to keep her vision from fading, Liana forced herself to focus on the path before her. Sweat beaded on her brow and her body shook with every

The Light Within

movement. She shifted along the wall and steadily moved into the branching corridor.

The patrolling guard turned as they caught sight of her and approached. Just as they reached for Liana, Casimir appeared and lifted a hand. He waved the guard away and turned to follow behind her.

"Come now," he taunted. He walked leisurely beside her, crossed his arms over his chest, and, with a small internal laugh, prodded her again, "Don't you want this to be over already?"

Her staggering steps, weighted as though she trudged through a pit of tar, carried her through the castle at an agonizingly sluggish pace. She brushed back tears and turned her face from him as his continued taunts became increasingly harsh. Raspy, uneven breaths filled her lungs as she pulled herself through the massive, unoccupied kitchen, to the stairwell in the back.

"What are you doing? Come on!" he shouted as he reached for her.

Liana staggered to avoid his grasp and, as her heart skipped again, her shoulder collided with the frame of the stairwell and sent her tumbling down stone stairs. She reached in vain for the walls or anything she could grab to slow her fall. As her head struck the cold floor at the base of the steps, the enclosing darkness swallowed up her vision.

Just let me die, she thought feebly to the tiny light inside while it urged her forward.

Every fragment of her body ached and with each sharp pull of air, the pain intensified. Though she couldn't see, she knew she wasn't done. She drove herself with her knees and crawled along while she felt for the walls. Like fire, the poison lashed through her muscles and gradually restrained them. Tears streamed down her cheeks as she fell one last time to the floor. She reached out to pull herself along the hall but with each movement, it was harder to breathe. Further effort felt pointless; she could no longer move much of anything. Using the last of her strength, she rolled to her back. With a final heave of her chest, she dropped her arm above her head to the ground.

Something immediately grazed her fingertips and drew the last of her attention to her lingering state. A moment later, she felt it again. Only this time the touch was undeniable. As their fingertips gripped hers, they yanked her closer, then adjusted their grip again. Liana's vision steadily returned and the blurry stone ceiling above her came into focus. Her weak smile woke her spirit and urged her to her feet.

"Arietta!" she cried out thankfully.

Arietta gestured at a black glass panel on the wall as her disgusted face peered back at her through a set of thick iron poles.

"What the fuck was that?" she asked while she shook her hands out in front of her.

Liana looked to the smooth, buttonless panel, confused as she absently responded to Arietta, "*That* was Casimir. I know the way out if I can just..." She trailed off as she examined the panel.

Suddenly, her words hit her, and she turned towards the hall just as Casimir appeared. His suffocating grip was instantly under her chin and lifted her from the floor. Whispers sounded distantly in the shadows behind him. Liana kicked out frantically but came up short with each thrust.

Casimir dropped his head and after a moment, shifted his bright red eyes to Liana. As she gasped and

The Light Within

choked for air, she couldn't help but stare on in horror. Arietta screamed suddenly from behind Liana when a dark mist slowly emerged from Casimir's skin. It gathered along his bicep and twisted into a large striking snake. The creature slithered around his arm, toward Liana and abruptly stopped short as it hissed in her face.

She turned just as it struck out, and sunk its long, dripping fangs into her cheek. She cried out in agony as its venom seeped into her flesh. Instantly, the creature slithered to her open mouth and as it moved to strike again, she sealed her lips. The snake struck at her lips several times while she fought to seal her screams.

"Please!" she cried out but just as she opened her mouth, the shadowy serpent struck again and slithered inside.

Casimir set her to her feet and released her. Eyes never leaving hers, he lifted his hand to the glass panel and pressed.

A hiss of air as the cell door unlocked brought a smile to his face and he whispered, "Try to cure that."

Liana doubled over and clutched her chest as the shadowy serpent wriggled through her. Her raspy breath came in short bursts as the creature wrapped around her heart and penetrated her mind. Numbness spread through her body; it called her attention to the futility of her struggle and caused her to cease. As she accepted the lifeless sensation that filtered within her, she turned toward Arietta.

Tears gathered in Arietta's eyes as she bowed slightly before Liana. "My Queen," she whispered.

Liana's eyes wore the pain that her face would no longer carry. She shook her head as her whispers brought

168

Nightmare Realized

a chill to the air, "I'm fine." She smiled feebly and reached for Arietta, "It's okay."

In one swift motion, Arietta grabbed Liana's outstretched arm and pulled her into a resuscitating kiss. Liana instantly felt the lifeless void of Casimir's beast pull from her. Tears streamed down her face and as she opened her eyes, she cried out.

Arietta smiled faintly and collapsed in Liana's arms. The weight of her fading form sent Liana to the floor. She knelt and held Arietta to her chest while Casimir loomed dauntingly behind her. As Arietta's last thoughts played across their connection, Liana bowed her head and wept.

"Alright, alright," Casimir urged.

He shifted uncomfortably and nudged Liana with his boot. Liana lifted her head and watched momentarily as her glistening tears cascaded down Arietta's cheek to her lifeless lips.

Casimir gripped Liana's bicep as he urged her, "Come o-"

A sudden gasp of air cut off his words. Casimir and Liana turned their stunned expressions on the stirring form of Arietta as the color rose in her cheeks. Liana jerked from Casimir's hold and squeezed the blinking Arietta in a solid hug.

"You're alive!" she shouted as Arietta sat up and returned her embrace.

Liana turned her attention just as Casimir exchanged looks with someone in the branching hall. Before she could react, the Commander yanked Arietta from her grasp. As she reached out to intervene, Casimir restrained her.

The Light Within

"No!" she cried out just as Darkness grabbed a fistful of Arietta's hair, lifted her head, and ran a blade across her neck.

Casimir held Liana in place as she desperately reached for Arietta. He gripped her chin and held her gaze on Arietta's choking form. Hopeless tears streamed down her face, but her cries weren't enough to stifle the gurgling struggle before her.

"You did this," he hissed into her ear.

His words struck deep in her mind and sent her retreating to its furthest corners.

How could I be so careless, the thoughts echoed in her mind.

Liana turned suddenly and buried her face in Casimir's torso and as she did, his hands moved to her exposed arms and pulled her in. She squinted suspiciously as she felt the connection between them open and as her mind began to wander, she understood.

Images flashed quickly in her mind, rewinding the morning's events in distorted fragments. She guided her thoughts from Arietta's death to the King's Chamber where she searched for the stashed blade. Back further her mind wandered as she watched Arietta dragged off by Darkness and at last settled on the open column in the bright room where she once hoped to secure the blade for her safety.

Though, she thought intently, *my regard for my own safety seems to cost everyone around me theirs. Selfish*, as the word echoed in her mind, she shook her head.

While she let him into a fragment of her thought, she searched his and prayed he didn't notice. Dark whispers occupied the recesses of his mind. They lashed

Nightmare Realized

out in fear and brewed in hatred the further she sought for understanding.

Shuddering, she pulled her mind from his and, as she tried to push him from her own thoughts, grew weary and collapsed in his arms. The room spun around her as he lifted her and carried her back through the castle.

Chapter 8
Just A Peek

Leaves of orange and red shuddered as an enchanting wind danced playfully through the creaking boughs of the trees that held them. The cool breeze whipped across Liana's neck before it left in a gust and sent a shiver through her entire being. She lifted the cup of hot cider to her lips and breathed in its heavenly aromas. As she sipped, the chill left her body and she relaxed into the hard iron chair.

At W's urging, Liana, accompanied by a select group of Casimir's choosing, infrequently met in the orchard for conversation. Just outside the castle walls, the orchard stood as one of the last food sources of the Kingdom and was heavily guarded. Though everything was heavily guarded anymore.

As the rustling of the wind grew distant, the mindless chatter broke through her meditative state. She shifted uncomfortably in the hard chair while the ladies around her conversed. Her chest raised as it filled with the sweet air around her and for a moment, she was alone again. She enjoyed this time more now that the group rarely attempted to involve her in their conversation.

It wasn't that she disliked them; rather she cared for them quite deeply. Though she wasn't sure why. She didn't understand the internal pull to protect those who allowed their disgusted gazes to linger on her as though she were a deadly parasite. Perhaps it was the need to protect any life or her drive to fulfill her role. Whatever the reason, she treasured any moments outside of the King's Chambers, even if they were riddled with nonsense small talk.

Just A Peek

The sun momentarily broke through the gloomy overcast that regularly suffocated the sky. It spread across Liana's face and brought a settling warmth that reached across her skin. She closed her eyes and soaked in its rays for several peaceful moments. A growing eerie silence around her prompted her to open her eyes and she resumed the staring contest with the cup in her hands.

"Liana?"

Liana immediately lifted her gaze from the cup in her hand to the curvy blond who sat nearest her. Her inquisitive glare fixed on Liana. As she uncomfortably cleared her throat, Liana looked around to find the others gawked curiously at her.

"I'm sorry," Liana said before she cleared her throat, turned her attention to the woman, and attempted a small smile. "What were you saying?"

The woman heaved a massive sigh and, with an eye roll, sat back in her chair. She raised the cup in her hands to her lips and stared into the trees. Across the table from her to Liana's right, huffed a green-eyed woman with closely cropped hair.

The green-eyed woman leaned across the table to Liana as she spoke, "How has your health been lately Hun?"

"Oh, I'm doing well, thank you. How about you?" Liana asked and she gestured to the woman's knee.

She nodded slowly and turned her gaze to the ground as she replied, "Oh, hanging in there."

The woman laughed reluctantly but it was quickly cut off when a young, dark-haired girl stepped between them. The young girl sat her cup forcibly on the table with a loud clamor that made Liana question the cup's chances of survival. With a snap of her fingers, a chair was beneath her and as she sat, she turned her attention to Liana.

"That's great, that's great," she said through a large smile that twisted with disgust as though she had sat on a pile of manure.

Liana straightened in her chair uncomfortably and turned her focus on the young girl.

As she spoke, her stare traveled up and down Liana in a scrutinized search for flaws as she carelessly discharged her words, "So that means you should be expecting soon then?"

"No," Liana replied softly and turned her attention from the woman as she began her usual assault.

"Oh?" She drew her hand to her chest in a mock concern before she stood. "You may want to start soon."

Liana's face remained the unyielding vacant appearance she had adapted for quite some time now. She got to her feet and turned from the misguided girl as the others slowly stood to join her. As she walked up the orchard path towards the gates, the guards turned and followed alongside the group.

"It's really not that hard; I've done two myself." The girl boasted from behind Liana as they walked along the path back to the castle. "I'm just saying." She chuckled and continued, "Before you get any older is all."

Liana sighed and tried to force the incessant girl from her mind while she droned on about something she knew nothing of. Her step lightened when she caught sight of the gates to the Kingdom. Several agonizing moments later, she turned and nodded to the group of ladies as the gates closed behind them. They turned from her and went their separate ways.

Just A Peek

As Liana turned from the group, several guards from the orchard moved into a circle around her. She redirected her attention to the ground and traced her steps. They moved in unison with her until she reached the entrance to the castle. The massive castle doors creaked open steadily as she approached. The surrounding guards suddenly parted in front of her and allowed her to pass into the castle. As the doors shut behind her, another group of guards approached her.

Led by the elven guard and dressed similarly were several additional guards. As he gestured for Liana to lead, they moved to her sides. She dropped her head again and examined her folded hands that dangled at her waist while she moved mindlessly through the castle.

Before long, she paused in a hall, in front of a simple wooden door. The guard moved from behind and approached the door. He knocked twice then reached for the knob and pushed open the door. She didn't bother to turn her attention to the room, for the scene regularly played on repeat.

Casimir stood, brooding over stacks of parchment strewn across a darkened table. He spent the majority of his time there now, in constant conversation with various faces, most of which Liana did not know. He waited with his hand in the air for her to speak, so he could wave her away. She no longer minded his impersonal interactions. His presence was increasingly unsettling; it weighed over her like a suffocating shadow that drained the hope from her core and constantly fought to stifle the flame within if it so much as dared to flicker.

"I have returned," her words lifted across the space to him and concealed the deadened expression glued to her face.

The Light Within

"Good. How was it?" he mumbled.

"Good," she replied as previously instructed.

Liana waited in silence for the usual nod and wave of his hand. After several moments of stillness, she shifted and glanced in his direction. She froze momentarily at the sight of Casimir, who watched her from the doorway. Instantly, she cleared her throat, dropped her attention to the floor as she turned to him, and bowed slightly. She did not dare lock eyes with him anymore, for when she did, the darkness behind them sent a shudder through her core. As he neared her, she tensed and tried not to shiver from the chill that crept in the air along with him.

"Have you thought about what we spoke on?" he inquired in a calm tone.

She cleared her throat and kept her eyes fixed on his chest as she spoke, "Yes, my King. I've been contemplating how I was unable to serve you previously. Perhaps if you could have someone train me to use the power properly, I would be better able to serve you. I understand this is a lot to ask and if you will not allo-"

He raised his hand and instantly she clamped her mouth shut. She watched as it lingered and waited patiently while his unnerving presence persisted. Even the air about him drained the life from her the longer she remained nearby. After several agonizing moments, he waved his hand dismissively, turned, and slammed the door behind him.

Liana continued up the hall, along their usual route. She crossed her arms over her chest as they walked along back to the King's Chambers. While she stared at the floor before her, she considered the misled words of the young girl in the orchard. With a shake of her head, she attempted to dislodge the confusing, hate-filled commotion that swirled within. Slowly, her hand found her chin.

Her thoughts centered on Casimir as she replayed their encounter. Over and over, she relived each tiny detail, until the pits of her stomach twisted. She reached up from her chin and covered her mouth. As she walked along, she redirected her thoughts to her slow, deep, breaths, and gradually, she calmed the churning panic.

She looked up abruptly, brow furrowed at a sudden commotion that sounded around the nearby corner. Liana jumped back as the hand of one of the nearby guards reached for her. She looked at it, then to the guard, with an offended expression plastered across her face. As the guard moved to block the path before her, they lifted their open palm and gestured to a hallway that branched off nearby.

Liana glanced over the guard's shoulder before she turned and followed their suggested route. Her hand absently rubbed along her arm where the guard almost connected. She found now, even the thickest of garments couldn't shield her from a connection and hated even the slightest touch of anyone. She threw a hateful glare to the elven guard behind her who was well aware of her distancing preference.

The elven guard tucked his hand to his chest and, with his words, bowed slightly, "Greatest apologies, my Queen."

She glared at him for a moment, then turned and tucked her arms across her chest again. As she turned, she let out a massive gasp and stopped in her steps. Liana stood, mouth gaping and wide-eyed, before a vast library. Two massive pillars marked the open entrance and reached several stories high. To each side of the entrance,

The Light Within

several cushion-strewn openings in the wall reached through to the other side. She stood and gawked in the entrance. Completely unaware of its existence, she couldn't help but marvel at the grandeur of the infinitely stretching shelves and the countless tales they contained. The guard behind her cleared his throat and she instantly turned to continue their journey. In a half-hearted attempt, she tried to contain her excitement.

o   o   o

With a loud smack, Liana's fingertips hit the glass high above her head before she dropped to her feet. She took a deep breath, squatted down low, and jumped again. Reaching up, she smacked the balcony glass just above her previous target. With a smile, Liana stood back, placed her hands on her hips, and admired the smudged-up glass while she caught her breath. She nodded absently to herself and approached the stone wall next to the glass.

Liana turned, placed her back against the wall, and slowly slid herself down until her knees bent at the perfect angle. She placed her palms together in front of her chest, closed her eyes, and concentrated on her breathing. Her muscles ached and screamed out in protest as she focused on ignoring them.

As she exhaled calmly into the quiet, she heard an increasing thud of heavy boots when they echoed off the stone floors in the approaching hallway. Liana pushed from the wall and darted for the sink. She quickly splashed the signs of sweat from her face and blotted herself with a nearby towel. As the doors to the King's Chambers flew open, she pulled a light gown over her hips and adjusted her hair.

"There you are," he said with a huff and reached for her.

Just A Peek

Liana withdrew her arm before he could take hold of her and glared at the Commander. His massive form filled the door frame and forced him to duck as he entered the washroom with her. He glared back for only a moment before he gestured for her to move. She held his stare and edged around him into the open room beyond.

Liana paused when she stepped from the bathroom and adjusted her gown. As she turned toward the King's Chambers, she took a deep breath and straightened her posture. When she turned, her eyes landed on the back of Casimir, who stood at the hearth of the fireplace deep in thought. While she crossed the room to him, she dropped her head and fixed her eyes on her hands. He looked up when she neared and nodded as he turned to her.

"Come," he began and opened his palm to the doors. "I have something for you."

She nodded to him and approached the doors. As she neared, the Commander reached from behind her and yanked them open. They walked on in silence for several moments before he brought her to a stop in front of a large oak door. An uncomfortable silence lingered while Casimir stood and stared at the door; his face riddled with the internal war that surely took place before her. Suddenly, he lifted his hand and gestured for her to come closer.

Once she was within arm's reach, he tilted his head to the ceiling and spoke, "I must know something." He dropped his head to stare at the door again and continued, "Before I can give you what you've asked."

Her jaw clenched, as did her hands as she fought to control her frustrations. *Why*, she wondered, *must he always speak in riddles?*

The Light Within

Without waiting a moment longer, Casimir gestured to the Commander, who reached out and grabbed the large black hoop at the edge of the wood. With a huff, he hauled the heavy door along its tracks to the side. As it opened, Liana immediately contained her confusion, adorned the familiar stone-face mask, and retreated within to prepare for whatever it was he had planned.

Her eyes instantly landed on Khius. He stood shirtless, in the middle of a sizable room with his hands crossed behind his back. He smiled as he caught sight of them and bowed low. When he straightened, Casimir gestured for Liana and approached Khius. She looked around while they crossed the room and noted several weapons along the wall. The floor seemed softer and slightly springy beneath her feet as she walked along. Her attention quickly returned to Khius when they stopped in front of him. They stood for several agonizing moments while Liana glanced between the two for any sign of what was to take place.

Finally, she could take no more, and blurted out, "What is this?"

Casimir took a deep breath, faced Liana, and carefully placed each word before her, "I know, I have called into question your relationship, but I have a solution. You say your power is mine; that it is mine to command." Casimir took another deep breath and continued, "So, if you are truly mine, you would do anything I ask without hesitation?"

She nodded and replied, "Yes, my King. What is it you ask of me?"

"Kill him," Casimir said casually and gestured to Khius.

Just A Peek

Without a second glance at the fear-struck Khius, Liana raised her palm to his chest and released the strongest pulse she could. She stumbled backward as Khius' lifeless body dropped to her feet. As the room spun, she reached for Casimir, but he lifted his hand to the Commander, who instantly caught her. The Commander gripped her arms in a crushing hold and steadied her for longer than desired while she desperately clung to consciousness.

"Yes," he whispered in her ear. "Gather your energy, my Queen."

Gradually, the room came back into focus and as she stood, she shoved the Commander from her. With a shudder, she frantically rubbed at her arms and moved away from him. As she shifted, she immediately looked to Khius. She stared on with a remorseful pity at what her power had been reduced to. Not one tear, not even an empathetic sob would she allow to escape her carefully walled-up composure. As her sights lingered on Khius, she took notice of Casimir who studied her at her side.

Liana turned towards Casimir, clasped her hands in front of her, and quietly, yet steadily asked, "Is there anything else I can do for you, my King?"

While he continued to study her, he placed his hand on his chin and after a moment he flicked his wrist casually in Khius' direction and muttered, "Bring him back."

Bring him back? She agonized internally, *Right, that would be easy if I could bring myself to weep for him as I had for Arietta.*

Deep in the sealed recess of her mind, her heart feebly cried out. She knelt next to Khius and sighed. As she examined his peaceful face, she leaned over him and

The Light Within

imagined her King as he would lean over his brother. Her eyes closed and as the image flashed before her, a small tear dropped from her lashes onto the forehead of Khius.

Instantly, he gasped, and his eyes shot open. He looked up at her in amazement, but it was quickly replaced by anger as he got to his feet. Casimir jerked Liana to her feet and stood in between her and Khius.

He lifted his hands out to them both as he spoke, "K has trained you previously, he is best equipped to train you currently. I simply had to ensure there wouldn't be any," he paused and turned his hand in the air as he searched for the word. "Issues."

Stunned, Liana stood silent and stared at the ground as he spoke. It had been weeks since her proposal, with not even the slightest hint of a reply. *I assumed*, she thought to herself, *it was a no. Now he wants Khius to train me?* She glanced back at Khius and wondered, *can I even trust him to let him in, enough to train this power?*

Casimir sighed and crossed his arms over his chest. Liana looked up from her thoughts and cleared her throat as she turned towards him.

"Thank you, my King." Liana bowed slightly to Casimir before he lifted a hand and walked from them.

o o o

Can't you show me, Liana thought intently to Khius, *some of those fancy moves.*

Her memory flickered to their sparring match in the center of a crowd with Antonio, ages ago. Khius instantly jerked his hand from her and disconnected her thoughts. He sighed when Casimir sat up in his chair, suddenly interested in their training progress.

Liana immediately reached for his arm and, as he yanked it out of her reach, she firmly gripped his shoulder

Just A Peek

and reasoned through their connection, *it's been weeks now! Every single day! Don't you think he's going to get suspicious if he doesn't see something?*

Khius turned his attention from Liana to the ground before him and heaved another sigh. *He's not going to allow me to train you to physically fight. Besides,* he concentrated on his thoughts and urged her to understand, *that isn't the battle that lies before you.*

She sighed. *Come on, it's only,* she deliberated through her connection to him, *a few feet.*

Khius shook his head with a smile and crossed his arms over his chest. With a snort, he stared at the floor before him and thought to her, *it's hardly about the distance. Please, I urge you to reconsider the use of this power he's asking from you.*

"K?" Casimir questioned, suddenly directly behind Khius.

Khius instantaneously replied, "Yessir?"

"What seems to be the problem?" he asked, annoyed.

Khius cleared his throat uncomfortably and responded, "Sir, I." He cleared his throat and started again, "I just don't want t-"

Casimir moved to the opposite side of Khius from Liana and lifted his hand up to silence Khius while he spoke, "Yea, that's kind of the point. *Your* job is to train her," he gestured across Khius to Liana and continued, "to convince anyone to do anything, even if they *just don't want to.*"

"Yessir," Khius mumbled as he dropped his head.

"Focus on your job, not the pain before you," Casimir said with encouragement as he raised his eyebrows and eyed them both.

The Light Within

"Sir." Khius shook Liana's hand from his shoulder and continued, "Perhaps she is weakened by the constant use o-"

Casimir waved his hand to silence Khius and looked to Liana. Her eyes instantly fell to the ground and, as his gaze lingered, she crossed her arms over her chest and waited.

"Perhaps, or perhaps you're not *actually* training her!" Casimir shouted.

Khius countered confidently, "Sir, I assure yo-"

"Again!" Casimir shouted and waved his hand to Liana. As he walked from them, he lifted his hands above his head and yelled out to the walls, "I want to hear you actually training her!"

Khius cleared his throat, took a deep breath, and nodded to Liana. As she approached him and raised her hand to his shoulder, he muttered, "Imagine the task at hand as a favorable one and believe it so much, that it," he cleared his throat again and continued, "convinces me."

"Right," she responded and nodded her head.

As she turned her eyes to the several feet of burning coals before Khius, all she could imagine was his immense pain. She cringed when she envisioned him falling along the way and being engulfed in the coal's fiery sting. Khius suddenly yelled out and jerked his shoulder from her reach.

Confused, she threw up her hand and questioned him, "What?"

He brushed at his chest and arms, then turned to her with an angry glare and yelled out, "That didn't feel very favorable!"

"I'm sorry!" she shouted back.

Just A Peek

Liana rubbed her forehead and agonized within, *did he just feel what I was thinking?*

As Khius regained his composure, Liana reassured him, "Well, you aren't *actually* on fire, right?"

Casimir snickered and leaned back in his chair while he watched the two. She glanced in his direction with a grin but, as their gaze connected, she quickly turned her attention back to Khius.

"Right, so that makes it okay," he said while he rolled his eyes and approached her again.

She sighed and with the shake of her head, responded, "No, I- look, I really am sorry, okay?"

"It's fine. Try again," he reassured her.

As she lifted her hand to his shoulder, he turned to her, threw up his hands, and shouted, "Wait!"

Her brow instantly furrowed as her glare burned into him. After a moment she flipped over her outstretched hand questioningly.

"Close your eyes."

She laughed as she questioned him, "What?"

"Come on," Khius urged her.

Liana sighed and closed her eyes.

"Focus first, then make the connection."

She took a deep breath and as she imagined the burning coals laid out on the floor, she pictured Khius skipping merrily across as though his feet were fireproof. She replaced the pain she anticipated with pleasure and giggled at the image in her head as she shifted her hand to Khius.

Her hand connected with his shoulder for only a second before he moved away. She opened her eyes in frustration, and as they landed on Khius, she reached for her mouth to stifle her reaction. Astonished, Liana stood and silently watched as Khius hopped awkwardly over the hot coals. When he reached the halfway point, he turned to her and gave her a thumbs up, but his expression immediately went flat.

She felt the gentle rush of air across her neck as Casimir neared and dropped her attention to the floor. As she did, Khius immediately cried out in horror and jumped from the coals to the floor nearby.

"Interesting," Casimir whispered from behind her.

He caressed her neck as he moved her hair to the side and questioned with another whisper, "Did your mind wander?"

As the room spun around her, she leaned into Casimir and nodded.

Khius looked up from his wounds and, seeing Liana's state, ran to her and frantically asked, "Is everything okay?"

"Just tired," she said with a nod.

"What did you do to her?" Casimir lashed out angrily at Khius.

Khius moved closer and scooped Liana up into his arms as he responded to Casimir's accusations, "I did nothing. I'm certain she's exhausted from overuse of her powers."

Casimir shoved Khius from Liana and lifted her into his own arms with a grin. "It's fine," he spoke to Khius over his shoulder as he turned to leave the room. "I've got her."

As the walls of the halls around her slowly faded, she felt the excited frenzy that stirred within Casimir.

She can grow her power as much as she likes, she heard the whispers of his mind cheering one another, *so long as she remains in our control.*

Just A Peek

The murmurs of his misguided psyche penetrated her furthest thoughts and, as she tried to force him from her mind, her vision faded. The swaying of his body as he carried her along was all she could decipher. Liana reached up and rubbed at her eyes, begging them to function. She looked up from her hand and gradually, the blurred light around her manifested into shapes. She shook her head as her vision fully returned and looked to her side.

"What th-" she whispered aloud.

As she pushed off Casimir, she felt something rough where his shirt was and looked at her hand. Liana found herself leaned into a colossal murky oak that dripped with a dark sap. When she lifted her hand from its bark, a faint stain remained. She instantly bent down and wiped her hand on the bottom of her dress but as her touch glided across the fabric, it felt off. She glanced down and noticed she wore thick leather pants. Further down her legs clung a pit of tar-like goop.

With an angry growl, she threw her fists to her side. At her voice, the air about her stirred. Liana looked ahead of her to a river only a short distance away. She drudged along in the muck and with each step, the once delicate breeze whipped into an angry whirlwind. As she neared the edge of the bog, a massive gust of wind knocked her from her feet, headfirst into mud. Liana pulled herself to her hands and spit out a mouthful of the disgusting ooze.

The wind ripped across her and with it, came a voice, "You must find her!"

Liana crawled to the edge of the pit and pulled herself onto the rough, scorched grass. As she climbed to her feet, another gust of wind rushed past her and knocked her to the ground again.

"Find her!" it screamed out.

"Find who?" she screamed back to the forest around her.

The air whipped angrily around her, uprooted a tree, and hurled it in her direction. Liana ducked and narrowly missed the massive trunk but as it passed over, a trailing branch knocked her in the head.

As the branch connected, the air about her screamed out again, "She can hold the light. Find her!"

Desperate to stop the assault, Liana raised her hands over her head and cried out, "Okay!"

At her word, the winds ceased. Immediately, debris that spun about her dropped to the ground. As the dust settled, she noticed a bright field of flowers across a surging river. She reached for a nearby tree and steadied herself as she got to her feet. Looking about, she snapped her head back just as something moved in the field before her.

Liana peered around the trees that stood between her and the field. Instantly, she covered her mouth to stifle her gasp as her sights landed on her own face. She moved around the trees, closer to the flower field, and watched, as a young Liana laughed obliviously in the field before her. Liana looked down at her hands to find they were no longer her own.

Her face lit with the sudden realization, *this must be Casimir's memory!*

She looked up from herself and the field was gone. Far before her in the distance stood a darkened home with only the flickering of a candle that lit a small room. Liana looked down and found herself crouched in a tree. When she looked up again, she was suddenly next to the house. Her brow furrowed suspiciously as she edged along the branch to look through the window. Liana strained to reach a little further and peered through the glass. A small child sat on a cushion on the stone floor, lost in a daydream, while her mother ran a brush over her hair.

"Mom?" Liana called out from the branch with a look of horror.

Liana reached up to wipe the fog from the glass and gasped. The mother's face was missing, as though it melted into her flesh. The mother brushed on, unphased and unaware of the growing darkness that loomed behind her. Liana lifted her fist and as she swung to bang on the window, something restrained her. She looked to her wrist and cried out at a shadowy serpent that slithered up her arm, toward her face. Instantly, she reached up to shove it from her and, as she did, lost her balance and fell from the branch.

She screamed out as she fell through an endless darkness. Countless murmurs stirred around her; each snatched and ripped at her flesh with such horrifying hunger she feared her heart would cease. Liana pulled her arms over her head and clenched her eyes shut. Slowly, the chaos around her dwindled and, as the light behind her eyelids grew, she opened them and found herself in the King's Chambers.

o   o   o

Rain hit the glass in rhythmic sheets while a grumble of thunder rolled into a crescendo. A massive crash of thunder rang through the air. Liana leaned against the balcony's glass and closed her eyes as she listened to nature's orchestra play a soothing melody for her. Just as the thunder cracked through the air again, a bright light surged across her eyelids and, as she opened them, she caught the end of a sharp bolt of lightning against the darkened sky.

As the storm diminished, Liana pushed herself from the window and paced about the room. She remained out of step with time with this weather that constantly blocked her only means of measurement. Her mind swarmed while she circled the chamber until two sharp knocks sounded at the door. Liana stopped in her steps and looked up suspiciously.

she questioned within, *The elven guard*? Liana looked to the windows where the storm picked up again, then walked to the door as she wondered, *can't be the orchard on a day like this.*

A rush of air from the massive door blew her hair from her shoulders as she yanked it open. Her eyes landed on the elven guard, unaccompanied by his escorts. She glanced behind him, then looked at him with raised eyebrows.

The guard turned from her and waved his hand for her to follow.

Her quiet, yet stern voice echoed down the silent corridor, "No."

With a heavy sigh, the guard turned to her and examined her with a glare.

Liana returned his expression and with a hurried whisper explained, "I'm not getting caught out running around with anyone should anyone come searching for me."

His expression softened as he explained, "They won't come for you today." He lifted his hand to the hall.

Just A Peek

"How can you be certain?" she asked and as her arms folded over her chest, the elven guard dropped his hand to his side.

He shot a glance over his shoulder, stared for a moment, then turned back to Liana and whispered urgently, "Come please, the Elder instructed me to bring you but you mustn't let," he paused and looked up the corridor again before he finished his thought, "others know."

As he turned back to her to enquire why she remained, she caught his gaze and held it with her angry glare as her words bore into him, "This very conversation is enough to end us!"

He gulped, yet held her stare firmly and after a moment, she smiled and turned from him. Liana quickly yanked the door shut and proceeded up the hall past the dumbfounded elven guard. After a few strides, he was at her side again and motioned her along their way.

Liana folded her arms over her chest as she wondered, deep in thought, *the Elder told him to bring me. Where?* She sighed as she reflected on a final thought, *what could he want?*

Suddenly, the guard cleared his throat from behind Liana. She looked over her shoulder to him and as he peered around her and gestured, she turned back around to find they stood in front of the library. Her eyes opened wide, and, without hesitation, she pulled the guard into a secure embrace. Almost immediately she realized what she was doing and released him. Liana cleared her throat as she smoothed out her gown and smiled at the guard.

"Thank you," she whispered excitedly. With a nod, she added, "and him."

The Light Within

She spun from the guard and skipped excitedly into the vast, open library. Liana glanced back at the elf and found he pulled a chair near the doorway to wait patiently. With a huge grin, she turned again and shuffled down a bright blue carpet that led into countless rows of shelves. Her eyes followed the shelves as they stretched far above her. Their frames, lined with ornate green and gold accents, reached like branches towards the sky to an open glass ceiling.

Tiny flames contained in decorative glass lamps hung periodically along the shelves and danced as Liana neared. She wandered in amazement for quite some time before she paused and went down a row. Her brow furrowed as she examined the countless aged books carefully set before her. The majority appeared to be written in a language she couldn't decipher.

"They're easier to read when you open them," a soft voice, followed by laughter rang next to Liana.

She jumped slightly at the interruption but joined their laughter and replied, "Yea that's the thing. I can't really," she waved her hand at a few of the indecipherable books and continued, "understand these."

"Not yet."

Liana turned and smiled at a shrugging, dark auburn-haired woman who stood in the walkway near her. The woman gestured for Liana to follow. She willfully hopped from the shelves and followed along behind her.

"Looking for anything specific?" she asked.

When she realized Liana was not beside her, she slowed until she walked next to her. Liana smiled at her and looked up to the shelves as they each passed.

"No, not really," Liana replied, absently.

Just A Peek

The woman chuckled and after a moment spoke softly, "Then let your mind wander and I will be around should you need me."

She turned to the woman with a smile. "Tha-" Her face lit up and instantly she asked, "Actually, do you have anything on trees? Plants?"

The woman pulled a small silver pen from the pocket of her silk blouse. As she lifted the pen in front of her face, she clicked the side and out popped a tiny magnifying glass. She turned about with the glass to her eye.

"Ah yes!" she called out to Liana.

Instantly, she took off with a quick stride and placed the pen back in her pocket. Liana kept in step, just behind her as they twisted and turned through the shelves. Before long, she stopped abruptly and gestured up a row.

"Thank you," Liana said with a smile and nodded to the kind woman.

"I am known as L, my Queen, should you need me," she said while she bent slightly and nodded to Liana.

In one quick motion, Liana and L turned from one another and disappeared into the bookshelves. With pursed lips and a fist on her chin, she examined each book. As she strolled along the shelf, her hand wandered behind and slid along the rough spines on the solid wood ledges. She stopped periodically and pulled a few books from the shelf. Before long, she turned with a sizable stack and wandered back through the bookcases.

The stack's weight became more apparent the further she traveled. She sighed and steadied the books against a nearby bookcase. As she looked around, her eyes wandered to the transparent ceiling. The distant tinkle of rain against the far glass echoed off the stone walls. As the

The Light Within

melodies played across her consciousness, Liana couldn't help but close her eyes and get lost. She took a deep breath and pushed off the shelf.

Liana looked to the ceiling again while she followed along the maze of twisting bookcases toward the front of the vast room. After a short distance, she caught sight of a small area of tables. She shuffled through the shelves and quickly dropped the stack down on the closest table. The elven guard set his chair on all fours and peered at her from across the rows of tables. His eyebrows lifted as he examined the stack and, as she noticed, she quickly turned their spines from his view.

With a content smile, Liana plopped down on a nearby cushioned chair and raised the first book from the stack. As the storm intensified above, she found herself lost further in the pages. She could've sworn it was only a matter of minutes when the guard appeared at her side. Liana cleared her throat as she stood and placed the book face down on the table. As the elven guard gestured, she moved from the table and proceeded joyfully from the library; thankful for any time she was allotted.

o   o   o

Well, she thought honestly, *I just don't know how many times I can say sorry.*

Khius smiled and dropped his head with a shake before he focused his thoughts on Liana, *for literally killing me? I'll let you know; you didn't even hesitate!*

She sighed and dropped her head as her heart willed him to understand, *I couldn't hesitate. If I did, he may question my loyalty. I've been working diligently towards leaving no gap that would lead him to believe otherwise.*

Khius turned his attention to her and nodded with his response, *So perhaps now you understand, and we are even.*

Just A Peek

Liana cocked her head to the side but after a moment nodded to Khius.

"Come on," she urged him.

He shrugged and crossed his arms over his chest as he replied, "I've trained you to use this power, now you must perfect it."

Liana gripped his shoulder and sighed as she thought, *you know that's not what I'm talking about.*

He shot a glare at her, then turned his attention back to the floor.

Yeah okay, she thought convincingly to Khius through their connection, *he might not allow you to train me to physically fight buuut.* As he sighed, she insisted further, *hear me out! Maaaaybe you just replay some of the techniques, slowly in your thoughts, and I can pick up on them?*

Suddenly, she felt the connection with Khius become distant and before long, she could no longer feel or hear him. When she tried harder, it was as though she bounced her thoughts around in her own mind. She swayed as she searched for him and immediately, he reached out and caught her.

Liana blinked back the foggy darkness that crept up in her vision and pulled away from Khius. She stumbled a short distance, leaned into a nearby pillar, and focused on breathing. After a moment, the room stopped spinning and Liana could once again hear over the rush of her heartbeat in her ears.

"Let's go!" barked Casimir from the corner of the room.

Liana jumped slightly at the sudden reminder of his presence; she had nearly forgotten him, quiet and brooding in the shadows. He rose from his reclined state and walked in her direction. Liana pushed away from the

The Light Within

pillar and rubbed her forehead while she crossed the short distance back to Khius. He looked at her questioningly as she took a deep breath and grabbed his wrist.

At least, she urged through her connection to Khius, *show me how to fight against this exhaustion from using my power.*

Khius snorted, crossed his arms over his chest, and thought intently, *but you haven't even mastered this power yet.*

"Come on," Liana whined and, as her shoulders drooped, she heaved a sigh of annoyance.

Suddenly she felt the icy presence of Casimir next to her. He gripped her wrist in his crushing, bony clutch and yanked her from Khius. After he hauled her a short distance away, he released her hand and rounded on her.

"What's the issue? What's going on here?" he questioned as he gestured rapidly back and forth from her to Khius.

"I..." Liana paused and dropped her head as she fiddled with her hands in front of her and searched for the right words. "It's just," she paused and cleared her throat. Liana straightened herself and began again, "He is being difficult."

Khius snorted from across the room and just as Liana turned to shoot him a glare, Casimir caught her chin and turned it back to him. His gaze locked with hers and instantly it was as though she were stone. The only muscle she could move was her heart, but even that pumped speedily out of her control. She gulped as he released her and slowly, crossed her arms over her chest.

"Stupid girl, of course he's being difficult." Casimir almost laughed as he spoke, "You should be growing your power to overcome the most difficult individuals. Or else," he paused and turned from her. As he walked back to his

Just A Peek

chair, his voice carried across the room, "how could you possibly serve me?"

Casimir nodded and waved his hand at her. He returned to his recumbent state as she turned from him. She lingered and stared at the ground for several moments until she noticed Khius' lingering gaze. Immediately, she straightened her posture and approached him. She lifted her hand to his shoulder and lingered just above it. Liana sighed, reached down, and grabbed Khius' forearm.

Can't you wear something with an open shoulder, she lamented as she eyed his sweater with frustration.

Remember, he rolled his eyes as he concentrated on his thoughts, *you don't need a flesh connection anymore and besides that, it's freezing around here!*

How did you, she questioned him through their connection, *force me from your head like that?*

"Focus my Queen," Khius whispered.

She stiffened and looked at his face. The glowing embers before him warmed his otherwise frozen expression. She nodded and closed her eyes. Instantly, she envisioned a spot on the wall across from Khius. Liana opened her eyes and focused on the spot on the wall. Suddenly, Khius left her grasp and walked out across the hot coals. When she felt Casimir approach, she kept her sights fixed on the wall.

"So, you just needed a little pep talk?" Casimir asked from behind her.

"Perhaps," she said with a chuckle and held her focus on Khius until he stepped from the coals.

Her confident smile quickly faded as the room around her spun. Casimir sighed when she reached out for him and caught her just before she hit the ground.

The Light Within

As he lifted her to her feet and steadied her, he grumbled, "Still weak I see."

"Here," Khius arrived at their side and reached out for Liana. "Let me-"

"No!" Casimir shouted.

Right before Khius could reach Liana, Casimir jerked her to the side and swooped her up into his arms.

"Just," Casimir cleared his throat and continued, "move on to the next phase. I've got her."

Apprehension laced her face as she looked over Casimir's shoulder to Khius, who stood perplexed in the open room behind them. Liana grew nauseous as Casimir bumped and jostled her about in his hurried pace. Before long, she could take it no longer; she pushed away from him and fell to the floor of the King's Chambers.

Chapter 9
The Mountain

The tiny flame of a candle flickered its dwindling light across the rosy cheeks of Liana. As she flipped another page, the burst of frustrated air from another hasty turn almost extinguished the light of the candle. When the small flame gently swelled in the stillness, the growing light suddenly illuminated the face of another near Liana.

A serene voice shifted the stillness of the air, "If you're searching for something, perhaps I could help you find it?"

"Yes. Well, sort of," Liana trailed off as she focused on the page before her.

After a moment she looked up to L who stood patiently nearby. She looked through the distant shelves to the elven guard who lounged at the entrance. She watched him for a moment as he stared down the hall with his back to her before she turned back to L.

In a lowered voice, she continued, "There's this strange... sickness spreading in... my garden." She nodded to L and gestured to the stack of books before her. "I thought one of these would have the answer but," she trailed off with a shrug.

"Hmm," L leaned in and examined the book before Liana. "No, that looks like the one, but you don't see anything like it there?" She gestured to the pictures on the pages as she questioned.

Liana shook her head.

"Perhaps the problem you're up against isn't in any of these books, yet." She smiled down at Liana.

The Light Within

Her brow furrowed and she shut the book quickly as she spoke, "Then how will I know how to fight against it?"

L tapped her finger to her lips for several seconds before she quietly responded, "It's usually best to look at the root of the issue."

Liana nodded and turned her attention to the table before her, lost in thought.

"Maybe if you can get a sample? We can take a look?" L added.

"That'd be great." Liana turned her smile to L for a moment before she got to her feet.

L nodded, returned her warm smile, and turned from Liana.

"Only," Liana paused as a scowl crossed her face. As L halted her steps, Liana continued, "I can't… really touch the tree." She tapped her chin, deep in thought.

L chuckled softly. "I'm sure you'll think of a way," she said as she walked off.

"Wait!" Liana called to her and drew the guard's attention.

L stopped abruptly and turned to Liana.

"If," Liana slowly approached L and continued in a whisper, "If you saw this surmounting… sickness that was consuming everything, what would you do?"

"You cure it," L said quietly, yet sternly. She closed the distance and held Liana's stare as she spoke, "You fight with every fiber of your being, until your very last breath. You fight with all your knowledge, all your skill, and all your resources, until the very end." She swallowed slowly and backed away from Liana.

The Mountain

Liana shook her head as she dropped her sights to the floor and uttered a tiny whisper, "What if you're too weary to fight?"

"Then fight against that," L said while she reached forward, held Liana's shoulder for a moment, and bowed her head.

L then turned from her and walked off into the maze of shelves. Liana's gaze lay fixed on the dimming bookshelves as a faint whisper danced through the nearby shelves. When the murmur swirled familiarly across her ears, she glanced over her shoulder to the elven guard. His attention was consumed with W, who whispered enthusiastically. Liana crept to a nearby bookshelf and watched intently through the tightly packed tomes. A slight look of annoyance periodically crept through W's multifaceted expressions while the elven guard gradually got to his feet. After a moment, W crossed her arms over her chest and went silent. The guard tucked his arm to his chest, nodded slightly to W, then he turned and disappeared.

Liana's brow instantly furrowed as she backed away from the shelf. She crossed her arms in front of her and contemplated the details of their conversation while her feet carried her through the towering shelves. Suddenly, Liana stopped in her steps, closed her eyes, and took a deep breath. The absolute silence, accompanied by her draw of air, interrupted the dark spiraling thoughts that fought viciously for her attention.

As she opened her eyes, she looked to the glass ceiling above with a smile. The sun fought to break through the dismal gray clouds that blanketed the cool autumn sky. Several glowing beams of far-reaching light tore through the darkened heavens. Liana reveled at the breathtaking scene. After only a short moment, the ever-changing blanket of clouds shifted again, and the sky went cold.

Her focus transferred back to her surroundings and the sound of approaching steps instantly drew her attention. Liana turned just as W rounded a bookshelf. Her face lit up when she stepped into the aisle and caught sight of Liana.

"Oh, thank heavens Liana!" she exclaimed as she half skipped, half sped-walked up to Liana, and wrapped her in a warm embrace.

"W!" Liana shrieked and gratefully returned her affections.

After quite some time, Liana released her and backed away. Lately, it was rare for Liana to get the opportunity, let alone the desire, to be near anyone. W was the only one whose touch didn't drain her. In fact, her presence alone seemed enough to recharge Liana. A sigh burst from her when she realized this probably was why she didn't see much of W anymore.

"I missed you!" Liana said with a grin as W linked arms with her and they walked together through the shelves.

"Ooh, I missed you too." W let out a short sigh and quietly continued, "They keep me so busy. How are things with Casimir?"

Liana huffed an annoyed sigh and turned her head from W.

"Hmm, maybe some air would help," W said with a nod and steered Liana toward the front of the library.

Liana instantly perked up and hugged W's arm with her response, "You know just what to say!"

The Mountain

Their laughter echoed warmly through the dim halls. Liana's steps felt light as air once the emerald doors came into view. With one quick motion, Liana tugged a heavy cloak from a hook near the doors and swung it over her shoulders. After W heaved the doors open, Liana stepped out into the frigid air and stifled a gasp.

Even the garden wasn't safe from the wrath of Casimir. Extraordinarily little life shone anymore. Liana closed her eyes and filled her lungs with air as they walked along. The quiet crunch of gravel beneath their feet set a rhythmic melody that eased her mind. Gradually, Liana opened her eyes to find they were further into the garden. Small blooms of pink and red fought back a dark red, glistening vine that slowly consumed everything in its path.

W prodded Liana, "How have your moments been going?"

"They haven't been."

W raised her eyebrows and tilted her head as her stare bore into Liana.

Liana sighed and crossed her arms over her chest. "It's not like I haven't been trying. He's always gone and when he *is* around..." Liana went silent; her blank stare fixed on the distant path before them.

W let the silence linger for a moment before she cleared her throat and urged, "Liana."

Liana closed her eyes and shook her head. "Sorry. He," she briefly paused and with a sigh continued again, "he just isn't there. I'm trying but I can't get through. I'm done with this nonsense." Liana's skin flushed red as tears of frustration welled in her eyes.

W stepped in front of Liana and blocked her path. "Okay, first of all, take a moment and just breathe."

The Light Within

W put her hands in front of her chest and gestured up as she took a deep breath. Liana rolled her eyes but joined in. As the air around her filled her lungs, her sights fell to the ground, and she began to calm down. W stepped to her side, locked arms with her, and steered her through the garden.

"Maybe it's time for a new approach," W began.

Liana heaved another sigh and turned her head from W. As she looked off into the distance, she stiffened and gripped W's hand tighter.

No worries, W's voice echoed in Liana's thoughts, *he can't hear us.*

W adorned a charming smile and turned Liana to face the direction of her gaze. They bowed briefly to Casimir who glared out from the King's Chamber balcony. Liana pushed forth an earnest smile before she waved a playful goodbye to Casimir. As they turned from him, she let the smile linger and dropped her head.

"Remember, it is not Casimir you fight against," W spoke softly as they walked along the large steppingstones that lined the pebbled pathway.

Liana's brow furrowed as she contemplated W's words, *but it is Casimir I'm fighting against. He's to blame for the desolation of the people.*

W shook her head and released Liana. She walked a short distance to a small stone bench that lay beneath two twisted, dark red trees. With a wave of her hand, she shooed a few fallen leaves from the bench, turned, and sat with a satisfied groan.

As W spoke, she patted the bench seat next to her, "Think bigger Hun. You're fighting for the *Kingdom* against the *evil* that is threatening it."

"Yea, Casimir," Liana retorted and glared at W.

The Mountain

When W shook her head 'no' again, Liana heaved a massive sigh, dropped her head, and trudged over to W. She plopped down on the stone bench with another sigh and let her head fall into her palms.

"I must leave," with her words, the thought of giving up, of failing everyone, consumed her and forced tears to burst forth.

"You must stay and fight!" W urged her.

"I *have* been fighting!" Liana lifted her head and in frustration, let her words fly. "I have given it *everything*. Yet he still remains closed." Liana shook her head. "I..." she trailed off and after a moment of silence continued, "I cannot bear this much longer."

W embraced her and let the silence linger. After a moment she released Liana and sat back.

With a gentle tone, she prodded Liana, "Much longer means one last try then?"

Liana sat up straight and wiped the tears from her face. She debated within, *and if he still can't be helped, are you willing to go through more torture for nothing?*

Liana nodded absently to herself as she spoke aloud, "It's not for nothing. I will give every last effort left in me to help The Kingdom."

W clapped excitedly but suddenly stopped as Liana turned to her.

"However, if the Light leads me elsewhere, I *must* follow."

W nodded once and whispered, "I understand. Now," she sat up straight and looked to the sky in thought, "maybe if we could rekindle the affection he once had for you." W distractedly bit her index finger and went silent for several moments.

The Light Within

Liana closed her eyes and listened to the air as it filled her lungs. She willed it to fill more with each breath. Gradually, she opened her eyes. Her focus wandered around the withered garden and stopped on the tree next to her.

Her eyes went wide with the light of an idea, and she whispered excitedly, "I'll need a distraction; a big one."

W turned on the bench to face Liana and her face lit up as she spoke, "Oooh we should have a feast!"

"A feast?" Liana's expression shifted from doubt to certainty in seconds as she thought aloud, "Yes perfect! The people *are* starving. Let's feed them!"

W bounced on the bench and clapped her hands together as she spoke, "Yes! With big dresses and gorgeous hair and ooh *your* gown."

W was silent again. Her eyes fixed on Liana, clearly deep in thought. As her stare traced Liana's form up and down several times, her scheming expression grew.

"But wait, you seriously want to bring a bunch of people right in the middle of this crazy mess?" Liana asked, suddenly uncertain about such an ordeal.

W shot Liana a deadly glare and clicked her teeth before she responded, "Hun, you're missing the point. You need a distraction, right? What's more distracting than 'a bunch of people right in the middle of this crazy mess?'"

Liana laughed as the reality of what W was saying hit her and questioned, "Okay, so how do we get him to go for something like that?"

W's wide grin shone brightly against her soft, earthen complexion and elevated her words, "Trust me, he wouldn't say no, if it's his idea!"

The Mountain

Liana's brow furrowed and she lifted her hand in front of her as she thought out loud, "I can try while he's sleeping."

W instantly reached up and pushed Liana's hand into her lap with her urgent words, "My Queen, I would always caution against altering a person's will this way. It is not using the power for the Light and can lead down a dangerous path." She released Liana's hand and after a brief pause, began again, "It's easier than that though. Here," W stood and turned toward Liana. "Practice on me. What would you say?"

Liana stared at her hand for a moment, then cleared her throat and sat up straighter. Slowly, she pieced together her thoughts aloud, "It would be a… smart idea… to host a feast… to celebrate the… unification of the Kingdom."

"What about me? Waaaa!" W cried out as she balled up her fists and stomped her feet in the gravel like a child.

Liana burst into laughter but quickly cut it short and whispered, "Right. Okay then." She took a deep breath as she reconsidered and after a moment, spoke again, "It would appear most gracious to host a feast to honor the King for returning the Queen to his Kingdom so we could… ugh!"

"Okay, okay. We'll get there," W said before she gave an airy laugh and invited Liana to join her.

L nodded with a smile and stood with W. They linked arms and slowly followed the steppingstones along the garden's path.

The Light Within

○   ○   ○

"Please strengthen me," she whispered through the air with her extended exhale.

Liana drew in another long breath of air as she concentrated on the Light that grew within her. She focused on the darkness of her eyelids and as she tried to clear her mind, an image of Khius crept up. Liana shook her head, opened her eyes, and stared out over the garden below her. With a sigh, she rose to her feet and braced herself as the distant clunk of boots neared. Her thoughts flickered to Khius again.

Instantly, she snorted and whispered to herself, "of course."

The door of the King's Chambers flung open violently and drowned out the sound of her voice. There was no need to look to confirm who interrupted her extended moments of peace. His boots thundered heavily as he hastily crossed the distance between them. In one swift motion, Liana stepped to the side and turned to him just as he reached for her shoulder.

"We had an understanding," she muttered and glared at him while he circled behind her.

With his words, he lifted his arm out beside her and gestured to the door, "Yes, I know."

They walked on silently for a short distance. Periodically, the Commander waved his arm and gestured for Liana to take a different direction. Before long, they stopped in front of a simple door. The Commander moved before her and blocked the door frame with his arm. Beyond him, Liana could hear a clamor of shouting, amongst other noises.

"You must remain in steady silence, careful not to disturb the flow of thought and you must never recount anything that occurs once you have left. Do you agree?"

The Mountain

She studied him for a moment and as he prodded her for a reply, she nodded apprehensively. Without hesitation, he thrust open the door and shoved her through. When she turned to scorn him for touching her, he slammed the door in her face. Instantly, she whipped around and found a table full of individuals gawking at her.

With an awkward smile, Liana lifted her hand to wave. As though she resumed a movie, they all turned to each other and continued squabbling amongst themselves. W appeared at Liana's side and gestured toward the table. Liana shot her a nervous look, to which she smiled and gently guided Liana. They made their way, careful to avoid the few stray objects that were thrown, intended for another target.

Before long, W moved aside and gestured to a seat next to Casimir. Liana studied Casimir for quite some time before he glanced in her direction and waved her over. She shook her head, frustrated at herself for lingering, and moved to the seat as he turned his attention back to the table.

She sat slowly and watched the chaos unfold before her. After quite some time, she pieced the various arguments together and before long, she followed the shouts across the open stone table.

A voice cut through the crowd, "My Queen, surely you have some insight?"

Liana sat up straight in her chair as the individuals at the table slowly turned their attention to her. While their murmurs died away, they took their seats and eventually a stillness rested in the air. She turned her focus to Casimir. His glare burned into her, as though she, herself had uttered the words.

The Light Within

After a tense moment, the Elder spoke up from the other side of Casimir, "Morale is at a desolate low. We must act to spare the few remaining lives. Our recent attempts to mediate have calmed the direct attacks against the castle but there remains a small resistance. What is it you suggest?"

Her focus remained on Casimir as the Elder's words formed a list in her mind. Fear flitted across her eyes as she wondered how one person could be expected to resolve such a list in a matter of seconds. To her horror, Casimir nodded at her and opened his palm to the table before him. She turned her attention forward and instantly, her sights rested on W.

W stood in the far distance and waited against the door. Her absent stare fixed on Liana for just a moment. She gave a short nod before she turned her attention to the ceiling.

Liana cleared her throat and as she did, heard a small voice from within whisper, *breathe.*

She sat up straighter, took a deep breath, and spoke out, "I'm certain the King's plans will take hold with tim-"

Murmurs instantly cut across the table and interrupted her.

She shook her head and spoke out over them, "I'm certain the King's plans will take hold with time. However, the King would appear most gracious and could improve his position by opening the gates. It will show we can be civil to feed the needs of all his people and there is no longer a need to fight. A celebration to honor him for returning the Queen safely to our Kingdom, ensuring prosperity and safety for all."

Their murmurs grew to a roar with her words, only this time, they were shouts of excitement. Liana smiled and sat back. Slowly, she turned her attention back to Casimir and, to her despair, was met with a suspicious stare. Liana locked eyes with him as the grin remained on her face.

"We can barely feed ourselves and you're suggesting what exactly? To host a feast?" Casimir's shouts boomed across the room and drew everyone's attention but didn't stifle their excitement in the least.

"What about a ball instead?"

Several voices cheered from across the table, "What a great idea your Majesty!"

Liana's eyes, locked on Casimir's, went wide with the words. Unsure of her growing concern with the slight change in plans, she shrugged innocently to Casimir. His glare softened, and as the excitement around them grew, he closed his mouth and sat back.

The shouts continued across the table, "That way it's only a little food to shut them up but not enough to break us."

"Yes, great idea My King! Let's do a masquerade!"

"Ooh yes, we can break out the good wine."

Casimir threw his hand up playfully to the affectionate council and, as he spoke, his tone shifted, "Come now. Surely, my radiant gem," he gestured casually to Liana and continued, "is my inspiration."

She smiled and nodded to them as she tried desperately to stop her eyes from rolling out of their sockets. When they continued in the excitement of the details, Casimir flicked his wrist dismissively to Liana. Almost instantly, W was at her side and pulled the chair back from the table. Liana stood, bowed slightly to an oblivious Casimir, and turned from the group.

The Light Within

They crossed the room quickly and as they reached the door, W reached up, knocked, then opened the door. When they stepped from the room into the hall, Liana passed by the Commander. He leaned against the wall and fixed his stare on them until they were out of his sight. After they put some distance between them and the rowdy council, W turned to Liana and gave her the thumbs up excitedly. Liana smiled half-heartedly in return.

"What? Come on! That went great!" W reassured Liana as she bounced with an enthusiasm that almost boiled over.

"I don't know." Liana shook her head and continued, "It did go better than I thought it would but..." Liana trailed off as her stare fixed absently on the ceiling in the distance.

W clapped her hands together in front of her as she spoke, "Okay, so it's not a feast, but we can still work with this, right? Still get an awesome dress!"

Liana stopped in her steps and gestured behind to where she thought the council chamber may be.

Quietly, yet feverishly, she let her words fly, "They turned a gesture of goodwill into this grandiose event to feed their own flesh." She shook her head and lowered her voice as she continued, "Sorry. I know we can make it work. It's just..." She paused, shook her head again, then looked back to W as she spoke quietly, "I don't know. I just have this terrible feeling. I can't explain, sorry."

W shook her head and embraced Liana. After a moment she stepped back and whispered sternly to her, "Then we will do our best to prepare."

They nodded at each other and turned to continue to the King's Chambers. W was kind enough to take Liana a longer route; she claimed to have forgotten where she was going. As they approached the narrow hall back to her room, Liana sighed. W turned to her and embraced her again.

"Don't worry. Just think about the upcoming chocolate and wine," W said with an earnest smile.

They both burst into laughter.

After a moment, Liana whispered, "Thanks."

Suddenly, the doors of the King's Chamber burst open, and before them stood Casimir. Liana and W immediately dropped their arms to their sides and bowed slightly.

"Don't you two look awfully friendly?" he asked suspiciously as he crossed his arms over his chest and stepped from the room.

"Yes, my King, you have chosen a great advisor. I was merely enjoying light conversation before I returned to await you." She smiled at him but when he returned a scowl, she lowered her head.

He wore a suspicious glare while he circled them and lingered behind for a moment. The silence lingered until he stood before them again.

"Off with you," he said and flicked his wrist in W's direction.

W bowed, turned from them, and hastily made her way up the hall. As soon as she turned, Casimir gripped Liana's arm in a crushing hold and pulled her into the King's Chambers. Once in the room, he slammed the door shut behind her. He steered her across the room and shoved her down on the couch.

He shouted and pointed at the door, "Don't ever speak to me like that in front of anyone!"

"Like what?" she questioned him through narrowed eyes.

The Light Within

He growled and threw his hands in the air before he unexpectedly turned and paced with his shouts, "You know exactly what I'm talking about! Stop being stupid."

Liana crossed her arms over her chest and with a glare she replied, "I-"

Casimir instantly stopped in his steps, turned to her, and shouted, "Stop interrupting!"

She uncrossed her arms and lifted them open to him to continue. Slowly, Liana sat back against the couch, rested her hands in her lap, and fixed her gaze on his feet.

He let out a massive breath of air and lowered his voice, "Always getting us into these impossible messes. Why do I continue to save you?"

Casimir shook his head and reached up to shove his hair out of his face. With a sigh, he turned and walked towards the balcony.

After a moment he spoke out again, "Another escape plan perhaps? You must think I'm blind... or stupid."

She huffed and hoped he could hear the eye roll he wasn't able to see. As the silence lingered uncomfortably, Liana sat up and turned toward Casimir. He stared out through the balcony glass over the garden apparently lost in thought.

"Why was he looking at you like that?" With his quiet question, a scowl developed across his previously blank face.

Gradually, she stood, took a step towards him, and timidly asked, "What are you talking about?"

He turned towards her suddenly, as if he just realized she was in the room. Casimir blinked rapidly, then fixed his stare on Liana. "A feast, by the way? What were you thinking! So stupid." He shook his head and continued on his rant, "We're desperately low on food, that's why the citizens are starving! Now you want to offer up what's left to those people? I suppose you would have *me* starve then?" He crossed the room to her as his words flew.

Her blood boiled over at his selfish remarks and she instantly pushed back, "We have plenty of food within these walls. If my people are starving, shouldn't I be as well?"

"I can arrange that," he scoffed.

Liana rolled her eyes with her reply, "That's hardly what I mean."

"Then what *do* you mean? Always speaking in riddles, can never get anything out of you," he spat back at her.

Still as a statue, she stood, mouth open at his ironic accusation. He let her marinate in frustration until her tiny voice finally whispered, "I was just trying to help bring the Kingdom together."

"Shh, don't worry my beautiful gem," he said while he lifted his hand and, as his fingertips stroked her cheek, she closed her eyes. "I won't let your careless plans ruin us."

o   o   o

"Did he mention *why* you're taking me... wherever it is you're taking me?" Liana prodded.

"Must you always ask questions?"

Annoyance laced the elven guard's hushed reply and brought a wounded silence to Liana. She crossed her arms over her chest and slouched back against the cushioned carriage seat. As her stare fixed on the floor at his feet, her mind raced with one torturous idea after another for what lay waiting for her at the end of the ride.

The Light Within

Finally, the carriage lurched to a halt. The elven guard moved instantly to the door and waited in silence. Liana studied him while he lingered with his head tilted slightly. As he glanced back at her, she could've sworn he felt sorry for her. She gulped as he opened the door and jumped lightly from the carriage. With a gesture, he held the door open. She stepped out to a dark and desolate mountainside.

As her leather boot hit the dark and dusty rock, a wall of guards immediately formed around her. She clicked her teeth when her tippy toes weren't enough to warrant her even a glance over their shoulders. Liana looked upward and basked in the shadow of the mountain as they marched her closer.

After only a short distance, the guards parted in front of her and shoved her through an open doorway in the mountainside. She turned but not quick enough as they slammed the door shut in her face. She shoved against it and cringed as she heard a loud click, followed by rattles from inside the door. With a sigh, she leaned her forehead against the cold stone and closed her eyes.

"Our guest of honor has arrived!" Casimir's voice echoed from Liana's left.

She sighed again and turned her head on the stone wall towards his voice. Liana immediately stiffened and with wide eyes, she examined her surroundings. She stood on a small stone ledge with only the door in the wall next to her. Before her was a vast, dark pit and beyond that, was Casimir. He paced on the balcony of an open patio that occupied several of the individuals he usually kept close by. They sloshed their drinks into one another and cheered indiscernible snide remarks at Liana's sudden arrival.

The Mountain

"Great," Liana mumbled to herself as her heart sunk.

Just then, a door opened behind Casimir, and in walked his Commander. The group cheered him as they shoved a large stein in his fist. He nodded to Casimir as he joined the others. Instantly, Casimir turned back to Liana with a grin.

"Now then, let's get started," Casimir said excitedly as he walked to the stone banister at the edge of the platform he stood on.

"K, would you join us for training?" he called out over his shoulder.

The group behind him erupted in thunderous laughter.

Once the group subsided, Casimir called out again, "K? Let's go!"

The rowdy group burst into laughter again. Several banged the table with their fists and mugs in a boisterous display. Casimir raised his drink to the group, then turned back to Liana. When he was met with her unamused glare, he smacked his hand against his forehead.

"Oh! That's right!" He chuckled lightly and turned to the group again before he turned back to Liana and called out, "He's already here."

He shook his head and reached for the closer of two large, wooden levers on the wall next to him. As he yanked the lever down slightly, a loud clicking sounded across the pit from Liana. She sighed and turned from him; ready to be done with his latest game. The stillness in the air crept across the abyss as the rowdy crowd stifled their commotion and watched Liana in anticipation.

Gradually, a glow emitted from a cell carved in the mountain, far across the dark pit before her. As the light

The Light Within

rose, Liana squinted into the distance. She could barely make out Khius, who shifted along the wall and groped in the darkness until the light rose around him. He immediately spun, took in his surroundings, and stopped when his sight rested on Liana. With a small nod in her direction, he kicked the chain that tangled at his feet and crossed his arms over his chest.

Liana's face remained flat as the latest training ordeal materialized before her. She studied the chain at Khius' feet and quickly found it secured around his neck. The other end of the chain snaked along the narrow cell and down into the abyss. She crossed her arms over her chest and turned to Casimir.

He glared at her, unamused by her lack of amusement in his carefully constructed plan. As murmurs and grumbles rose behind Casimir, Liana raised her hands out before her with a shrug. When she saw the anger rise in his face, she cleared her throat, suddenly reminded of her situation.

Liana bowed slightly to Casimir and as she rose, called out to him, "and how may I serve you, my King?"

A mixture of reactions boomed from the crowd behind Casimir and his expression softened slightly.

He cleared his throat and called back, "Ah, ah, my Queen. We must give our other guests a chance to arrive."

He lifted the index finger on his drinking cup out to her and waved it as though he scorned a child. Her jaw tightened instantly at his words. She turned from him, back to Khius as Casimir jerked the lever down. One by one, cells to the left of Khius' illuminated.

As the occupants of each cell became aware of their conditions, their mixture of emotions swelled into a fury that reached across the abyss to Liana in a flood of angst

The Mountain

and fear. Liana pulled her hands to her chest and diverted her attention to the endless dark pit before her.

Annoyance laced her shouted words as she stared down into the abyss, "Okay…What do you want me to do?"

"You'll want to make note of the chains on their necks," Casimir said before he cleared his throat and placed his hand on the second lever.

Liana rubbed her temple as an irritated sigh escaped her form and she muttered, "You always make things so complicated."

"What was that?" Casimir called from across the open pit.

"Ready!" she shouted and waved with an awkward smile that instantly turned to an inquisitive scowl as the grin on Casimir grew.

"Thanks for reminding me," he murmured.

He raised his hand and snapped his fingers. She opened her mouth to question what he'd said but her voice failed her. Liana reached for her throat and looked back to Casimir in shock. He burst out in laughter that was immediately echoed by his group and as her expression turned to a glare, his laughter increased.

After a moment, he took a breath, then called out to her, "I can't have you cheating, Now, can I?"

She sighed and turned from him. Liana drew in a breath of air and closed her eyes.

Has he always been able to do that? The questions crashed in her mind and drew her attention from the scene around her, *wouldn't he do that when he first told me to keep silent? Are his powers growing as mine are? Surely, he wouldn't leave me like this.*

The Light Within

Her hands lingered on her neck until a loud clunk, followed by metal clinking pulled her from her internal spiral. She looked to Casimir, his grin wide and the second lever halfway down. She glared at him and instantly turned to the wall of frantic prisoners. Her eyes darted to the chains again. She followed them down into the dark abyss. Instantly, she shook the image from her mind of what their fate could be. Liana paced the tiny platform.

Her head shook as the thoughts swirled, *he didn't even tell me how to unlock their chains. What could I possibly do?*

She looked up from her spiral and squinted across the dark abyss. The light shone out from their cells, reflected off something on the stone wall just outside of Khius' cell, and immediately caught Liana's eye. Quickly, she picked up her gown and sat, cross-legged on the cold stone floor. She leaned against the door and concentrated on Khius.

Focus, Khius' voice, fuzzy at first, grew to an echo as she searched for his thoughts.

Liana pictured the glint of metal in her mind and searched for Khius again. Suddenly, he bolted across the long, narrow cell. He poked his head around the edge, reached out along the wall, and grabbed at something. When he turned to Liana and held it up, he almost lost his balance on the ledge. Khius quickly jumped back and looked at Liana. She nodded slightly to him and let out a small breath of air in relief.

With his question, laced a sinister laugh, "Time's ticking. Will you only save K?"

Liana looked at him in horror as she pondered how long they truly had. She turned from him and studied the row of individual souls still bound and needing to be released.

She shook her head with the realization, *he wants them all at once.*

A shiver crawled down her spine at the thought of what he'd do with such a power. Worry laced her face, but she bowed her head and with a sigh, closed her eyes. She searched for the thoughts of the prisoners across from her. As each of their frantic views crossed her mind, she showed them the glimmering wall from her perspective.

One by one, they rose; some quickly, others with fearful apprehension. They retrieved their keys and unlocked their chains. Some cast them down and others kicked them into the pit. After a moment, Liana opened her eyes and looked down the wall. She could see two cells where the occupants remained in the shadows of the furthest corner, still bound. She quickly closed her eyes and searched for their thoughts.

Focus, she heard the voice of Khius whisper to her from across the void.

She lashed out, *I'm trying!*

Liana shook her head and looked up to Khius with a glare. He threw his hands up and paced in his cell, head down. With a huff, Liana turned her attention back to the remaining individuals. She closed her eyes and searched for them again.

They lashed out in fear and anger as she tried to convince them that their freedom was within reach. She slumped to the side, exhausted as she pushed harder. When she reached for their thoughts again, she showed the others released. One of them lashed out again as she showed the glinting key at the edge of their cells. The other was completely walled away in fear.

The Light Within

She heaved a sigh and opened her eyes. Her heart felt as though it may cease with how frantically it pumped, but her mind was at a loss. Suddenly, her sight was drawn to their chains. They snaked along the cell, and it was only a short moment before all slack was gone. Liana reached forward and tried to shout, but her voice failed her. Instantly, her display was met with obnoxious laughter from Casimir and his audience.

She shook them from her head and drove one last thought to anyone that would listen, *it's not too late.*

She collapsed on the cold stone floor, her face at the ledge. Her shallow, uneven breath kicked dust up in her face. She lay for a moment as the screams of the lost souls scraped at the inside of her bones while they were dragged away. When their cries cut off abruptly, Liana sat up, her sight set on Casimir as she wept silently.

"What's that?" He put his hand to his ear mockingly before he tilted his head back and shouted to her, "Oh! That's right!"

He snapped his fingers and instantly, her cries echoed through the cavernous mountain. She stood and staggered desperately close to the edge of her platform as though she tried to reach him. Her eyes landed on the lever, where his hand remained from pulling it down.

"You monster!" she screamed at him.

When she lurched, hoping to jump the enormous cavern, several hands from the guards behind her, gripped her in a secure hold.

He pulled his hand from the lever and placed it on his chest with a look of offense worn across his face and replied, "Me? You're the one that let them die."

Her mind exploded with a million replies, each of them lethal should even the thought be unearthed. As her mouth lingered open and her exhaustion set in, she gave in to the guards that drug her away from the horrific scene. They pulled her out of the mountain and shoved her towards the carriage. Liana stumbled as she turned and fell to her knees. As the cold wind whipped across her face, her tears intensified.

The elven guard, previously leaned against the carriage, was quickly at her side. He offered her a hand and when she refused, he grabbed her arm and hauled her to her feet. She stumbled as the ground before her spun and reached forward. Quickly, she hauled herself inside the carriage and collapsed on the plush silk seats. The elven guard slammed the door and thumped the wall before he sat opposite her. Instantly, the carriage lurched and signaled their departure.

They rode on in silence for quite some time. Before long, Liana noticed the guard's curious stares that lingered increasingly. She pulled herself up and leaned against the wall of the carriage.

"What?" she asked quietly.

The guard uncrossed his heel from his knee, sat up while his sight remained on her, and he inquired, "Are you okay?"

She nodded with a shrug.

The guard huffed and sat back, though his stare fixed on her. She swung her feet up on the plush bench next to her and leaned back, her eyes locked on him. Her mind reeled on; she wondered if the clamor of the carriage ride was enough to conceal their conversation. She studied him, concerned for his safety regardless, and cleared her throat.

"Do you know of this power of the Light?" Her whispers, barely audible over the grumbles and groans of

The Light Within

the carriage, shook with the anticipation of this knowledge.

The elven guard gave her a short nod, sat up, and leaned closer to her.

Liana continued, "Using my power is too draining." She shook her head and stared into her lap.

The guard shook his head and whispered back, "Don't rely on *your* power. Tap into the Light."

The elven guard sat back and pulled a small, wooden flute from his vest. He reached up and pulled off his mask. She couldn't help but stare at his beautiful face as his words flitted past her.

"Focus on the Light. Allow it to strengthen you," he said as he lifted the flute to his lips.

She turned from him, closed her eyes, and listened. His smooth, gentle melody whispered over the clunks and clamor of their ride. Her breathing slowed as she focused on the song and before long, she felt renewed. Liana opened her eyes and kicked her feet from the seat as the elven guard tucked the tiny instrument away.

"Thank you," she nodded to him.

He nodded back to her and secured his mask. She wondered again what purpose his mask served but her thoughts shifted when the carriage lurched to a standstill. The elven guard moved to the door as he had before. Liana tensed, reminded of the mountain.

Her face fell as she recalled the previously failed event of Casimir's. In somber anger, she stepped from the carriage as the guard gestured for her. With a clenched jaw, she walked silently as the guards escorted her to the King's Chambers.

Chapter 10
Let's Have A Ball

A brilliant ray of sunlight reached through the high-paned windows on each side of the hall and wrapped Liana in a warm blanket of light. The beading and fabrics of her gown reflected a brilliant array of colors along the walls around them. She closed her eyes and walked arm in arm with W while she soaked it in. After a moment, Liana looked about and, as she took another deep breath, found that W's stare lingered on her.

"What?" she asked with a laugh.

W shook her head and with a grin, replied, "Look complete. That's the smile that matches."

Liana chuckled again and countered, "Great, I'm sure he'll hate that too."

W laughed with her and before long shrugged as she sang out, "I don't caaaaaare! You look amaaaaazing!"

"I missed you," Liana laughed and squeezed W's arm while they walked.

"Me too, Hun. We go far too long without seeing each other," W said as she stopped and turned to Liana.

W wrapped Liana in her arms; in a warm embrace that lifted her spirits and lightened her step. Too quickly, she stepped from her and was lost as she meticulously adjusted Liana's gown. She studied W for a moment before she looked up around them. The narrow corridor was eerily quiet, absent of any guard or guest.

"W, please," Liana whispered and pulled W's hands from her gown.

Liana caught W's attention and quickly focused her thoughts, *how do you energize me like that? When I use my power, it drains me. How do I stop that?*

The Light Within

She swallowed nervously as she waited in the silence, eyes locked on W. After a moment, W dropped her head and closed her eyes.

Liana mirrored W and, as she did, heard her voice echo in the distance, *Stop trying to use your power, tap into the Light. Light strengthen me, energize me.*

Suddenly, W pulled her hands from Liana and backed away. Liana lifted her head and took a deep breath. She tried to recall the warm smile from moments ago and, after another breath, her smile shone radiantly as ever.

Her gaze fixed on Casimir as he strode down the hallway to her, the Commander in tail. From a distance, he was more than enough to make anyone swoon. His recently trimmed hair, each set perfectly in place, accented his clean-shaven, chiseled chin. Her heart raced as he crossed the hall.

He tugged at the sleeves of his carefully pressed royal garments before he rested his hand on a jeweled sword at his hip. As his stare lingered on her, Liana nervously turned her gaze to the floor. The look of disgust securely fixed across his face tarnished his handsome figure and threatened to steal her smile.

"What is this?" he spat at W and threw his open palm up to gesture at Liana.

W laughed slightly with her response, "I really tried for blue, but the dye came out kinda purple."

He spat back, "You think this is funny? You thought this was acceptable?"

"Actually, I..."

Liana nervously interjected from behind the two, "Please, Casimir. I love it and honestly, we don't have time fo-"

"Take her!" He motioned the Commander to W.

Let's Have A Ball

Liana shouted, "Wai-"

"Enough!" Casimir yelled over her and waved the Commander away.

Liana turned to W, who traced a smile and pointed back to her. Liana shot the Commander a glare before she turned to Casimir and bowed her head.

"My King, please. I thought you may like your… gem to stand out." She swallowed slowly against the lace of the gown that gripped her neck and remained still.

He scoffed at her, "Go chan-"

Without notice, the double doors beside them swung open. Her grin grew as she tilted her head toward the roaring crowd. Casimir lifted his arm up to her and immediately, she wrapped her arm in his. Liana shifted the fluffy fabric that flowed from her waist, behind her where they naturally fell, and carefully descended the massive staircase with Casimir.

"As though the color weren't hideous enough, you've gone and covered all the good bits." Casimir shook his head in disbelief and continued to rant under his breath, "Uck and left your hideous back wide open for all to see your scars." He gestured to her form while the complaints carried only slightly over the roar of the crowd to her ears alone.

With the roll of her eyes, Liana gradually diverted her attention from Casimir's fear-fueled attacks to the sea of blue before them. The vast ballroom stretched on; infinitely packed with smiling faces, all clad in various shades of blue. They neared the extravagantly embellished throne chairs that sat on a marble platform in a break of the sizable staircase. Casimir paused and smiled down at Liana. He turned to her and gripped the sides of her arms roughly.

The Light Within

He leaned in and quickly, yet quietly, let his words fly, "Yes, every citizen is here. So, give that fancy speech once again and move your people to love me as they love you. This is what you've been training for after all."

Her smile quickly faded as his words sunk in. He placed a quick peck on her cheek and stepped from her.

She bowed slightly with her words, "Yes, my King." As she rose, she smiled at him and added, "you look very handsome."

Immediately, Liana turned from the stunned Casimir. The look on his befuddled face from her oddly timed compliment drew a sincerity to her smile. She willed her lungs to fill with a deep breath of the sweet, energetic air. A hush fell over the crowd and the tinkle of Liana's bangles rang out as she lifted her arm up slightly.

"Good evening!" she called out. With each word her confidence grew, "Our generous King has seen the needs of his people and been so moved that he invites you into his home tonight. Please, come drink, dine, and dance in celebration to honor King Casimir for returning the Queen safely to our Kingdom, ensur-"

"Ensuring prosperity and safety for all!" Casimir shouted over Liana and pulled her into his side with a playful tug.

With his words, the guests roared thunderous cheers of approval. Liana flinched as the magnitude of their support hit her. Gradually, soft music queued up around them. She pushed from Casimir and fell into her seat as the room spun around her. The floor before them instantly erupted with dancing.

As Liana watched the swirls of fabric and faces, she felt renewed. Along the walls to either side of them, stretched tables embellished with delicately designed and decorated foods, and fancy drinks. Liana looked to the ceiling and took another breath as the music caught her attention. The once soft melodies grew as she concentrated on their intriguing rhythms.

The dancers twirled and spun before them in an array of beautiful gowns, glittering jewels, and painted faces. Each was adorned with an ornately decorated mask, designed to impress. They all moved in unison to the music and created an enchanting show.

Liana sighed as a frown crossed her face. Frustrated for never allowing herself to enjoy a moment, she crossed her arms over her chest and let her thoughts spiral, *A tragic playlist for their dance. All for show.*

Suddenly, Casimir stood before her and opened his palm. She blinked repeatedly, confused at the gesture.

He cleared his throat, pressed his hand closer, and with a seductive tone, said, "My Queen, may I?"

Liana cleared her throat and as she took his hand, her cheeks flushed. He lifted her grasp as he guided her down the set of marble stairs before them. When they reached the dancefloor, he dropped her hand, spun to face her, and bowed. She smiled and bowed slightly. They rose together and locked eyes. As an earnest smile crossed his face, he gripped her around the waist and guided her over the dancefloor.

"Your beauty is most enchanting this evening," he called out to her over the music.

Her smile grew while she stared into his chest and quietly replied, "Thank you."

The enchanting melody swirled about them and drew them closer. Liana was instantly swept away in the sweet aromas and beautiful tones. She hadn't seen him smile like that in a long time. With a pang of guilt, Liana

The Light Within

had to admit, it was slightly intoxicating. She recalled each sinister smile and devious grin until she landed on the pleasant ones, so long ago, when they'd first met.

She lifted her wrist to Casimir's shoulder. The tinkle of her bracelets as they clinked against his decorated neckline drew her attention. She frowned at her heavily jeweled wrist and turned her attention back to Casimir. His magnificent royal garments accented his frame perfectly. When he smiled, she was instantly lost in his gorgeous cheekbones and, as she found herself blushing again, she turned her attention back to his words.

"The most radiant in all the Kingdom surely," Casimir said and spun her about.

An unnerving feeling crept up inside the pits of her stomach and sent a scowl across her face as she searched for the cause. Her wary gaze was drawn behind Casimir where several ladies stood. They grouped along the edges of the dancefloor, hands clasped at their chests as they gawked in admiration of Casimir and Liana. As he let another perfectly timed compliment fly, Liana watched the instant swoon of all who were close.

Liana sighed and turned her attention back to Casimir. With a slow swallow, she returned his stare and, as her eyes locked with his, she was lost in his dark pools. Her heart raced on as a strange remembrance of this moment muddied her thoughts. Suddenly, her mind flitted to Arietta and her tragic end. Casimir instantly dipped her and planted an incredibly hard kiss. As he pulled away from her, she heard the deafening crowd about them and looked around to all the spectators.

Casimir pulled her back up to his side and, as the dancing resumed, he quietly muttered to her, "Make your rounds my Queen. Ensure the message is set."

Let's Have A Ball

She instantly snapped her head towards him but kept her eyes on the ground. He lifted her hand and placed it in another's, who appeared before them in the crowd.

As he turned to leave, he called out over his shoulder, "I'll have W fetch you something to cover."

Casimir gestured to her open back just as her partner turned her and moved her to the dance floor. She sighed, already exhausted from the night's beginnings and desperate to slip away. Immediately, her exuberant, masked, dance partner twisted and steered her enthusiastically across the dance floor. Liana diverted her attention to the melodic tones about them as she twirled through the other dancers.

Before long, the whirlwind of fabric and faces slowed as the music calmed to a gentle pace. Her dance partner released her hand and bowed low. She nodded to them and with a smile, turned. Instantly, her face went flat. Liana filled her lungs with a deep breath and edged along the tables of lavish desserts.

With a grateful exhale, she popped a dark chocolate truffle in her mouth and attempted to skirt around the group of ladies who stood whispering to one another at the edge of the dance floor. Suddenly, one laughed obnoxiously loud and, as she did, took a step back right into Liana.

"Liana!" they all cried out.

She cringed and after a short moment, adorned a smile, and turned to the ladies.

"I'm so sorry, I didn't see you there," the curvy blonde said as she reached sympathetically for Liana.

Liana backed away from her grasp and smiled as the woman scowled at her. "It's okay, honestly."

The Light Within

"So," the spritely brunette began. She shrugged off the woman next to her, who continued to poke her, "What's the big celebration for?"

Her brow instantly furrowed at the question. After a moment of silence amongst the group, Liana cleared her throat and replied, "What do you mean?"

"I mean, it's a pretty big celebration. Is there some announcement you're going to make?" she questioned as she pointed to Liana's stomach.

Several of the ladies hushed her and instantly, Liana understood. She rolled her eyes and coldly replied, "Sorry, did you miss the King's speech?"

The girl huffed and crossed her arms over her chest. Liana nodded to the group with a smile and turned to leave. Just as she passed them, the curvy blonde sneezed obnoxiously and bumped Liana with her rear. She stumbled onto the dance floor and was instantly caught up with the dancers again. As she turned to shoot the group a glare, dancers blocked her view, and her hand was snatched up by someone nearby.

In an instant, she was pulled in another direction. She turned her attention to the dancer and was hit with an overwhelming aroma. Scents of pine and cedar danced playfully about her as she swirled around the dance floor. Her eyes closed while she drew in the air and allowed herself to get lost in the moment.

Without notice, her partner spun her and pulled her back into his chest. She laughed as she stumbled slightly. Her partner laughed with her before he resumed the tempo and cautiously steered her around the dance floor. As they moved about, Liana's gaze landed on the throne. She smiled up at Casimir, who watched her like a hawk with his arms crossed over his chest.

Let's Have A Ball

Slowly, her smile faded, as she worried, *he might get the wrong impression.*

Her attention slowly shifted to her partner before her as he carefully guided her through the sea of dancers on the floor. She took another deep breath and caught the familiar scent again. As her mind wandered back to memories of Nicolai, her partner cleared his throat. She instantly shook her head, diverted her thoughts, and withdrew inside.

How careless, she thought, *to lose control of your thoughts around so many.*

Suddenly, her partner spun her again, though this time she was ready. She twirled out and let her free hand linger until he pulled her back into his chest. A small, coy smile danced across Liana's lips as she placed her hand back on her partner's shoulder. When the familiar scent crept up again, she turned her sights to the dancers about them. Her eyes wandered and searched the guests' faces. She longed to rip their masks off and demand they show themselves.

There it was again! No, she checked her thoughts, *don't be stupid, he's gone.*

The tinkle of her bangles drew her attention but as she turned her head, her sights fixed on her dance partner's beard. As they danced, she glanced over him again and again. Had she not seen Nicolai shot down before her very eyes, she would've sworn he danced with her now. She shook the idea from her head and looked back to the throne again. The Elder leaned in at Casimir's side, listening intently as Casimir spoke and made sharp gestures with his hand.

The Light Within

As the melodies swelled, her partner spun her again, and the music cut off. She turned back to him just as he bowed low. With a warm smile, she nodded to him.

"My Queen," a voice sounded from behind her.

Liana spun and as her sights landed on the Elder, her heart sunk. She glanced over her shoulder to find her previous partner had disappeared. With a sigh, she turned her attention back to the one before her.

"Elder," she said with a small bow as she kept her warm smile fixed.

He extended his hand to her and, as she took it, he yanked her firmly into his chest. Liana stumbled slightly and cleared her throat. She straightened her posture as his hand slid low on her hip and roughly guided her through the other dancers on the floor. Her focus turned to those around her; careful to smile at each as they looked at her. As she skimmed from mask to mask, she glanced at the Elder. His dark, silky robes shimmered between charcoal and navy. The high collar accented his long neck well and matched perfectly with the small mask on his flawless face.

As his grip adjusted uncomfortably around the folds of her dress at her hip, he spoke out and drew her attention, "How goes the-" He paused for a moment to clear his throat before he continued, "task at hand?"

A small smile formed at his thin lips as if amused by his own words. With a heavy sigh, accented by a lengthy eye roll, Liana turned her attention to the throne. Her brow furrowed as she noticed Casimir's focus lay on a group of ladies to the side of the dance floor who waved and giggled at his sudden interest. Immediately, the Elder turned and blocked her view of Casimir. She turned her glare to him and was met with an amused grin.

Let's Have A Ball

Annoyance laced her words when she asked, "What?"

He let a small chuckle out and, as he continued to harshly steer her away, spoke in a hushed tone, "You're invisible to him right now. Isn't that what you want?"

Her glare intensified as she met his question with silence.

"I'm just saying," he said with light laughter. Slowly, he pulled her against his chest and whispered into her ear, "He's so consumed in himself that, in this moment, you could do whatever you wanted, right in front of him and he'd never be the wiser."

Her mind raced along and threw her heart into a frenzy as she wondered, *what is he talking about*?

She gulped when he leaned his cheek into hers and inhaled slowly. With another soft chuckle, he spun her and gently shoved her past a group of standing ladies. Liana turned around several times, but the Elder was suddenly nowhere to be found.

A sudden chill sent a shiver down her spine. Liana adjusted her gown and looked about again. Everyone around her was wrapped up in the events of the night and completely oblivious to her. It was as though she really was invisible. How she missed the days of being another face in the crowd. With a grin, she turned and sauntered off into the gathering.

Her thoughts swarmed as she carefully navigated the passageways, *could the Elder be trying to help me, or is he with Casimir? What if that really was Nicolai?*

As she rounded the entry hall, Liana quickly shot down a small hallway. She pressed herself against the wall and waited to see if anyone noticed. After she caught her breath, she darted down the narrow passageway.

The Light Within

Her heart leaped when the scent was instantly before her again. She stopped in her tracks and glanced down a branching corridor. After a short pause, she shook her head and crept along her way, determined to return to the ball before anyone noticed.

Don't be stupid, she let logic piece the puzzle together, *he's gone, it's a trick. Don't lose focus.*

Again she nodded to herself, lifted her gown, and hurried up the passageway. In a matter of minutes, she came to a short stop in a spacious foyer. Dread filled her face as she took in the state of the massive tree before her. The once beautiful, aromatic boughs were now fully encased in a dark, tar-like substance. It no longer bore any leaves; even the ones at its base were gone and the previous stench had rescinded.

With a downtrodden heart, she approached the tree and reached for one of its branches. As she tugged at a tiny offshoot, she ripped it from the larger branch. Upon inspection, she found a small sliver of greenish-white at its core.

There's still time, she thought excitedly.

Just like my people, she laughed to herself as the thought entered her mind. Instantly, her thoughts were drawn to the group of misguided ladies, and something stirred within her.

She shook her head as she spoke the words aloud and willed the light within her to comply, "There's no way I'd bear him a child. I'd rather *never* experience motherhood than bring a soul into this world of hate and for *him*."

Tears trickled down her face at the thought of what that could mean. Liana allowed a deep breath to fill her lungs and, with a massive sigh, opened her eyes. She quickly wiped the tears from her cheeks and knelt at the base of the tree. For a moment, she fussed with her dress, until she was finally able to pull the quartz-like dagger from the hilt on her thigh. As the light blade connected with the dark substance, the tar-like goo around it sizzled. With haste, she stabbed and dug at an exposed root until she wrenched a piece free.

"Sorry," she whispered up to the tree before she carefully stashed the sample in a small vial and tucked it away.

Liana held the blade out for a moment and inspected it. A grateful smile held firm on her face as she recalled W's perfectly timed recovery and stashing of the blade. She shivered abruptly as an icy wind whipped across her neck. She hurriedly tucked the blade back into the strap on her thigh.

As she stood, the familiar alluring aromas that teased her earlier in the evening taunted her again. Liana snapped around the corner where a darkened corridor stood and pursued the strange scent. When she rounded another corner, the shadow of someone further up the hall, shot around a bend in the distance. Her heart thumped as she raced in pursuit. Once she neared the end, she whipped around the corner and found an empty, far-stretching passageway.

With a heavy sigh, Liana shook her head and turned back. Her mind fought her aching heart and demanded her to be rational, *you're crazy, he's gone! Get back before it's discovered that you're missing*.

Slow steps retraced their way, carrying her back to the ballroom. She twisted and turned, gaining haste until she suddenly hit the overpowering fragrance again. Just as she shook her head and picked up her pace, she caught movement out of the corner of her eye. Liana immediately stopped in her steps and glanced down the branching hall to her left.

At the end of the darkened corridor before her, the soft glow of candlelight flickered over the silhouette of a man. Liana's heart skipped a beat as he turned suddenly and bolted around the corner. With his movement, the light flickered over his masked face and revealed the same dancer she had so desperately hoped for another run-in with.

Liana immediately pursued him, determined to see who he truly was behind the mask. She rounded corner after corner, narrowly missing him until his laughter made her slow. Without warning, he stepped from the shadows with a coy grin on his face. With a glare, she shoved him against the wall.

"What are you playing at?" she questioned.

His enchanting grin intrigued her and fought to distract her from the moment. She pressed his shoulder into the wall and reached for his mask. He lifted his hands defensively but didn't stop her as she ripped the embellished cloth from his face. Liana gasped and staggered backward.

The man before her looked exactly like Nicolai. She shook her head, confused. Though she had hoped it was truly him, she couldn't believe what she saw. He took a step towards her and immediately she stepped back again.

"No, it's..." her voice shakily whispered as she choked back tears, "it's a trick. You can't... you d-"

He shook his head and took another step towards her while he spoke, "I thought I did but," he shook his head and laughed awkwardly, "it did hurt a lot. Casimir was a poor shot thankfully. Right in the neck. Arietta showed up just in time." He smiled earnestly as he recounted his plausible story, "she had a funny way of doing that."

Liana stared silently at him for quite some time before he tried to step towards her again. She instantly backed away. He sighed and lifted his arm out for her to see. She squinted at the tiny scar on his wrist and remembered it so long ago as though it were another lifetime.

"Look, it really is me. Please believe me, Liana I... I've been waiting so long to..." his voice cut off as he choked over his words. He stood there silent, mouth open, arms out, and stared at her.

Liana agonized internally wanting it so much but still, something tugged within her. As he drew closer, she found it harder to step away, and suddenly he was face to face with her. Her fingers twisted in his beard as he wrapped her in his secure arms. For a moment it felt like she could finally breathe. As she turned her gaze upward to him, he locked her in a secure kiss.

Her heart danced with excitement and yet, almost instantly her mind begged for her to reason again. She pulled from him and stared in silence.

Liana jumped as a voice cut unexpectedly through the air, "What have we here?"

She spun around and bowed her head as Casimir strolled down the hall. Her blank stare secured the panic that clawed frantically within her.

"She was at the tree, with this."

The gruff voice of the Commander boomed from directly behind her where moments ago Nicolai had stood. He reached by her in the same garments and tossed the light blade to Casimir.

The Light Within

Casimir's sinister laughter echoed hauntingly around them with his words, "Finally, and she's almost ready."

Her shock painted across her face and, as Darkness laughed, Liana's stomach instantly turned. She had no clue what they had in store for her and the disgust in herself for embracing him weighed like an anchor in the pit of her soul. The only thing she was certain of is that she wasn't certain of anything anymore. Liana shivered as she reverted to a familiar blank stare and fixed her focus on the floor. Casimir slowly approached her. He toyed with her hair as he circled her.

His whispers crept across her cheek, "Perhaps there never really *was* a Nicolai."

Chapter 11
Story Time

Liana's eyes shot wide open. The canopy of twisted curtains stared back from above her while a moment of confusion passed.

Just a nightmare, she repeated in her head.

A deep breath filled her lungs and she attempted to sit up. In an instant, her heart raced on uncontrollably as her other muscles failed her. Rapid gasps filled her chest as she tried to shift her arms and legs in vain. It was as though an impossibly heavy blanket rested over her entire body and pinned her in place.

The icy discomfort from the dream lingered in her foot and radiated painfully through her leg. After a moment of panic, Liana shifted her focus upward and concentrated on the curtains as she tried desperately to keep from hyperventilating. When she slowed her breathing, the pain receded. Gradually, she was able to lift her arms. She froze, for just as she moved to sit up, a low growl rumbled from the foot of the bed.

A sideways glance found a sleeping Casimir and pushed a frustrated sigh from her. Another deep grumble sounded right at her feet. Liana tried to kick, but her legs still refused her commands. Her heart threatened to jump from her throat as she turned and sat up. Instantly, a dark shadow pulled from her and stood just beyond the foot of the bed.

Liana stared on, eyes wide as the shadowy creature lingered before it suddenly shot off into the darkness. She pulled her knees into her chest and wrapped her arms around her legs. Her unblinking gaze fixed on the door; in

The Light Within

wait, should the creature return. She stared on, stiff as a statue as the night hours crept by.

When the light of the approaching dawn slowly filled the sky, her mind eased, and she debated going back to sleep. A cool wind crept across her open back and sent a shiver up her spine. With a sigh, she laid back, rolled to her side, and pulled the blankets to her chin. After she wiggled into just the right spot, she opened her sleepy eyes and was met with the stare of Casimir. He sat at the edge of the bed near his nightstand and faced her with a glare that burned the longer her stare remained.

"Morning," she whispered with forced enthusiasm.

"Good morning?" he questioned with a huff. "Are you just getting to bed?"

"No," she replied slowly and matched his glare while it lingered on her.

He threw his hands up and turned from her. While he walked off to the shower room, he mumbled, "You wonder why you're always so tired. Been out late, doing what?"

An utter look of confusion set over her face the longer his ramblings continued. As the light peeped over the tree line and shone into her eyes, Liana huffed and rolled to her other side. She pulled the blankets over her head and tried to block him out.

"Thinking about me? Plotting my demise?" he questioned loudly over the running water.

She heaved a sigh and threw the blankets from her form. Quietly, she rose and readied herself. Just as she sat on the ornate sofa, Casimir sauntered from behind her. He moved quickly and stood in front of the chamber doors for quite some time.

Story Time

Suddenly, Casimir heaved a massive sigh and called out, "I'm waiting!"

Liana's stare burned into the back of his head as she crossed the room and stood behind him. With a deep breath, she bowed her head and followed along quietly while Casimir guided her through the castle corridors. Liana looked up as they entered the small, dark room with the black and gold, marbled table.

A chill in the air sent a shiver through her entire being. Liana tugged the sleeves of her gown down to her wrists and adjusted the bangles. When she looked up, the few individuals that sat scattered at the table rose from their seats and stared at her. She cleared her throat and quietly sat next to Casimir.

As the doors opened and several individuals fussed about, Casimir leaned towards the Elder. Liana strained to listen but the clanking of dishes and murmurs of the few that sat amongst her drowned them out. She turned her attention to her plate and sighed. As she looked up to Casimir, she found his attention rested on her. She returned his look with a questioning stare that intensified as he spoke.

"My radiant gem," he said as he reached for her. He ran the back of his hand up her cheek while he spoke, "What do you have planned for your day?"

Liana cleared her throat and forced a smile as she replied, "My day is open to you, my King."

"Perfect," he said with a grin.

He tapped his hand against her cheek once and turned from her to attend to his breakfast. She swallowed the knot in her throat and raised her cup to her lips.

The Light Within

From across the table, she barely heard the mumbled remarks of the Elder as he leaned into Casimir, "She's nearly ready for the ritual."

Casimir waved his hand dismissively to the Elder and shot a strange look at Liana. She stiffened in her chair, yet her expression remained flat.

"What ritual?" she asked; unamused by their secretive talk.

Casimir cleared his throat and leaned his elbow on the table as he shifted towards her.

"My gem," he said with a smile.

Her expression remained fixed as she instantly recited her rehearsed lines, "Yes, my King?"

His smile grew with her reply. After a moment he cleared his throat and responded, "How would you like to explore the Kingdom today? Let your presence uplift our people; possibly heal some of our wounded soldiers?"

"What ritual?" she asked again and, as her expression remained stone, his smile dissolved into a scowl.

He turned quickly and shot the Elder a glare. The Elder's gaze remained fixed on Liana as he observed her. Silently, he lifted his hand out to her. Casimir instantly turned back to her and sighed.

In a hushed tone, he let his words fly, "A ritual to increase your power."

Her eyebrows raised with his words and immediately, she fought to control her expression. She nodded once and turned to her plate. As she placed her cup on the table, the clamor of her bracelets drew her attention. She nodded to herself and shifted her gaze to Casimir.

Story Time

"My King," she said with a small smile. "I would love to visit our soldiers. What a wonderful idea! Surely that would uplift their spirits and encourage them to keep fighting for the Kingdom."

"Perfect!" Casimir's voice rang out.

"Only," she paused and cleared her throat as Casimir shifted with irritation. "I wonder how many more I could help if only my restraints were lifted?"

Casimir's face flushed red, and his hands instantly balled into fists on the table.

Instantaneously, Liana sat up and reassured, "Temporarily, of course, my King. Merely a suggestion."

She shrugged and placed an innocent smile on her face. As she turned her focus to her breakfast, Liana let her noisy bangles clank and clamor against the table.

Suddenly, Khius spoke out and threw the brakes on her plan, "I can assure you that's not necessary, my Queen."

Her eyebrows knit together as she leaned forward and glanced around the Commander. Khius sat near the end of the table, a distance from Liana. He ate quietly with two others.

"If you pace yourself, you can fulfill the King's request. I could accompany her, your Highness, at your command. For more extensive training on this, of course." Khius spoke quickly, then immediately turned his attention back to his plate.

She opened her mouth to interject and, at that moment, felt the tinge of a voice unlike her own instantly caution her, *be still, now is not the time.*

Liana glared into her plate, frustrated that she was so close to slipping out of her bindings. She let her stare linger as she heard Casimir's voice echo across the open table.

"Fine."

Casimir waved to Khius and returned his focus to his breakfast. As he finished his plate, the Commander grumbled next to Liana. Casimir stood suddenly and shoved his chair back.

"Commander. Escort Liana to the areas most affected," he said sternly, then approached Liana.

As she moved to stand, he placed a hand on her shoulder and pushed her back into her seat. Casimir stepped closer to her and lifted her chin in his hand. He held her face firmly while his glare burned down into her.

"You are to remain with your escorts. You will only heal who you are instructed to. Understand?" he demanded.

"Y-yes," she replied in a tiny voice.

Casimir nodded once to her, then turned and marched from the room.

o   o   o

An exaggerated sigh left Liana while she marched next to Khius and slowly but quietly, timed her words to their steps, "I was so close! You just *had* to open your mouth."

"Please, I saved you," Khius boasted next to her. "The only thing you were close to, was a dirt nap."

Liana huffed and crossed her arms over her chest. After a moment of her silence, Khius looked sideways and rolled his eyes at her.

Khius nudged her with his elbow as he spoke, "Look on the bright side."

"I can't look on any side," she said with an eye roll while she walked on her tiptoes for a moment.

Story Time

He laughed and immediately drew the Commander's attention. He glared down at Khius over the wall of soldiers that surrounded Khius and Liana. After a short distance, he turned his attention from them and continued to lead the group. Shortly after, Liana made out a set of decrepit stone gates that loomed high above them. When they neared, they paused for quite some time.

Khius shifted uncomfortably back and forth on his feet while they waited. Once he noticed Liana's stare, he perked up and tried to make conversation. As soon as his mouth opened, she hushed him. Khius shot Liana a glare but she pointed her finger up as she craned her neck to listen. After a moment, he shook his head at her and moved in closer.

"The bright side is, they think your biggest weakness is the shackle situation," Khius pointed to her bracelets as he spoke. He looked up for a moment, then continued to whisper feverishly, "use that as your strength."

"Use the thing that cuts my power off?" she asked and shot him an irritated glare.

"No, lo-" Khius immediately cut his words short and moved away from Liana when the gates before them creaked open.

As the gates parted, the soldier wall that surrounded them did as well. One by one, the escorting soldiers broke off and scattered around the small encampment before them. They revealed a cramped and chaotic mess of soldiers. Crumbling walls lined the small enclosure and broke away in one area to reveal more soldiers beyond.

Liana swallowed the knot in her throat as she examined those around her. When she slowly spun, she saw face after face calling out and countless more barely clinging to life. Her eyes lingered over the Commander while he spoke heatedly with a highly decorated, uniformed individual.

Without wasting another moment, Liana broke away from the small group that remained near her and walked the encampment. Khius followed closely behind and muttered directions that Liana refused to hear. As she walked about, her focus on the essential drowned out the chaotic commotion that surrounded her and melded the cries into a tragic symphony of emotion.

Gradually, she made her way by each warrior and tried to soothe them. Some she offered water and others she paused longer to attend to their wounds. Murmurs spread quickly through the camp as she used the power within her to heal those suffering. Suddenly, a frail young lady in a black dress gripped Liana's wrist and yanked her to stand.

"Please!" Her voice shook as she pleaded with Liana, "Please help, he's almost gone!"

Liana yanked her wrist from the girl's clutch. As Khius stepped between them, Liana nodded and gestured for the young girl to lead. With haste, they jumped over red-stained rocks and around the groups of gathered soldiers, to the furthest side of the encampment. The weight in the air shifted as she approached and made it increasingly harder for her to breathe. She watched the small girl drop next to the man on the ground in between others who assisted him.

"No!" he shouted as the individuals around him tried to help.

Liana approached cautiously and when she met the stare of the young man, he shouted louder. He continued to shout until his gurgling coughs broke his words. Instantly, Liana rushed forward and reached for him.

"Please," he managed to whisper in between coughs. "Please let me go."

"I can help. I..." Liana trailed off and let her mouth hang open while she studied the man's torment-ridden face.

"Heal him," the Commander boomed suddenly from behind her.

She jumped at the sudden company and instantly reached for the man's chest.

"Please," he begged her.

As her eyes connected with his and she saw the sorrow in his story, she couldn't help but sympathize with his wishes. She shook her head and pulled her fist into her chest as the man took his last breath.

The Commander's boots clunked off the broken stone ground as he approached Liana and slowly his grumbles rose directly behind her, "I told you to heal him."

"Too late," Liana whispered as she rose to her feet and dropped her head.

The Commander circled around her and gestured to the man at her feet, "Then bring him back!"

"Bring him back?" someone questioned from behind her.

She glanced over her shoulder and noted the decorated soldier that the Commander had previously been in conversation with, had joined them. With a second glance, she realized several others stood behind him and watched in silence. The Commander cleared his throat and immediately, Liana turned to face him.

The Light Within

"Yes. My Queen, show him," with his words he gestured to the lifeless man at her feet.

She glared up at the Commander just as the man behind her spoke up again, "He is one. This way. Let us truly see what she is capable of."

Liana turned just as the soldiers formed a path in the crowd for them to walk through. When she lingered, the Commander nudged her in the back with a growl. She sighed and followed along in silence as she tried to mask the small grin of triumph. When the man leading them stepped to the side, her smile instantly dissolved.

They stepped through a break in the wall. As her view opened, she stopped in her steps and her knees went weak. Her tear-filled eyes landed on the infinitely stretching forest floor littered with piles of lifeless bodies. Liana gripped her chest at the unbearable pain and dropped to her knees. As she fell forward to her hands, the Commander heaved a sigh and reached for her.

Khius quickly called out, "I wouldn't-"

The Commander shot him a glare and turned back to Liana. As he reached for her arm to pull her to her feet, a large zap sounded. He pulled his hand back and shook it as his eyes lingered on the electrical shield that shone around Liana.

"All those lives," Liana whispered to herself, unaware of anything that took place around her.

She sat back on her heels and gripped her chest again. It felt as though a searing spike ran through her heart. Liana cried out, leaned forward, and slammed her fist into the grass in front of her. A small wave of blue and teal electricity pulsed from her. The pulse rippled through the grass and over each body and tree that lay before her.

Story Time

Just as it left her body, she toppled forward. Khius was immediately at her side and caught her right before she hit the ground. The grass and trees spun all around her while she clung to consciousness. Liana focused on Khius's face as his words echoed in the distance. She stared on confused as his focus shifted away from her and his expression changed.

After what felt like an eternity, the trees above her finally came into focus and seemed more vibrant than ever. Liana pushed away from Khius into the grass and slowly lifted herself to her feet. She rubbed her pounding temple and slowly looked around. Her eyes instantly went wide as she stared in stunned silence.

Before the Commander turned her from the area and shoved her hastily through the camp, she caught sight of the most wondrous scene. The once dull and scorched lawns now shone a vibrant emerald that bloomed with thousands of tiny, colorful flowers. They reached as far as the eye could see in a vibrant display that stretched up to the trees, now in full bloom. The piles of soldiers beneath the fruitful trees, unfolded themselves, slowly stood, and looked at each other in amazement.

Her eyes remained wide with excitement and a small grin settled in as they marched quickly away. Liana kept her eyes fixed on the ground and tried to regain strength. After what felt like an eternity of travel, she turned her attention to Khius. When she saw his face was wrought with worry, she turned her focus back to the ground.

That was amazing, she thought to herself. *What could he be so concerned about?*

She glanced back in his direction. He took no notice of her lingering stare as he remained deep in thought. Just as she opened her mouth to inquire with him, shouts broke out from a distance to their right. The Commander grumbled something from in front of them and suddenly, several soldiers broke from the circle that surrounded them. When the remaining guards shifted, Liana's view improved.

Gates to the Kingdom stood in the distance, across a field of tall grass. The path they walked, continued far around the fields into the distance. The Commander threw his arm up and halted the group at the edge of the grass. A scowl formed as she watched him examine the path and the field, back and forth several times while he weighed his options. The Commander turned suddenly and faced her. Liana could've sworn a look of worry crossed his face but before she could be certain, he shook it away.

"Quickly," he grumbled.

Immediately, he turned from the group and shot off into the field. Liana stood stunned for only a moment before the wall of soldiers around her shoved her on. The look of bewilderment remained glued to her face as she ran along with the group. Just a short distance into the grass, the blades shifted beside them. Without warning, one of the individuals surrounding her was yanked into the grass. They all stopped in their steps and adjusted tighter around Liana. As they waited, no movement in the grass, or even a fateful scream, indicated the lost soldier's fate.

The Commander shot a look over his shoulder to Khius, then turned and took off again. As they ran, another was pulled from the circle. The group adjusted without losing pace, even as a third was pulled away. Khius reached for Liana, grabbed her arm in a painful grip, and pulled her forward at an increasing speed. Once they reached the break in the high grass, they paused in a row of trees, just outside the gates. They all looked around as they caught their breath and before long, the Commander pressed forward.

They were at the entrance in no time and, as they approached, the gates creaked open to greet them. Just as they stepped inside, the gates closed with a loud clamor. Liana jumped slightly and noticed her arm remained in Khius' clutch. She cleared her throat and yanked her arm away.

"Back to the castle, no stopping," the Commander barked at Liana.

"Gladly," Liana muttered as she fell in step with the group around her.

Not far into the streets of the Kingdom, the citizens caught sight of Liana. The whispers grew to murmurs and before long, they had a large group of curious people that followed them.

"Move along!" the Commander shouted when a little girl reached through the soldiers and yanked at Liana's gown.

Liana smiled down at the young girl and gently nudged her from the group. As her arm reached outside of the soldier wall, someone grabbed her wrist and yanked. She was instantly pulled away from the group into the civilians just beyond.

The Commander drew his sword and lifted it high over his head as he shouted, "Release her!"

"Wait!" Liana shouted and raised her hand to him.

She looked down to the frail, sickly woman, whose stern grip had pulled her such a distance. The Commander sheathed his sword and moved between the two.

"Please," the woman whispered shakily.

The Light Within

"Move along! You were not instructed to heal these people," he said to Liana as he shoved the two of them apart.

Liana angrily shot back, "These people are also my people."

"The orders were for soldiers only," he grumbled and nudged Liana back to the group.

Wait, her mind raced as she stared back into the Commander's glare, *he only wants me to raise his army...* Her eyes widened in horror with the realization, *all those soldiers... ready for battle again.*

She swallowed the knot in her throat and replied, "We must go this way. I will help those on our way back."

Her quiet, yet stern voice reverberated through the atmosphere. After quite some time holding his stare, the Commander nodded once and stepped aside. He grumbled something indiscernible and stood at the front of the group of soldiers.

Liana quickly turned to the woman, took both her hands into her own, and bowed her head. She touched her forehead to their hands and urged the light within her to help the woman. Almost immediately, she lifted her head and released the woman. The woman stumbled back in amazement as the life seemed to flow back into her flesh.

All those nearby instantly shouted and reached for Liana. Khius placed his hand on her back and urged her along. While they walked, countless citizens continuously reached for her. She took each of their hands and prayed she could bring them any comfort. As the outside foyer of the castle came into view, Liana sighed and leaned into Khius for a moment.

She pleaded to the light within her, *please give me the strength to make it to the end.*

254

Story Time

With a deep breath, she stepped away from Khius and with each step, she felt rejuvenated. They quickly closed in on the courtyard but as Liana moved to climb the many marble stairs, a hooded individual broke through her escorts and blocked her path. Liana patiently stared at the figure. They carried a bundle of blankets at their chest and hunched over in an exhausted manner.

"Come on," the Commander shot at Liana through gritted teeth as his patience thinned.

Liana glared at him, then turned to the citizen and quickly urged "Please, how can I-"

Her mouth fell open as the cloaked individual turned the bundle of blankets to reveal a small, pale child.

The Commander shouted and instantly stepped between them, "Enough!"

Furious, she stepped around him and let her words fly, "It's one child. What kind of King wouldn't want me to save one child?"

She carefully gripped the blankets at the woman's chest and pulled them to her own. Her face instantly went flat as she eyed the small child.

"Liana," Khius cautioned quietly from behind her.

The Commander warned her, "You weep for this child as if it's your own? Stupid girl, these people are beneath you. Put it down. You are directly violating the King's order."

Ignoring the chaos about her, she looked to the child and wondered, *why would I bring you back into this cruel place?* As she questioned herself, her mind settled, *you deserve a fighting chance.*

Liana ignored the shouts around her and closed her eyes.

The Light Within

She called to the power inside her, *please restore and protect this child from any harm the enemy may intend against it.*

A shudder ran through her body as a small tear fell from her cheek onto the child's forehead. As it landed, it chased the icy grips of death from the infant's face and suddenly, tiny cries called out. The woman grabbed her child with a thankful bow. She instantly turned and ran from the group. Liana stood confused for a moment until Khius grabbed her arm and pulled her up the stairs. She instantly shot him an angry glare and pulled her arm from his grip.

"Come on!" Khius shouted and gestured behind her.

Liana turned and immediately ducked as the Commander's blade cut the air above her. She stumbled back and turned as the Darkness around the Commander overtook him. When she neared the top of the steps, she reached for the guards.

Stall him, she urged them.

As she concentrated, they shoved her through the door and slammed it shut. The guards immediately secured several locks just as Darkness pounded. Liana let out a relieved breath and turned from the door to find an angry Khius. He stood, arms crossed over his chest, with a glare that burned into Liana.

"Always have to push it too far," Khius started in on her in an aggravated tone.

She sighed and shoved by him. She was determined to give Casimir her side of the story before Darkness could cloud his mind.

Khius shook his head and clicked his teeth as he followed along behind her and occasionally muttered,

Story Time

"Just couldn't stop while you were ahead. So, what's the plan now?"

She turned to Khius and asked, "Do you know anything about a ritual to increase my power?"

Khius's eyes narrowed. Liana heaved another sigh and turned from him to continue down the hall.

"Look, Liana..."

His words trailed off and he halted in his steps. She paused but didn't turn as he pleaded with her.

His remarks, so certain at first, shook the further he continued, "I know you want to grow your powers but please be careful...Where you get them. How you use them...it, it can change you."

With a half-laugh, she waved her hand dismissively and assured him, "I know, I know Khius."

"I'm serious Liana, I-"

"I know!" she cut in.

He cleared his throat and resumed their walk. They walked on in silence for a short time before Liana moved in front of him and blocked his way in the corridor.

She questioned curiously, "But what is this ritual? Like what does it involve?"

Khius scowled at her, pulled his arms over his chest, and immediately shot back, "If it's coming from Casimir, almost certainly nothing good."

Her question cut in quick, "Maybe I can use it to fight though?"

He threw his hands up with a loud groan and lifted his voice, "How much more will you appease him and risk completely losing yourself to the Darkness?"

"I'm in control!" she shouted angrily. "I don't care. I'll be fine!"

"You need to leave this place," he urged her.

The Light Within

Something inside her stirred at his words and she wondered if he was right. Liana shook her head and pushed back, "No, I have to stay and fight!"

"Why?" Khius questioned.

Liana turned and shot him an angry glare with her retort, "Clearly, he's the winning team in this one Khius. We must work with him, look around you. We're only here because he allowed it. Look at all the times he's spared my life."

Khius let a long sigh go and, as he spoke, crossed his arms over his chest, "Liana, come on; look again. It's that Power, the Light within you, that has spared your life. If you cling to him, he'll continue to bring only death."

She sighed and after a moment spoke quietly, "Sometimes death is necessary. I don't need all this philosophical, counseling bullshit. I must stay and if you aren't here to fight, then leave."

His eyes narrowed suspiciously at her, for the voice that spoke was hers, but the remarks were unlike her. His words almost failed him as he replied, "As you wish."

Suddenly, Darkness lumbered from around the corner and crashed into the wall. He growled as he laid eyes on her.

"Okay, you want a fight, fight him then," Khius said with a hearty laugh as he took off down the hallway.

Maybe I really could fight him, the thought flickered in her mind for a moment.

Liana turned to the stumbling beast that lumbered towards her and felt a strange triumphant sensation rise within. As he neared her, her confidence shook, and so did her head.

"Maybe if you would've let them take the shackles off," she jabbed at Khius, yet still, she didn't move.

Story Time

Khius slid to a stop further up the hall and shouted to her, "What are you doing?"

Fight, a tiny voice urged within her.

She shook her head and convinced herself, *I can't.*

Just as Darkness heaved his blade above his head, he paused. Liana looked up and slowly backed away. He gradually sheathed his blade and nodded his head. Suddenly, the dark cloud of black mist that surrounded him receded behind him. He let an frustrated growl burst from his chest and drove a fist into the wall next to him. With a deep breath, he turned to Liana, gripped her wrist, and pulled her through the corridors.

They neared the throne room in no time. The Commander lingered just outside the door for quite some time. He turned his head to Liana slightly and let out an eerie chuckle. He opened the door and shoved Liana through. She immediately caught Casimir's attention. He lifted his head, and, with the wave of his hand, the door slammed shut and locked the Commander and Khius on the other side. Liana spun from the door, back to Casimir, and lowered her head.

"Come, my Queen," Casimir called to her from the center of the throne room.

Slowly, she made her way to him. As she approached, she could hear the laughter of children. She glanced up from the floor and watched while Casimir playfully wrestled and fumbled with a group of several children. Something stirred within her, and once Liana drew closer, they all settled into a circle around Casimir.

"Story! Story!" the children shouted.

He grinned up at Liana and cheerfully asked, "My Queen, would you join us for a lesson?"

Liana nodded apprehensively.

The Light Within

"Good," Casimir replied shortly and waved his hand.

Instantly, she was yanked off her feet and shoved into the throne quite a distance away. She looked down frantically as several dark shadows twisted around her and held her in place. The children around Casimir clapped their hands excitedly, then all settled down as he raised a finger to his lips.

"Once, there was a beautiful Queen," Casimir began.

"Casimir, please, let me expl-"

"Shh," he lifted his finger to his lips and looked at her.

Slowly, Liana closed her mouth and stared helplessly. She searched the face of each child, but none were the one she'd saved earlier; the only positive she could cling to at this moment. Her mind raced over the fates of the children before her as Casimir recounted his tale of a selfish Queen who risked the lives of others to do as she wanted.

Liana lurched forward as she saw dark mists forming at the children's feet. She pushed with all her power and yet the shadows around her held firm. A shiver crawled up her spine and she noticed a beast lurking over her shoulder. The shadows that bound her tightly to the throne slowly rose into a gurgling, fanged monster that gripped her face. It clamped her mouth shut and turned her attention back towards the more horrific scene.

Dark shadows materialized from the mists at the floor where the children sat. The children, so captivated by the storytelling of Casimir, took no notice until one suddenly cried out. Instantly, the shadows reached out and stifled the child's cry. Chaos immediately set in as the other children took notice and scattered.

She pulled her eyes from the screaming children and fixed them on Casimir as he got to his feet. Casimir walked from the group while the encircling shadows snatched each fearful child until it devoured them all. He slowly approached her and just as the last scream cut off, he came to a standstill in front of her. Liana gasped for air when the beast released her. After a moment, she slowly lifted her face. He caught her chin in his hand and jerked it upwards.

Through gritted teeth, he spat his angry whispers at her, "Simple orders, my Queen."

As her blank stare met his, the grin on his face made her stomach turn. He released her chin and gave a quick pat on her cheek. His eyes lingered on her as he took a few steps backward. Casimir glanced up to the shadowy beast that loomed behind her. With a shrug, he turned from her and slowly made his way from the hall.

"Casimir!" she cried out.

"Shh."

Once his hush echoed across the open room, the beast behind her reached its claws over her mouth and held it closed. She flinched as its gurgling jaws clamped shut next to her ear. Instantly, she closed her eyes and lowered her head. She could care less what happened to her at this point. All she could think of is how she had failed each child.

"Stupid girl," the beast growled from over her.

Tears streamed down her face and, as they washed over the beast's bony grasp, its tar-like flesh sizzled. It howled and instantly released her face. She gasped for air and wiped her face on her shoulder.

The Light Within

It wrapped around her torso and squeezed her tighter as it hissed into her ear, "Weak girl… Why do you weep for them? They are nothing. You are nothing."

She remained still and silent as the beast tormented and taunted her. Before long it threw its head back and let out a thunderous roar. The room shook while dust and bits of rock fell from the ceiling The beast drug her from the throne. It pulled her along the halls and as they reached the King's Chambers, it wretched open the doors and tossed her through. She slid across the floor and stopped abruptly against the bed.

As she lifted herself to a shaky elbow, the beast roared at her and instantly, the shadows around it pulled the doors shut. With a tiny grin, she collapsed to her side. The shallow draws of her breath lulled her into a painfully short rest.

Chapter 12
Seek The Truth

Her eyes wandered from the page before her and rested on the clouds that swirled in the stormy sky. The distant melodies of droplets against the glass ceiling drew her attention and held it for quite some time. While her mind wandered, it tortured her with the laughs of the children she couldn't save. Her chest tightened as the tears welled in her eyes. She shook her head and diverted her focus back to the task at hand.

"There has to be something here about a ritual," she mumbled as she flipped through page after page.

Several moments later, she let out a frustrated sigh, closed the book, and tossed it on the stack next to her. Liana leaned back in her chair and crossed her arms over her chest. As she eyed the large stack of discarded books, L appeared next to her. She always had a way of showing up when Liana needed her most.

"Haven't found what you're looking for?" L asked curiously.

Liana shook her head.

L lifted her hand to her chin and after a moment, asked, "Do you know what it is you're looking for?"

Liana sat up in her chair and scowled at L but almost instantly her face softened, and she asked, "Do you know of the Power we possess?"

L nodded, "I've studied it closely for years."

Liana's face brightened as the spark of hope reignited and instantly, she inquired, "Do you know of any way to amplify or increase my power? Using my power is draining; there must be a way to stop that or increase the Power perhaps?"

The Light Within

L nodded to Liana and after a moment she quietly replied, "Your issue may not be the Power but rather the source. Tap into the Light, instead of your own power. Perhaps during the drain, so you are restored by the Light and your strength doesn't deplete."

Liana stared quietly at the table as L spoke and took in every word, careful to digest each individually before she considered a reply. After quite some time, she mumbled absently, "Something similar has been suggested by others."

"Perhaps you should listen," L said with a laugh.

Liana let out a chuckle and replied, "Perhaps."

o   o   o

Liana shielded her eyes from a bright lawn that stretched out before her. She shivered and looked around herself.

As she turned, her mind raced, *where am I? This seems so familiar.*

A shudder rose from her core and instantly, she pulled her arms around herself. The shadows whipped around her in every direction. As she turned her attention ahead, the wind gushed from behind and shoved her forward. She climbed a few steps of the crumbling, stone staircase that twisted into the shadows before she paused.

The strange sensation of familiarity rose again. She scowled and looked to her feet but the harder she concentrated, the foggier the world around her grew. Liana narrowed her eyes and searched around.

As she craned her neck to see what lay beyond, the shadows surged around her and whipped into a frenzy. Liana cried out as they sliced across her flesh and shoved her down against the stone. She pulled herself over the last few steps to a landing where the stairway turned to her left. The shadows whipped in every direction and pulled her hair with them. Liana blindly pulled her arms over her head.

A frustrated growl escaped her and suddenly she shouted, "Enough!"

With her word, the shadows instantly receded beyond a crumbled wall that lined what remained of the stairwell.

Liana blinked several times before her mind reasoned, *it's your dream, you have control.*

With a nod to herself, Liana bounded up the next several stairs. As she reached the top, she squealed and rocked back as her feet met the edge of the stairs. The deteriorating stone crumbled away right in front of her step. Instantly, Liana jumped back to another stair and watched as the stone dropped into a dark abyss. She looked over the large gap and noticed the platform continued.

On the other side of the bottomless chasm stretched a rough stone block. Liana held her breath and jumped the gap. As she landed on the other side, the sting of the hard stone shot through her feet and up her legs. She drew a sharp breath inward between her teeth and shakily stood.

Her sight set on the stone altar at the center of the platform and instantaneously, the shadows whipped about her again. They stirred with such fury around her that they stole the breath from her lungs. Liana flailed her arms frantically but one by one, the shadows secured her limbs to her sides.

"Stop," she whispered with her last breath.

She felt her head spinning, as though she'd pass out, and suddenly, like a light bulb going off, the thought illuminated, *it's a dream.*

The Light Within

Frustrated at herself, she closed her eyes and concentrated on the thought. After a moment, the deafening roar of the whipping shadows dwindled. Before long, she could hear the rhythmic pulls of Casimir's breath beside her. She opened her eyes but the suffocating darkness around her remained.

Liana took a deep breath and pushed to roll herself from her stomach. When she tried to move her arm, she felt it restrained at her side. She pulled her face from the pillow and turned her head. As her sights rested on Casimir, she felt something heavy press into her back. She tried to call out, but her voice failed her and though she fought to get free, she didn't move even the slightest.

A deep, gurgling, growl rose from above Liana. Her eyes went wide as she struggled futilely against its grip. She squeezed her eyes shut and focused on calming her racing heart before it seized. After only a moment, she felt the weight lift from her and instantly rolled over. The dwindling shadows of the rising dawn filled the room before her and revealed nothing there. Still, her eyes darted around several times before she could convince herself she was safe.

o   o   o

"I believe the room you saw houses the veil," L said with excitement painted across her face.

Liana nodded to her as she thought to herself, *that's exactly what Arietta called it.*

"What do you know of it?" Liana asked curiously.

L pulled a chair out at the table that Liana had stacked high with discarded tomes. She sat and leaned across the table towards Liana as she recounted her knowledge on the matter.

"It is rarely discussed as *usually,* no one can locate it." She studied Liana for a moment in silence, her eyes wide with wonder before she shook her head and continued, "It is a crossover point between realms; similar to the one that transported you here. Only... it doesn't go to the mortal realm."

Liana leaned in curiously and asked, "Where does it go?"

L stared blankly ahead and whispered, "It isn't meant to be seen until the end of times."

The fear painted across L's face stole Liana's curious smile. L's lingering silence made her uneasy, and she worried about what could possibly lay beyond. After a moment longer, Liana drew in a big breath and looked back to L.

Liana cleared her throat and asked, "Why are the daggers there?"

L's eyes went wide again, and she leaned closer into Liana, "You've been inside?"

"Yes..." Liana drew out her reply with a furrowed brow.

L scooted closer yet again, shoulder to shoulder with Liana now. She lowered her voice and with a feverish pace, spoke quietly, "The daggers are vessels that can house the power of the Light. We all bear a small amount of the Light's power naturally, but when fused with the power housed in the dagger, it is amplified. When the Light is withdrawn back into the dagger, the essence of who you were with the Light is drawn back also. Your memories, powers, abilities, essentially who you are, are intertwined with the Light's power. If the dagger remains in the realm with you, it will, in a sense, search for you until you are reunited. They are stored in the veil because the crossover makes it unable to locate the soul it was tied to."

The Light Within

Liana stared back blankly.

L cleared her throat and with a smile, she continued, "So, when they banished you and pulled the Light's power from you if they would've taken the dagger back to the veil, then your memories of your time when you had the Light would've never returned. Also, no one may have been able to recover the blade since few can find the room. Then, no one would've been able to return the power, allowing you to return to your Kingdom."

Liana nodded and after a moment she looked to L and asked, "Why was I able to find the room then and you said everyone has the Light in them? Even Casimir?"

L stared blankly ahead to the bookshelves and after a moment, she quietly replied, "Some say only the worthy can find the veil; others say the Light chooses who finds it. Yes, somewhere in there I'm sure he does. Certain souls approach it… differently."

Liana stared at L and tried to understand what she couldn't say. After a moment, L broke her stare with the shelves and looked at Liana. Instantly, she rose to her feet, lowered her head, and backed away. Liana turned in her chair and stood when she saw the elven guard. She moved in between him and the table to block his view of the books. When she turned back to L, she was nowhere to be found. With a frown, Liana fell behind the guard as he led her through the twists and turns of the bookcases.

o   o   o

A fierce wind whipped across the back of Liana's neck and carried a shiver down her spine. She raised her hand to the blinding light that surrounded her. After several agonizing moments, the room materialized around her, and she met it with a groan.

"Not again!" she shouted with frustration.

Seek The Truth

The rough stone staircase that stood amongst the bright grass and dark shadows, the same one that had haunted her dreams night after night, materialized before her again. She heaved a sigh and moved towards it.

"No," she whispered to herself.

Liana instantly dropped to a squat, clutched her knees to her chest, and bowed her head. She squeezed her eyes shut and willed herself to wake. The wind thrashed about her and almost knocked her from her feet, but she kept her eyes firmly closed. After several moments, the stillness of the room about her registered in her mind.

Gradually she opened her eyes. When she was met with the ceiling above her bed, she let out a grateful breath of air. Liana lay there for a moment, lost in thought, and stared at the canopy above her. After quite some time, she rolled to her side. She eyed the empty spot next to her in bed where Casimir rarely laid anymore.

A small cracking noise drew her attention from across the room. She sat up slowly and squinted into the darkness of the night. Her eyes adjusted and settled on Casimir. He sat back in an armchair he had pulled from their seating area closer to the bed. One heel rested on his knee and his chin on his fingertips but the most unsettling was his stare and it fixed on Liana.

As she opened her mouth to speak, he instantly cut in, "Sleep weighed down by a guilty conscience?"

"Huh?" she asked and blinked back confused.

Casimir heaved a massive sigh and quickly responded, "Is there something you need to tell me?"

Liana racked her mind for what he was asking but stared back at him and hopelessly shook her head. Casimir instantly let out an angry growl and in one motion, stood and kicked the chair behind him. He lifted his hand to

The Light Within

Liana and waved her closer. Instantly, whispers surrounded her as the shadows yanked her from the bed and shoved her to the floor at his feet.

They left her shaking as they released her and retreated to the corners of the room to wait for his command. Eyes wide, she stared at the floor and searched her mind for the right words. Casimir circled her for quite some time while he examined her every expression. Suddenly, he stopped behind her and swept her hair from the back of her neck to one side.

"All I've given you. All I've made you," he said in an eerily calm tone as he circled her slowly. "Yet Khius still has your affection."

Instantly, her brow knit into an angry furrow, yet her silent stare lingered on the ground. Casimir's gaze remained fixed and his step constant while he slowly paced around her.

"You think I don't see what goes on around here?" He laughed as he continued, "I saw how close you two were, coming back from the war camps."

Liana opened her mouth to speak but instantly decided against it.

He let out another laugh at the sight of her and continued, "I should've seen it! The way he jumped at the opportunity to go with you knowing I wouldn't be there."

His pacing stopped behind her and the room grew quiet. Liana swallowed slowly as her mind raced through the misperceived details. After a concerning amount of silence, she glanced over her shoulder. He stood, head in hand, quite a distance behind her.

"May I speak?" she asked.

He laughed and quickly retorted, "Please, I'd love to hear this one."

Seek The Truth

Casimir crossed the short distance to her. He flicked his hand up and she felt a weight lift from her. She stood and lowered her eyes to his chest as he stopped in front of her.

She shrugged and shook her head as she replied, "Send him away."

He stared back at her, baffled by her words.

"My King," she took a deep breath and continued, "I was weakened from healing the troops and needed his physical support at that moment. As for his motive for accompanying me, I assumed it was for further training. If you are uncertain of him then who am I to question the King. Separate him from us." She shrugged and continued, "If you wish. Anything else?" Liana asked as she slowly shifted to meet his gaze.

A slight smile crept across Casimir's lips while he stared down at Liana and muttered, "That is all." He leaned down and before he kissed her forehead whispered, "Rest up; you'll need your strength."

Chapter 13
True Power

"Please," she whispered aloud to the Light within and prayed it would hear. "Please, save me."

She felt no response, no certainty that her words were heard, let alone granted. Liana sighed and stared absently at the tiny blades of grass that dared peep through the dirt path she trudged. A rhythmic tinkle accompanied her steps as her bangles knocked together at her hands clasped in front of her. Before long, the noise grew to an irritating mock and she threw her hands down at her sides.

The guard in front of her suddenly cleared their throat. Liana looked up and instantly the world around her spun. She dropped her sights to the ground again and focused on the grass before her. Slowly, she approached the stone staircase and blinked several times before her hazy vision would focus.

Liana stood on a stone landing that looked out over two forests. A small stream divided the two and pooled under a platform that stood high above her. She turned to the carved stone stairs and continued her climb. As she reached the top, her heart leaped, and she stumbled.

Instantly, her arm was in the Elder's clutch. He quickly yanked her to him.

"Watch your step," he cautioned.

She stared at him a moment and when he didn't release his grip, she looked to her arm, then back to him. The Elder smiled, released her, and turned her to the center of the platform. As her eyes landed on Casimir and his Commander, she tensed and drew her hands to her chest.

True Power

"Didn't you know? This is where you were to be from the start," the whispers of the Elder stirred in the wind around Liana.

He gripped her shoulders and firmly nudged her closer to the center of the platform where the other two stood.

"I've placed the path out before you this whole way. I sent Casimir for you." His quiet laugh sent a shiver down her spine as he continued, "I alone saved you from those that called for your head after *I* sent you to war over him. Even now as you try to undo all my hard work; I have planned for that too. Resistance is useless."

Casimir and his Commander stepped aside. Liana dug her heels into the cold stone as she caught sight of the bloodied altar that they revealed.

The Elder's whispers cut fiercely through the air, "Now all your suffering will finally pay off. Embrace who you were meant to be. Step into your true power."

Liana stared at the bloody altar before her and reeled at the horror of the carefully orchestrated plans the Elder set in motion. With each reluctant step closer to the altar, the shadows began to stir around them.

"It… it was all you?" she questioned shakily.

His whispers formed into words as he spoke out over the churning winds around them, "I led Casimir to you; to give you the power you possess, the Kingdom you have. Now, accept it."

The Elder lifted his hand up next to her and gestured to the altar. Liana kept her eyes fixed on the altar and slowly backed away from the three. She pulled her arms around herself as the winds whipped frantically and tried to make sense of everything.

The Light Within

How could he have planned for the King? I saw it, she thought to herself while she considered what Khius showed her. *Unless Khius altered the memory*, she contemplated.

Everything inside her was confident the King wasn't persuaded to pick her; she wasn't following along on someone's path this whole time. His love for her felt genuine, though cut short. She was convinced at least that part was true. Liana shook her head, lost in her thoughts until a chill in the air and a sudden voice brought her back to the urgency of the moment.

"I can sense the darkness in you," Casimir spoke from behind her.

She didn't flinch when his hands ran down her arms but kept her eyes fixed on the altar.

"Your hurt, anger, uncertainty. It all can be put to proper use. You must accept it. Then we can rule this Kingdom together, as equals," Casimir urged her.

"Equals," Liana whispered and edged closer to the altar as she considered the idea.

Liana shook her head and stopped in her steps, eyes fixed on the altar.

"Well?"

Casimir's irritation laced word cut through the air and startled Liana. She stared down at the bloodied stone next to her and as she hesitated, shook her head again.

"Liana." Casimir's whisper sounded directly from behind her and as he continued, his hand clenched her shoulder, "Get on the altar, now."

Please help, she pleaded internally.

"Let's go," the Commander grumbled as he reached across the large stone slab and snatched Liana's wrist.

True Power

"No!" Liana shouted and pulled at her wrist.

Casimir sighed and with an eye roll, snapped his fingers. Instantly, the lingering shadows about them reached for her and pulled her over the altar. Liana kicked out forcefully while Casimir climbed over the top of her. The shadows snaked around her legs and immediately secured her.

"No!" she screamed out.

"Your struggles are useless," he said with a laugh. "Open yourself to true power."

Liana struggled in vain against the cold stone while every grip on her held firm. Dark shadows whipped into a frenzy around the elevated platform, amplified by their shouts. Casimir reached over his shoulder and pulled a long, jagged blade from a sheath on his back. A dark mist formed around the handle and turned red as it neared the tip. As soon as she saw it, tears streamed down her face, and she kicked out more frantically than before.

A sadistic smile snaked across his face as he dangled the blade over her chest, "Stop your crying, it will all be over shortly."

"Please help," Liana whispered and turned her head to the side.

Darkness grumbled in her ear, "No one can hear you in this place."

"The Light can hear me anywhere," she said with confidence and closed her eyes.

"No!" Casimir shouted.

Liana instantly opened her eyes, but Casimir's hair shielded her view. He lunged over her and pinned her arms to the cold stone slab. She struggled against him and craned her neck. Over his shoulder, she could see the

The Light Within

Commander near the edge of the platform locked in a battle with two others.

The Elder quickly retreated down the stone staircase, eyes fixed on the struggle that ensued. Liana turned her attention back to the Commander until Casimir shifted himself over her. She looked to Casimir just as he heaved the blade above her again.

"No!" she shouted and jerked just as the edge came down and screeched across the stone.

Casimir instantly lifted the blade, this time with both hands, and aimed for her chest again. Liana yanked her leg free from under him and swiftly kicked his head. Casimir toppled off the side of the altar and revealed the struggle that took place behind him.

Liana sat up as her eyes landed on the Commander and those he battled. She blinked several times and rubbed her eyes as she watched. While Khius fought with the shadows creeping around them, Nicolai went toe to toe with the Commander.

"Liana!" Nicolai shouted and tossed something in her direction.

Her voice cracked as she called to him, "Nic? Is it real-"

The clamor of the object as it slid across the stone floor and hit the altar drew her attention. She looked down over the stone and her eyes grew wide. Instantly, she reached for the Light blade. Just as her fingers grazed the translucent stone grip on the handle, Casimir yanked her back onto the altar.

He grabbed her shoulders and slammed her repeatedly. The world spun above as she frantically blinked the darkness away. Casimir raised his blade again.

True Power

She shifted her arms shakily above her in a feeble attempt to block him. The blade instantly caught in her bracelets.

As his laughter echoed around them, she looked at the struggle at the edge of the platform. To her dismay, she saw the Commander topple over the edge with Nicolai on his back and Khius at his waist.

"Why couldn't you... just let me go?" she asked through weakened whispers as she turned her attention back to Casimir. "I would've been happy with The King."

He questioned her furiously, "How could you possibly be happy without me?"

Liana looked to his cold, dark eyes with a sense of sorrow and shook her head. The shadows circled above him as the anger grew in his face. Suddenly he twisted the blade, and several of the tiny bracelets snapped. He lifted the blade yet again as her shout of excitement stirred the shadows around them. As the blade came down, Liana caught his hands and pulled with determination.

"Just...give...into me!" he shouted as he pressed his weight over the blade.

She fought back with every ounce of strength left in her as the blade dangled dangerously close to her stomach. Tiny silver sparks licked across her fingers to his hands.

"Never," she whispered but with her breath, the blade pierced the flesh on her hip.

Instantly, the shadows from his blade poured into her flesh. Liana screamed and kicked frantically as the acidic material sizzled while it poured into her. The power raced through her veins and snaked into her being. She shuddered as the chill reached for her heart. His eyes grew wide with excitement as he watched the darkness creep into her skin.

The Light Within

Her hands shook on his as gradually, she ceased her struggles. Liana laid back on the altar and released her grip. He smiled and eased his grip, yet still, the blade poured its darkness into her. With a sudden movement, she rolled over, snatched the blade at the ground, and smashed the hilt across Casimir's face.

He shouted angrily as he toppled backward off her. She seized the moment, climbed on top of him, and smashed the handle of the blade across his head several times. When his blood poured out and her hands became stained, she stopped and stared down at him. Liana raised the blade above her head and locked eyes with Casimir.

"Please Casimir, let me heal this darkness in your heart," she shouted over the howling winds that whipped angrily about them.

A disturbed laugh traced his words, "I am the darkness."

Tears streamed down her face as she lifted the blade above her head. Just as she brought the blade down, he shifted and almost knocked it from her grip. She reached out and pushed his arm against his chest with her free hand. Quickly, she drew the blade to the side and plunged it through his ribs. Casimir struggled for only a moment as Liana laid over him.

"We... would've been...unstoppable together," his gurgling whispers taunted as he drew a sharp breath.

Liana sobbed into his chest, eyes clenched shut and unwilling to accept his words. Her mind raced through every interaction, the good and the bad, weighing them all unjustly. She shook as the exhaustion from her battle registered in her mind. When the roaring winds encircling her died away, an eerie stillness filled the air.

True Power

"Liana," Khius' voice echoed in the distance. "Look!"

She sat up at his words and looked behind her. A battle-worn Khius and Nicolai stood at the stairway, at the edge of the platform. When she looked at them, Khius lifted his hand and pointed to Casimir. She quickly turned back just as his chest rose and fell with a weak breath.

Liana jumped from the altar and stared at him. The Light blade that protruded from his side was no longer clear. It slowly filled with a black and red mist that churned inside. She grabbed the blade and yanked it from his torso.

"He's weakened now. Kill him!" Khius shouted and quickly made his way to Liana.

"No," she said calmly and held a hand up to Khius.

Instantly he stopped in his steps, as though he hit an invisible wall. Liana looked up from Casimir to Khius and dropped her hand. He moved closer to her; eyes secured on Casimir.

"No?" Khius asked in disbelief.

She shook her head with her response, "no more death."

Nicolai charged across the platform towards her and tried to reason, "After all he has done? To you, to the Kingdom?"

Liana stared down at Casimir for quite some time before she shook her head again. She looked at the blade in her hand and nodded to herself. As she walked to the stairs, she waved to Casimir dismissively.

"Relocate him to another realm. He's their problem now."

Chapter 14
One Last Thing

"I...I don't understand. You were dead. I saw you die but you're here. You and the Commander were right there together. So, he wasn't taunting me... again," Liana rambled absently.

She kept her eyes on her feet as they trudged along the heavily wooded path. As the grunts and sighs sounded further behind her, Liana stopped and turned. She let her mind swarm again as Khius and Nicolai struggled up the path. Nicolai kept his focus on the tree canopy and stumbled along while he caught every root and branch along the way. Khius grunted as he shoved Nicolai by Liana and pressed on. He shifted the weight of Casimir's limp form on his shoulder and gestured for Liana to follow.

"They really tried their best to keep me away," Nicolai said with a laugh.

Liana glared at the back of Nicolai's head and quietly questioned, "What happened in the woods that night?"

"Huh?" Nicolai mumbled.

As Nicolai turned around to view Liana, Khius shoved him forward again. Nicolai shot him a glare to which Khius merely shrugged and gestured at the path in front of them. When the path narrowed in the dense foliage, Nicolai stepped in front of Khius and led the way.

After a moment with no response, Liana sighed and lifted her voice, "Casimir pulled the trigger. What happened?"

One Last Thing

Nicolai cleared his throat and quietly responded, "Liana this is hardly the ti-"

Annoyed by his avoidance, Liana interjected, "What happened?"

Nicolai sighed and, as he walked along, periodically turned to Liana and recounted, "It all happened so fast. I saw Casimir over me. You only had one chance left to run. I looked up and he had the gun shoved into my forehead and the next thing I heard was a scream. The gun went off right as Casimir flew over my head and that's all I remember. I came to and no one," Nicolai paused for a moment and dropped his head. After a slow swallow, he continued, "No one around was alive."

Liana dropped her head and stared at the twigs beneath her feet as they continued their walk in silence.

"Was that really you?" She questioned quietly, "at the ball?"

An eerie silence lingered in the air momentarily before Nicolai replied, "I wish I could've stayed. I was afraid Casimir was on to me. That's why I left so suddenly after we'd danced."

She gulped down the lump in her throat while she repeated the encounter and cringed when she realized where Darkness stepped in. Before long, she looked up as they navigated through the increasingly dense slender tree trunks. As Liana glanced about, her sights fell on a thick wall of blue, and green vines. She stopped in her steps while the others continued.

It felt like a lifetime has passed since she slipped from the curtain of foliage that concealed the entrance to the cave. It seemed almost impossible that it was the same cave she had been exiled at. Almost as though those weren't even her stories anymore. She laughed to herself and shook her head. After quite some time, Khius and Nicolai emerged from the vines and made their way to Liana.

"Now what?" Nicolai asked.

Liana looked down to the blade in her hand and responded, "One last thing."

o   o   o

"I still think it's a little strange we didn't run into anyone," Nicolai whispered fervently. "Not even a guard?"

Khius retorted in a loud whisper, "You saw the Elder run for it. They knew it was over, the rest probably wised up and ran for it too."

"Still kinda strange," Nicolai grumbled.

"Please," Liana shot over her shoulder to the two.

She turned her attention back to the empty room, closed her eyes, and concentrated, *I must find the room, the veil. I must return this dagger, so Casimir's memory is never restored. Then he can never return.*

She nodded to herself and opened her eyes. Before her, materialized the narrow hallway she searched for. The frame of warm light illuminated her distant destination. She looked down to the blade in her hand and watched the shadows as they swirled around the tip. Her free hand absently reached for her hip. It still burned where Casimir had pierced it.

Liana took a deep breath and stepped into the hall. As she crossed the threshold, the quiet squabbles of the room behind her were stifled by the roar of a circling wind. She fixed her gaze on the frame at the end of the room and pushed through the gale of whispers and winds that whipped into a frenzy around her.

One Last Thing

As she stood in front of the door, she hesitated. Before she could convince herself otherwise, she reached her arm with the blade through the door. Instantly, the room about her went unnervingly silent. Liana glanced around her but saw nothing and turned back to the room. She leaned her shoulder into the frame but didn't move through into the room of Light.

Her eyes went wide, and she lifted her other arm up to the door. She pounded on the now solid surface with her fist and frantically pulled at her hand that clasped the dagger. Liana's heart raced on when she realized her arm remained trapped in the door's clutch. After a frantic second, she leaned her head against the solid wall and took a deep breath.

She could still feel the blade on the other side of the wall. Without a second thought, she released her grip and, as she let go, pulled herself free. With a smile of relief, Liana staggered backward. The frame of light before her drew her attention as it grew brighter with every moment.

Liana lifted her arms to block the light while she stood there in wonder. Suddenly, a pulse broke through the frame. The force broke the remaining bangles at her wrists and knocked her from her feet. It sent her sliding slightly down the hall. She was quick to her feet and as she looked over her shoulder, she saw the light fading from the frame.

The whispers about her quickly grew to a roar with each pounding step she took through the corridor. She could see Nicolai and Khius in a small frame of light in the distance and called out to them. They carried on with one another, unaware of her cries. Another pulse emanated from behind her and knocked her from her feet again.

The Light Within

She looked down at her hands as they collided with the floor and a small crack appeared. Slowly, she got to her feet and kept her eyes on the crack. It splintered out like glass and something stirred beneath it in the shadows. Liana instantly turned and sprinted up the hallway to the castle room in the distance.

A loud boom followed by an unnerving roar shook the ground beneath her feet. Liana jumped through the doorway as the floor shattered and a shadowy beast emerged. When she connected with the floor in the hallway, she slid a short distance. Khius and Nicolai immediately halted their conversation and ran over to her. Liana was on her feet before they could reach her. She shoved them aside just as the beast broke through the frame into the castle.

"Run!" Nicolai yelled.

Liana turned with the others and sprinted up the corridor. The dripping fangs of the shadowy beast grazed her shoulder as they snapped shut. She cried out as the burning substance it left behind sizzled across her flesh. Without notice, the beast leaped up, then dove down and disappeared through the floor. They all stopped in their tracks and caught their breath as they looked about.

"What was *that*?" Khius shot Liana a glare as he gestured behind them with his question.

Liana stood up from catching her breath and rubbed the back of her neck as she awkwardly admitted, "I may have broken something?"

With her words, the beast exploded through the floor beneath them. It snatched Liana's leg into its many claws and crashed through the ceiling above them. She kicked frantically but its grip dug deeper into her leg. She looked down only to find Khius and Nicolai fighting back

One Last Thing

a horde of shadows that poured from where the beast had just escaped.

The creature continued to carry her further and she could see several just like it as they burst through the castle. In a matter of moments, they swarmed the sky and blotted out what remained of the day. Liana pulled herself up and gripped the claws of the beast. She closed her eyes and focused on the Light within her as she let out a powerful zap.

Instantly, the beast let out an ear-piercing shriek and dropped Liana. As she fell, a blinding light emitted from the castle in the distance, upward into the sky. It burned every beast that neared it and shone like a beacon as the last source of light.

o   To Be Continued   o